The Day
of the
Lord

Dr. Terry Gage
&
Lyle A. Way

The Day Of The Lord

ISBN 978-1-4507-1681-9

Library of Congress Control Number 2010906744

Cover photographs - Arenal at night and Denver Lightning are used under the authority of the Creative Commons Attribution 2.0 generic license as attributed and documented at the following websites…
http://commons.wikimedia.org/wiki/File:Arenal_at_night.jpg
http://creativecommons.org/licenses/by/2.0/deed.en
http://commons.wikimedia.org/wiki/File:Denver_Lightning.jpg
http://creativecommons.org/licenses/by/2.0/deed.en

Cover design by Jonathan Gage
deepimpactdesigns.com

Printed in U.S.A.

Biblemystery.com Publishing
in association with Acts Ministry Press

Dedication

This book is dedicated to the Lord Jesus Christ, whose grace and mercy sustains us, and to the many whose assistance and prayers have been vital to bringing forth this work.

Chapter One

Sometimes in the course of human events, things that become earth shattering begin in small, out of the way places and are caused by men who remain unknown to history.

Two such men barreled down Highway 87, south of Yellow Pine, Texas in a crème colored 1956 Ford F-150 pickup, which could best be described as a "rattle trap." The driver of the mobile junk pile was Louie Sims, who considered himself to be the smartest guy in Yellow Pine. He was 24 years old but lied to everyone and told them he was 30. He had a plain, heavily tanned face with dark eyes. His light brown hair hung down to his collar, and a wisp of it was continually in his eyes, causing him to brush it back every minute or so. He was built with the bulk of a weightlifter in his shoulders, but his growing stomach protruded more than he liked.

Louie's passenger was Darryl Patoli. People unkindly called him "the lip" behind his back because his lower lip stuck out and hung down like the lower lip of a horse. Darryl was tall, around 6 feet 4 inches, and extremely thin. His shoulder bones stuck out so badly his shirt looked like it was hanging on a hanger. His face was so thin it looked like a skull with buck teeth and a hawk-like nose. He was a 29 year old Ichabod Crane. Long arms stuck out of every shirt he had, and his fingers were long and boney. He had light green eyes, causing him to look as if he had no iris at all, just black pupils in grayish white eyeballs. The lip always had drool hanging from the side of his mouth, especially when he was drinking beer, which he was now.

These two losers were on their way to the Donner Ranch just south of town. They were drinking cans of Bud Light and throwing the empties in the back of the truck, even though most of the cans blew out and ended up on the road.

"Com'on Louie, what's the big plan? We goin' to make any money?" Darryl queried while grabbing another brewski.

"My poor ignorant fellow, of course we're going to make money. It's the perfect scam. I got the idea from the latest National Geographic. The Jews over there in Israel are looking for red heifers; something to do with their religion. Seems they want to kill a red heifer so some big shot politician will get elected or something. Anyway, we're going to con old man Donner out of one of his heifers and sell it to Israel. Shouldn't be too hard to find out who's in charge over there."

"How we goin' to get the cow? We got no money," Darryl muttered.

"We'll tell Donner that we'll give him $500 as she stands in the pasture. I've got a few bucks saved. How much you got?" he asked.

Darryl was having difficulty focusing while drooling a steady little rivulet down his chin. "I got maybe $100, but that's got to last me to the end of the month," he added.

"Hmm. This ain't good. Oh well, we'll figure something out. I figure we can sell the critter for several thousand, maybe more," Louie said, ever the optimist.

"How do you know he even has a red heifer?"

"Cause he's got red cows, you idiot."

The old pickup wove its way into the driveway leading to the Donner ranch. They drove through groves of pines and pristine meadows on the way to the ranch house which stood on a slight rise in the land. It was made of red and black brick and supported an ancient cedar roof that had areas of moss because of the shade cast by huge cedars next to the building.

The two con artists decided to check the barn. Luckily, Donner was there cleaning the calf pens. Neither of the would-be business men liked the smell.

"Hi there, Mr. Donner. How you doin'?" Louie asked, smiling like a used car salesman.

Donner looked up from the pen and glanced at the two men standing behind him. One was weaving just a little. "Hello yourself. Who are you guys?"

"I'm Louie, and this here scarecrow is Darryl."

"Nice to meet ya. What are ya'll doing out here in my barn. You want a job shoveling this pretty stuff?" he asked, grinning.

"No thanks, that stuff stinks," Louie wrinkled his nose. "We could use a job but not that bad," he sniffed.

"Well, what do you want then?"

"We want to buy one of your red heifers if you got any," Louie said.

"I got a couple, but what in the world would you two city slickers want with a red heifer?" Donner asked suspiciously.

"That's our business. You got one that's all red, no other colors?"

"Got one, but she's just three weeks old. You guys ready to mix a bucket of Land O Lakes milk for her twice a day?" the old man asked, smiling and shaking his head.

"Sure we are. You ready to sell or what?" Louie was getting a tad testy.

Colin Donner had been in the ranching business for forty years and could spot crooks a mile off. He was tired of their little game and wanted them off his property. "No, I'm not going to sell her or any of my animals to a couple of losers. Now get back in your truck and take off."

The two entrepreneurs were taken aback. The alcohol in their brains slowed their thinking a little, but finally Louie realized his little game was over. "Hey, you can't order us around like that. We were going to pay you $500 cash money, but you can kiss that good bye. Come on Darryl, let's get out of this crap hole."

Donner roared with laughter. "Five hundred dollars you say. Man, you are a couple of high rollers ain't ya? That animal will sell for more than $3,000."

Louie sniffed, turned and stomped out of the barn. Darryl seemed confused and unsure of what had just happened. They got in their truck and swerved back up the driveway, nearly hitting the white fence on each side of the road.

"Who does that hot shot think he is, talking to us like that? Nobody talks to Louie Sims like he's a hired hand. I'm telling you, Darryl, I'm goin' to get even with that guy if it's the last thing I do." He stomped on the gas pedal, and the truck made an attempt to speed up but just kind of sighed. Darryl was asleep.

The next day the two wheeler-dealers were nursing a beer in the Cattle Ranchers Tavern. As they sat in a booth casually glancing around the room, a man came into the tavern causing everyone in the room to stop what they were doing and gawk at the stranger. He was tall, tan, very handsome, wearing Oakley sunglasses. Nobody had ever seen clothes like he was wearing. His suit was light beige, made of pure silk. It probably cost more than Louie and Darryl made in a month. His shirt was pale lavender, complimented by a tie that was a brilliant yellow/orange combination that seemed to light up the room. He wore brown Italian loafers with a gold chain across the arch. Louie was almost certain that the shoes had never seen the messy side of a cow pasture.

The gentleman came directly to their booth and sat down, pushing Darryl up against the wall, much to his displeasure. He took out a cigar, lit it, and blew smoke into Louie's face and said, "I understand you two fine fellows are in the cattle business," he said as the Oakleys peered at him.

Louie sat up straighter and put on his best business face and said, "You could say that, stranger. We dabble in the markets on occasion," he lied.

"I have a little job for a couple of good men. Wouldn't take but a few minutes, and I'm willing to pay $500 each." The fragrance from his cigar seemed to melt any resistance they might have. Louie thought he caught a whiff of sulfur, but then decided it must have been from the match the stranger used to light his cigar.

Darryl wiped the drool from his chin, and said, "Don't think I heard your name, mister."

"You're very astute because I haven't given my name. Some people call me Mr. Diablo. I'm rather busy…do you want the job or not?"

Louie felt that as the leader of the partnership he should be the one responsible for making any deals. "Sure, Mr. Diablo, we want the job; what is it?" he asked.

"I want you to kill a young cow for me," he said while the Oakleys eyed them closely.

"Want some veal do ya?"

"I don't want any meat; I just want a particular animal killed tonight. Can you do it?" he wasn't smiling now.

"Sure, we can do it, don't get riled up. Which animal is it, and where is she grazing?" Louie asked. He was getting a little nervous about such a strange request.

"It's the red heifer on the Donner ranch. The same one you tried to buy yesterday. It must be killed tonight because old man Donner is planning on shipping her out in a few days. All you have to do is sneak into the barn, shoot the calf and get back to town. I'll pay you $200 each now, the rest when the job is done."

Louie was curious now and asked, "What is so bloom'n important that the calf has to be killed tonight?"

Darryl was watching both men with bulging eyes and more drooling. He wanted to say something but was afraid Louie would hit him.

Mr. Diablo didn't answer. He took out an alligator skin wallet and put $400 on the table. "I'll be here when you finish," he said and got up and walked out of the tavern and climbed into a new, black Cadillac Escalade. Every eye followed him out and then turned to look at the town losers, wondering what a man like that would have to do with Louie and Darryl.

Suddenly they were involved in a conspiracy. Louie whispered, "We've got to be quiet on this job. We'll use my .22 rifle; it doesn't make any noise. Come on, let's get moving. It'll be dark in an hour. This will get us even with old man Donner, hey?" he laughed and dragged Darryl out of the booth, shoving him toward the door.

Two hours later they parked the Ford on the highway and cut across the pastures on the Donner ranch, heading for the barn. The two black ops pretenders stepped in every fresh cow pie in the field.

They got to the building without any problems, cautiously opened the barn door and went quickly inside. Louie was smart enough to bring a flashlight, and they soon found the little calf lying on a bed of straw. Suddenly a dog was barking just outside the barn. This unnerved Louie for a second, but he continued on his errand of death. Just as Louie was taking aim, the barn door flew open and Donner roared in followed by his hired hand.

"What are you fools trying to do?" he yelled. "Get out of here before I call the Sheriff," he shouted as he rushed the two men and grabbed at the rifle. Louie instinctively backed up and tripped over a bucket and fell on his rear end. When he hit the floor, the rifle went off; the bullet struck Donner in the forehead, and he dropped like a sack of grain. The hired man kicked the rifle out of Louie's hand, and then kicked him in the head, knocking him senseless. Darryl let out a whoop and tried to run in the dark. He barreled into a pen by mistake. When he tried to run out, the hired man hit him in the head with a board. He moaned and sank to the floor unconscious.

When both adventurers regained consciousness, they found that a deputy sheriff was there, and they were in handcuffs.

"Okay, boys, get up and get in the back of my patrol car. I'll Mirandize you on the way to the court house." Darryl was terrified. He thought Mirandizing must be some kind of terrible torture.

As they crawled into the back of the deputy's car, they could see other police cars with their lights flashing. They also saw an ambulance. Louie regained what little wit he had left and shouted at the deputy, "What you arresting us for? We didn't do nothin."

"You're under arrest for the murder of Colin Donner."

"Murder, we didn't murder anybody. He pushed me, and I fell. The gun just went off!"

"Save it for the judge. Now shut up and enjoy the ride. It's the last one you'll have for a long, long time.

The little red heifer, whom Donner named "Alice", had been terribly frightened by the shouting and fighting. She jumped from one side of her pen to the other, her ears pointing forward, then quickly back. Her little eyes bulged, and her heart pounded as she wanted to flee. Then things quieted down. Her peaceful barn was again a place of rest. Soon she lay down and returned to sleep, unaware that she had played a small role in the religious destiny of a far away nation.

Chapter Two

Late in the afternoon in Tehran, the summer heat was bearing down on the city mercilessly. Everywhere, there was the whirring of air conditioners. For the millions unable to afford such a luxury, it was necessary to seek some relief in the shade and a light breeze.

It was different in the presidential palace. The floor to ceiling windows that could be opened to capture a breeze from any direction were now covered in white chintz curtains which billowed gently in the moving air caused by the giant air conditioners.

President Hafez traced his ancestry all the way back to the ancient Persians and was very comfortable in a light breeze but allowed the conditioners for the people working in the palace.

Hafez was in the prime of his life at 42 years of age. Tall for a Persian, he was muscular and relatively handsome. His light brown hair was receding from a high forehead above dark, penetrating eyes. A carefully trimmed beard accentuated his face and slightly pronounced jaw, which betrayed a powerful personality and an iron will. He had almost no sense of humor and didn't tolerate much laughter in his administration.

Hafez was a driven man. He had worked and planned and campaigned on the passion of his life: to destroy Zionism and the state of Israel. He would not rest until all Jews in this part of the world were exterminated. He considered it his personal religious duty. Hafez was a violent, power hungry extremist.

The phone on his beautiful but modest desk purred gently. When he answered, he was told that Barrack Huesson, his Minister of Interior, was here for their scheduled meeting. Almost immediately, his beautiful secretary, Dannah ushered in the minister.

Barrack Huessen waddled into the tastefully decorated office. Vastly overweight, his collar was open under his tie to assist his breathing. He was perspiring heavily, with the moisture causing his scraggly attempt at the requisite beard to glisten like small diamonds on black velvet. His round face sported a number of chins, and his bald head gleamed as it reflected the light from the gold sconces on the wall. Small, close-set eyes peered through a pair of wire rimmed half glasses. He smiled, showing tiny, uneven teeth and collapsed into a green leather chair opposite the president. The man's comical appearance masked his astute political mind. No one in the administration knew national politics as well as he did, and his grasp of domestic politics was legendary.

Hafez, as was his habit, got immediately to the reason for the meeting. "Tell me, Barrack, why is it taking so long to get the uranium enrichment process moving faster?"

"Mr. President, the scientists are working at a feverish pace. We are held back, somewhat, by the Russian advisers. They cannot make a decision without checking with Moscow first. It can sometimes take days for them to get an answer. This holds up the progress in the critical areas of production. I am sorry to report, that at this rate, it may well take another year to get weapons grade uranium in sufficient quantities to make several bombs," he said quietly as he glanced furtively at the president over his half glasses.

Hafez's face seemed to drain of color. He got up from his chair and leaned over the desk towards the minister. "It is your job, Barrack, to keep this project on schedule. I am not going to wait another year because of your incompetence. Do you hear me?" He was seething with anger. Huessen shrunk before his wrath. He knew full well the whispered stories telling of the strange disappearances of people who disregarded the wrath of the president.

"Sir, I know of your desire to be ready for an invasion of the evil Zionists this year, but we depend on the Russians for critical information and direction in the production of the weapons grade material. They are slowing this process on purpose and for their own political gain. They can make the world believe they are helping us develop nuclear power for the cheap production of electricity. By forcing us to use their technologies and advisors, they can control the speed of the work, making us depend on them even more. They don't like the Zionists any more than we do, but they are not ready to be caught up in a war. They still respect the Americans' power and war machine," he said while mopping his brow with a handkerchief that had once been white.

"I know, you know, and our dear friends the Russians know that the new American President has no love for Israel and is working hard to convince the Arabs that he is their new friend."

"That is true, sir. Our information also says that their CIA has been cleansed of most of the old 'patriots' with the new people following the line of the President. Israel's pleas for more assistance are going unanswered. This will soon cause a financial problem and make it difficult to finance their military programs, particularly missile defense."

"All the more reason to move forward at the fastest speed possible. Now is the time to strike, not years from now. Blast you, Barrack, get this moving at top speed, and don't let up the pressure. I'll call Propochnik and light a fire under him. Now get out of here, and don't come back until you can tell me we are on schedule with the missiles and the bombs!" the president shouted.

The Minister of the Interior gathered his briefcase without latching the lid. Papers flew all over the floor. He dropped to his hands and knees to scoop the documents back into the case. His hands left wet prints on beautiful blue tile floor. Finally, he scurried from the room, dropping into a chair in the outer office to catch his breath.

"You pompous ass, do you dare to talk to me like I'm a peasant sewer worker?" he thought. "One word from me to the right people, and your whole plan is exposed to the world. That would probably cause Israel to attack us right away, with or without the help of the United States. You fool. Do

you think Syria is going to be pleased with the radiation fallout that will drift over their country? Yes, praise Allah, the right word, and I just might become the president."

He hurried on down the hall. His shirttail was out of his pants, showing below his jacket. The secretarial pool snickered and looked away.

As the Minister of the Interior waddled down the hall mumbling to himself as he seethed over the way he had been treated, Hafez's beautiful secretary glided into his office and told him that a strange man was waiting in the office, demanding to see the president.

"If he doesn't have an appointment, tell him to make one and come back at the proper time," he groused.

A man brushed past Dannah and entered the room, pushing her outside as he closed the door. He was very tall and very handsome, with a tanned face and sparkling white teeth. His eyes were hidden behind Oakley sunglasses. His suit and shoes must have cost a fortune. The man smiled and made himself comfortable in one of the chairs across the desk from Hafez. He did not offer his hand.

Hafez was stunned. He hadn't seen this man since he had been elected. In a secret meeting, the sinister stranger had shown him how to rig the election. He stuttered and cleared his throat. "Mr. Diablo, how wonderful to see you again. I thought you had forgotten me," he said lamely, trying to act friendly.

"I am afraid, Mr. President, it is you who have forgotten me." There was that blazing smile again. He took out a cigar, lit it and blew smoke in Hafez's direction. The president wrinkled his nose in displeasure.

"I do wish you wouldn't smoke that thing in here," he sniffed.

"Let's not worry about my cigar. Let's talk about the progress you are making with the Zionist problem. I gave you a good plan when I helped you get elected. Now, how is my plan working?" He sat back in the chair and studied the president closely, smoke curled toward the ceiling.

Hafez stuttered, regained his composure and began talking. "My plan, excuse me, your plan is going very well. We are within a year of having enriched uranium in quantity, enough to make at least two bombs. We are having some problems with the Russian consultants and engineers. They will not make a move without checking with Moscow, which slows down the process," he said, eyeing his visitor.

"That shouldn't be a problem. You're the president; make it happen. Get Moscow moving."

"I intend to make a call in a few minutes. I'll make sure they understand the importance of keeping on schedule."

"I think I have a better idea. Keep on developing the nuclear bombs as you have been. This will keep the Russians and our friends at the United Nations busy trying to reason with you, and they won't be watching other areas of preparation. I want you to contact the Syrians and the Jordanians and ask them to agree that, when you send in your new missiles that will be accurate enough to strike Israel, they will join you in invading the country. Tell them you will have your military man the machines if they get nervous about retaliation. This attack should turn the whole region into another holocaust." Diablo sat back in his chair and blew small circles of smoke toward the president.

"That will be a very difficult thing to persuade them to do. Neither nation is very anti-Israel in anything except the press. They both have active trade relations with the Zionists. It is disgusting!" He would have spat on the floor if he thought Diablo would be impressed.

"You will be ecstatic if there is a holocaust, will you not?" Diablo asked smiling.

"Ecstatic? How do you mean, ecstatic?"

"I mean when the world is in the process of destroying itself, the Mahdi will come back to earth. Isn't that what your religion teaches?" He was still smiling.

"Oh, yes, of course. I didn't catch your meaning at first. Yes, that will be a great and wondrous day."

Diablo got up and came around to stand beside Hafez. He bent down until he was eye level with the president, who found himself trembling. Abruptly, Diablo removed his glasses, as Hafez looked on in terror. His eyes were a blazing yellow!

"Listen to me, little man, you don't want to make me disappointed in the fact that I am trusting you to wipe out Israel. I trusted that incompetent Adolph Hitler to do the task. He started well and millions of people were killed, but he forgot the plan was mine, not his, so I let him be defeated. I was there in the bunker when he blew his own head off. It was pathetic. He only killed a portion of the Jews; you will eliminate the whole nation. There will no longer be a homeland for Jews to emmigrate to. Then, new pogroms can be started worldwide to sweep up the rest. Oh, my friend, it will be glorious!"

Diablo spoke as if he were in a trance. He put the glasses back on his head, and the bright light that had engulfed the whole office was dampened. Hafez thought he was going to vomit. His mind was swimming as he sat under the power of this strange man. Failure would mean certain death. He had to kill the Jews in Israel.

Muhammad Hafez was a trembling shell of a man, but with surprising strength and not a little courage, he faced Diablo and asked, "Sir, why is it so important to you that the Jews in Israel be killed? I don't believe your ancestors are either Muslim or of Arab descent so I fail to see any connection with the hated Zionists."

"Let's just say that one particular Jew has irritated me for a long, long time," Diablo hissed through clenched teeth, while he seethed with anger.

"Centuries ago, I had that fool Herod poised to kill him along with all the children of Bethlehem just to make sure he would not escape. But Herod was indecisive and kept putting off the job. Three unknown kings had come from the east to worship the little imposter. Herod should have acted immediately, but was weak willed. He decided to wait for the three kings to return and point the child out to him. But they went home by a different route. By the time he realized their trickery and sent troops into Bethlehem to slay the children of the city, the child had escaped into Egypt.

"I am the real power of this world, not that weakling! Christians proclaim that the pathetic Jew is coming back to rule as the Messiah of Israel. Some Messiah he will be...Messiah of the dead! He cannot come back as a triumphant Messiah if they are all dead.

"Every last Jew in Israel must die; do you hear me? I want them all dead! And as for you," Diablo whispered, grasping Hafez with razor-like fingernails, piercing deep into his throat, "you will never again question my motives, and you will see to it that every last Jew in Israel is dead. Do you hear me, Hafez?"

Diablo left the room like a fading whisper. The air was pungent with the smell of smoke and sulfur as Hafez rushed to the mirror on the wall to see if he looked like he was dying. There were only faint marks on his neck, but his tie and white shirt were stained with streams of his own blood.

Chapter Three

The President of the United States, Solomon Steinmetz was in a surly mood. At 35 years of age, he was one of the youngest men elected to the office of President. He had unruly, brown hair that was collar length, matching the well-trimmed mustache he supported. Solomon was a rather short man, standing just over 5 feet 6 inches in height. He had the personality and drive of many short men, wanting to prove that they could compete in a tall world. A daily work out in the White House gym kept him in good shape.

His azure colored eyes were a direct gift from his mother who was blond and blue-eyed as well. His heritage, however, was half Jewish, which he never mentioned. Newspapers had disclosed the fact during the campaign, but he never answered them and never introduced anyone to his father. The two men disliked each other with Middle Eastern passion.

Now that whining prime minister of Israel, Hiram Meier, was on the phone. He would probably cry about the way the world treated them and ask for more money from America to protect them from the always-ready-to-invade Arabs.

He picked up the receiver and forced himself to smile and say, "Good afternoon, Mr. Prime Minister. Isn't it a fine day?"

"Good afternoon, Mr. President. It is a fine day. I have just come from an orange grove near the coast. The trees were in blossom, and the fragrance was intoxicating. I wish you could share the experience with me."

"That would be wonderful, Hiram. We'll make it a date. What is on your mind?" he asked waiting for what surely would be a request for something.

"I wanted to ask if your CIA has received any new information about the centrifuges in Iran. Our intelligence tells us that this whole dance around United Nations sanctions is nothing more than a delaying tactic. With the help of the Russians, they are rapidly preparing to enrich uranium very soon. When that happens, then it is just a matter of time before they have a couple of bombs destined to visit our nation," the prime minister concluded.

This was the strangest of calls. If video cameras were running in each office, they would have the exact facial expressions of disgust on both men. Neither liked the other, and they had a hard time concealing it from the press.

"Now, Hiram. You know Hafez is just rattling the sabers to get you all worked up. My secretary of state is working with the United Nations to get another set of sanctions in place that will really punish Iran if they show any real aggression against your country. When the time comes, I will personally talk to Hafez and get him to calm down. Heck fire, I'll even fly to Tehran to do a face to face."

Meier's face was beet red. He couldn't stand the condescending attitude of the American President.

"Thank you, Mr. President, for this most generous offer of personal negotiations with Iran. But we both know that he is very unstable and difficult to deal with. He hears no argument but his own and listens to no one who doesn't agree with him. You know that we believe he is deadly serious about driving us into the sea.

"I am sure you agree we have to defend ourselves. We do not intend to just sit here while you or your secretary of state negotiate, and negotiate, and negotiate some more, giving him the time he needs to finish his weapons program," he stated emphatically.

He didn't care if the President heard the anger in his voice. He considered the American President to be as dangerous to the State of Israel as Iran's President.

Steinmetz's throat was filling with bile. His anger was roiling his stomach. He could no longer contain his emotions. "Mr. Prime Minister, I deeply resent your implication that our efforts on your behalf are anything but genuine. You will do well to remember that there is a new administration in the White House, an administration that reaches out to the Arab

20

as well as the Jew. In this new world order, the Jew can no longer count on being the only Middle Eastern state that will be supported by America. In fact, because of our new diplomatic direction, we will be unable to support the amount of money directed to go to your country as foreign aid. It is common knowledge that you are using this money, not to help your people or your economy, but to bolster your military and its aggressive plans against Iran and any other country that might be considered a friend of Hafez.

"Please consider this discussion as your notification that next year's aid to Israel will be reduced from 2 billion dollars to 20 million. That should be enough to keep your orange groves producing," he stopped speaking and tried to regain his composure. He was breathing hard with excitement and anger.

Hiram Meier was stunned into silence. He knew the American President did not especially like Israel but had no idea the depth of the animosity this man had for his country. He cleared his throat and spoke slowly in a whispered tone.

"Mr. President, since the rebirth of our nation in 1948, every American President has come to our aid and been our staunchest ally and friend. You are the first to break that longstanding relationship. You have revealed your true makeup.

"You are a traitor to the Jews in your country, and you are a coward, sir, bowing down to Arab kings and sheiks and that madman in Tehran. You think only of the oil he and his friends can provide for your refineries. You gladly pay them billions and insult us with a pittance. I believe God will punish you and your country for this despicable act.

"We will survive, Mr. President, which I am sure does not fill you with happiness. But we will be here when God weighs you in the balances, and you are found wanting," he roared into the phone and then slammed the receiver down.

He leaned back in his chair and closed his eyes, trying to recover from the shock of the phone discussion and

21

revelation. He rang his secretary and directed her to notify his cabinet that there would be an emergency meeting at 7:00 p.m. that evening.

Then, even though he was an avowed agnostic, he bowed his head and prayed to the great God of Israel, counting on the fact that, because he was a Jew, Jehovah might be listening. "Oh great God, hear the travails of your people, Israel. Our closest friend has turned against us, and great danger lurks just northeast of us. Your people need you in this hour of immense peril. Amen."

In Washington, just the opposite was occurring. President Steinmetz was so proud of himself that he had to tell someone. He asked his secretary to call a cabinet meeting for 7:00 p.m. that evening. But that didn't help his need to talk to a friend now. He called the man in charge of the Secret Service and asked for the "special detail and car" to be made ready.

In ten minutes, his phone rang, and he was informed that the car was ready at the rear of the White House. It was a beautiful spring day, and the cherry blossoms were in full bloom in Washington. This ride and the men riding with him were on a secret outing. He picked up the car phone and dialed a number.

In two rings, a sultry woman's voice answered and said, "Larry, is this you?"

"You little minx, I happen to know you have caller ID. You know who this is. I'm on my way to your house. I need some of your special comfort," he said, smiling with anticipation.

"Why, sure 'nuf, sugar. Come right over, but give me a few minutes so I can get the men out of the house," she teased while laughing.

"Morgan, what would I do without you? Bye."

"Bye, sugar, see ya in two shakes of a cat's tail. Bye now." Her drawl dripped with honey.

In ten minutes he was in her arms. He was too excited for romance; he wanted to tell her what a great statesman he was and how he had single handedly changed American foreign policy that had been in place for sixty years.

"Guess what I've just done?" he teased.

"What did you do, sic the dogs on some poor widow or orphans?"

"Stop it, you big kidder. I just told off that old Jew in Israel. Told him we were stopping almost all aid to his pitiful country. He wanted to tell me that would open the door for Iran to invade his country, and they would defend themselves. All I could think of was 'who cares, old man.' This will insure that Iran keeps selling us their oil and keep the American machinery running. He tried to tell me that God would judge me. Ha! He doesn't know I'm an atheist. Ha ha ha. He tells an atheist that God's going to get 'em. Ha ha ha!"

Morgan feigned no interest in his international politics, but she listened carefully. "Darling, were you too mean to the prime minister guy?" she asked demurely.

"Naw, who cares about Israel? This is a new age, new people in charge, working on a new world order. It's going to be wonderful. Now, let's not worry your pretty head over this stuff. Make me happy."

The beautiful presidential mistress could do that and do it well. Tall, not too thin with a beautiful figure and auburn hair that fell gently to her shoulders, she was a striking woman. Her emerald eyes missed nothing, and her pouting lips whispered desire when she spoke.

Now, with the presidential head on her shoulder, her demeanor changed slightly, as she stared out the window. Something important was on her mind, something very, very important.

Chapter Four

The Russian President, Andre Propochnik, was standing on the patio of his beautiful dacha, located about twenty miles outside of Moscow. He loved this place and loved the way his wife kept their garden beautiful in the spring. The long, cold winter was over, and new life was pushing its way into the world, although there were still patches of snow in the shaded areas.

Propochnik was just 50 years of age, a kid as far as the age of traditional Russian presidents was concerned. He tried to keep in shape, but the long hours behind his desk caused him to be 30 pounds overweight, which showed in his stomach and his fat jowels, causing him to look as if he was scowling.

His black hair was thinning, and there were already many worry lines on his pale forehead. Dark eyes betrayed his cunning, detail-oriented mind. He had a dark beard, which always looked as if he had a "five o'clock shadow."

As he was admiring the wonderful yellow in a cluster of daffodils, his wife, Dora, raised a window in the kitchen and said he had an important phone call on his "special" line. He grumbled as he made his way to the door.

Inside the beloved dacha, he grabbed the receiver on his Victorian style telephone and said, "Yes, what is it?"

"Mr. President, this is Muhammad Hafez. How are you?" he asked without caring.

"I'm fine, just enjoying a beautiful spring day," he replied, also without caring.

"That is good, praise Allah. It's very warm today, and we have a little sand mixed in our breeze. Do you have a few minutes for me?"

"I always have time for my friends. What is on your mind this fine day?" he asked, dreading what the response would be.

"Sir, I need to talk to you about your country's scientists and engineers whom you have so generously allowed to help us in our nuclear power program. We are falling behind schedule, partly because your people cannot, or will not, make a decision without checking with their people in Moscow. Sometimes it takes days for an answer to come back.

"I am wondering if possibly you could speak to the people you have in charge of the program and ask them to speed up the process of questions needing answers," he paused, already bored with having to ask the Russians for anything.

When he was producing his own enriched uranium, he wasn't going to ask them for anything.

"I feel positive our people want to make sure they are doing the very best job possible for your country. Mistakes with centrifuges and delicate engineering equipment can be costly and time consuming to repair."

"I understand completely and appreciate what your people are doing for us, but we have a very tight schedule to follow and I need your help in seeing that we stay on track," he said. The whining was back.

"Muhammad, what is so important that you have a time table that cannot be moved a day or two either way?" he asked, knowing what the answer would be.

"We scheduled the nuclear power plants to come on line in eight years; that was two years ago. We are no closer now than we were then," he moaned.

"I would appreciate your not trying to con me, Muhammad. What you want as soon as possible is enriched uranium so you can make a couple of nuclear bombs either to scare Israel with, or to actually explode them over the country. I understand you are receiving missile technology from the North Koreans, and you will have a delivery platform for the bombs very soon now. Is that not the truth?" he asked, smiling.

"Your intelligence is very good, Andre. We are making great strides in preparing to eliminate the hated Zionists from the face of the earth. But your people are slowing us down. Can't you speed them up?"

"Russia has no love for Israel, as you already know. If we did, we would not be helping you with nuclear engineering materials and trained experts. But quit complaining; we want to do the job right the first time. You should be pleased that we are doing a careful job."

"Thank you, sir, forgive me. I understand what you are saying. Good bye," he said, swallowing hard to keep from telling the Russian infidel where to go and how to get there.

Andre replaced the receiver, thought a moment, and then picked it up and dialed his secretary. "Arrange a cabinet meeting for this evening at 7:00 p.m."

"Yes sir, 7:00 p.m."

He walked back to his garden, thinking how foolish it was that his country had ever gotten mixed up with that fool in Tehran. He knew the tactic was a hold over from the Cold War and was intended to embarrass and frighten the Americans. But if that idiot exploded nuclear bombs over Israel, the United States would blame the Russians for being part of the attack.

He didn't want war with the Americans, although the new president was considered weak on national defense and intelligence. His people in the United States CIA and the State Department reported that Steinmetz considered himself a master diplomat, capable of persuading any nation to do his bidding.

"Good grief, I'm surrounded by idiots!" he thought to himself. *"If Iran drops nukes on Israel, a very wealthy country, it won't be free from radiation for hundreds of years. What good would that do anybody?"* He made a mental note to call the president of Syria and see what he thought about radiation drifting all over his country. Should be interesting.

On the same day many nations were calling meetings and discussing how to destroy Israel, a small freighter was working its way through the maze of off shore oil rigs in the Gulf of Mexico. Its course would soon be changed to one heading due east toward the Mediterranean Sea. She plowed slowly through moderate swells. The old freighter was hauling cargo for a number of different countries, but in the forward hold, where careful arrangements had been made to allow fresh air under the hatch cover to the hold below, the only cargo were three animals: cattle. The animals were from three states: Mississippi, Texas, and Montana. They were all Red Angus heifer yearlings. They were uncomfortable with the motion of the ship at sea and spent a great deal of time bawling, longing for their herd.

The one called Alice was fairly happy. She liked the good hay and grain they were given, but she didn't like the way the boss heifer kept bullying her. Soon she had enough of the persecution, stood her ground, and gave the bully a good head butt.

When the confrontation was over, she felt much better and lay down on her bed of straw to chew her cud and snooze a little.

She had no idea that the freighter was heading for Israel, where a special farm near Haifa had been built just for them and others like her, solid red without blemish. Alice didn't know about the future or what that word even meant. If she had known, she would have been doing some of her own bawling and mooing. Instead, she drifted off to sleep, proud of the way she had charged the bully, giving her a couple of good of head slams.

Chapter Five

Garrison Fong, director of the Far East section at Central Intelligence headquarters, was grousing under his breath as he headed for the Director's office. The Director of the CIA, Charlene Lewis-Sloden, had called and demanded his presence. His slender arms were pumping fast as he hurried down the hall. These kind of calls made two things happen in him. First, it made him want a Marlboro in the worst way, and second, it made his stomach turn flip-flops in anticipation of what the new crisis was about. He had been forced to quit smoking when it was discovered he had a stomach ulcer. Days of greasy hamburgers at his desk were also a thing of the past, replaced by bland food and milk.

He got to the office, knocked and rushed in without waiting for an invitation. Inside, he saw the director and a good friend examining a map of Iran on the wall.

"Good, you're here. What took you so long?" the director asked, grinning.

The stocky man with the shock of unruly brown hair, turned around, and his face broke into a wide grin. He charged the director of the Far East section and embraced him in a bear hug that took his breath away and made him think he might soon be joining his ancient Chinese ancestors. Now the man was pounding him on the back, removing what little air was left in his lungs.

"Help, somebody help me. An animal is attacking me," Fong yowled and then broke out in back-pounding laughter of his own. "Tuck, you worn out old spy, what in the world are you doing…wait a minute. You're the reason for this meeting. That means the world has gone to hell in a hand basket and this mad woman is intent on sending you to save us all."

"All right, you two guys, break up this 'mano a mano' stuff. We've got work to do. I have just been discussing with Tuck that I think we need him to go back into Tehran and see if he can get a cell of intelligence operatives started again. You know the one we had a couple of years ago was discovered and wiped out by Vevak. We lost some superb people to their torture chambers. But we have to learn how close Hafez is to getting the bomb, and we need to know as soon as possible," the director said as she stabbed the air with her right hand.

"Why? This administration isn't going to do anything about it. I don't want to risk good people's lives getting classified material just to have the White House leak it to the press, pointing out how 'out of touch' the CIA is to the real world. This President thinks he can talk any terrorist out of his bombs if given the chance," Tuck blurted out with real disgust in his voice.

"Easy, Tuck. You're right of course, but we can't forget we serve the people of the United States. Administrations come and go. We've survived some bad ones before, and we can again," Charlene said as she plopped down in her chair. Fong thought she might be putting on some weight but didn't dare say anything. The two men sat in chairs in front of the desk and waited.

"Tuck, forgive me, but I'm going to ask you to go back into Tehran and set up a reliable cell for us, not too big, but capable of getting some information out to us. Can you use some of the dissident students who we see rioting in the streets every few days?"

"Sure, we can find a few who might be effective, but they'll have to be very good to stay alive. Vevak is everywhere, and they are paying particular attention to the students they see in the streets. Many have already disappeared," Tuck said. "As you know, we have a young woman who works in the palace sending us information over a special encrypted cell phone. But she doesn't send much, afraid of being discovered. If she is caught, her death will be horrendous and take a long time. She is shockingly beautiful, and their agents will love getting their hands on her, if you get my meaning."

"I do indeed," Charlene said. She had been an active field agent or operative as they are called now and had seen the awful things done to captured spies. She shook old memories out of her mind and turned to Fong, "I want you transferred back to the Iran desk immediately. You will handle Tuck personally; whatever he needs. Give him a day to take care of things at home and then get him on a C-130 for Baghdad the day after tomorrow. I'll make arrangements with the Marines in the Green Zone to give him all of the assistance he asks for. Okay?"

"Ya, sure, but how are you going to keep this out of the hands of the White House lackeys who work here now? Somebody is bound to see the travel requests, vouchers for needed equipment, and encrypted phone, and, by the way, who would answer the messages that we can trust?" Tuck asked, his mind brimming with plans and doubts.

"Easy, Tuck. Give us a little credit, will ya? We know who our enemies are in the agency, but we also know of ways of working around 'em. Everything is going to go through Garrison. He's your contact. He will take care of all arrangements and get you the equipment you need.

"The plane will be carrying a load of replacement Marines; no one is going to notice you slip on, dressed as an officer on last minute assignment. Now get out of here and say good bye to Dorri. She'll hate me," the director said.

She got up, smiled the smile of an old, dear friend and gave Tuck a great bear hug and kiss on the cheek. "Be careful my friend," she said and turned away to hide the tears. Tuck did the same.

To keep things as normal as possible, Garrison remained at the Far East desk. He made special arrangements with a friend in the vast communications facility to have all of Tuck's messages sent directly to him, bypassing all normal administrative people.

In an hour, Tuck was ready to leave. He grabbed Fong again and said, "My life couldn't be in better hands, Garrison." Again the bear hug and the look in the eye of friends going into harm's way.

"Be safe, you big galoot. By the way, what is the name of your operative in the palace? When you get there, tell her to contact me and only me."

"Sure thing, her name is Summer Montabon. Found her at a pro-Iranian rally at Princeton. She's terrific and wants to do everything she can to help her nation become free. Oh, didn't I say, she's fifth generation Iranian. Her code name is Angel. Take care of her, my friend. She's a jewel."

"You've got it. I'll watch her back and yours. Now get out of here before I throw you out; and tie your shoe will ya?"

"Ha ha, yes, mother," he laughed as he ducked the eraser Fong threw at him.

When he was gone, Fong kind of wished he believed in some god. He didn't have a particular one that was more important than the others. If he did worship one, he would send up a prayer for his friend right now.

Chapter Six

It was a hot and dusty afternoon in Del Rio, Texas. The azure sky was tinted light beige near the horizon as dust, stirred by the westerly winds, moved across the landscape.

The city sat on Highway 277 not far from the Amistad Reservoir, which made it a destination city for tourists heading for the water.

South of Del Rio, just across the Rio Grande, was the sleepy Mexican town of Ciudad Acuna. Both cities had a population of good, hard working people, who just wanted to live their lives in peace and some happiness.

Unfortunately, international drug cartels had decided that these neighborhoods were perfect staging areas for moving cocaine shipments and illegal immigrants intent on entering the United States. They were carefully hidden in trucks which took them up Highway 277 to San Angelo, then on to destinations scattered over the north and eastern parts of the United States.

In the outskirts of this southern Texas town, a little church stood vigil as best it could next to a city park known for being a gathering place for young gang members wanting to get high on booze or drugs. The town's oldest and ugliest prostitutes hung out there as well, hoping for some business from kids bombed out of their minds.

It was a filthy place with beer cans and needles littering most of the area around bushes. The park employees had long ago given up trying to keep the place drug-free and clean so kids could play without fear. The park was the hangout of several rival gangs. Nights were often times of trouble, filled with fights and shouts of profanity, mixed with the spilling of blood. Several murders had taken place there within the last few years, and the kids were becoming bolder and more violent by the week. These same young people loved harassing the people who came to the church to worship, hurling insults and profanity at them whenever they were in the neighborhood.

The Jesus Chapel was small, seating about 100 souls, made of adobe and second hand lumber. Its part-time pastor took over a crumbling structure and built it into this church, with sweat, hard work, and determination. The pastor's name was Gabriel Townsend, and he was one of God's unsung heroes.

During the week, Gabby, as his friends called him, worked at a huge truck stop, pumping diesel and cleaning windshields for hundreds of eighteen wheelers a day. Gabby was a huge man, standing over 6'2'' and tipping the scales at a robust 276 pounds. He was nearly bald and his sandy hair was nearly the color of the dust in the air.

The really striking thing about this great bear of a man was his face, particularly his sparkling, emerald colored eyes. They were penetrating but kind and sympathetic. Coupled with his ready smile, a stranger was immediately at ease and comfortable with him. In a discussion, they would soon hear about his friend, Jesus.

On Sunday morning, Wednesday evening, and several nights a week, he preached a simple but riveting sermon from his well-worn study Bible or taught a Bible class to a few faithful souls, with the preparation and passion that would be necessary to teach thousands. He visited members of his little congregation in the hospital during his lunch hour or after work. Gabby spent many nights in hospital rooms so his friends would not be alone.

His wife, Evelyn, was just as faithful as he. She also visited the sick and taught a class for women at the church. Gabby nicknamed her "Eve" saying she was just as beautiful as the one in the Garden of Eden.

One thing the gangs of young toughs had learned was not to harass the people coming to the church when Gabby was there, as he became as dangerous as a mother bear protecting her cubs. Many a gang member had limped home with an aching head after a confrontation with Gabby protecting his flock.

Gabby and Evelyn were known and loved by the people in this part of the city. His hearty laugh and bear-like hugs were legendary, and their visits to the sick and lonely, many of whom were not members of his congregation made folks love them.

On this hot afternoon, Gabby had just finished at the truck stop and came to the church to try and coax some grass to grow in the Texas drought. He couldn't sprinkle very much water because neither he nor the church could afford to pay a high water bill to the city.

As he worked with his back to the park, a bunch of punks, high on coke and wanting to do him damage began creeping up behind him. They were bleary-eyed but organized. One creep had an old laundry bag. Two others were assigned the daunting task of grabbing his arms, while the rest had sticks and rocks ready to beat him to death.

They rushed him; the stumblebum managed to get the bag over Gabby's head as he roared his rage and tried to protect himself. The two twerps trying to pin his arms were swung around like rag dolls.

The gang started clubbing him without much success as he swung his great arms in circles, dispensing pain to anyone they hit. A board smashed down on his head, stunning him and bringing him to his knees. Another blow to the head and one to his kidneys nearly killed him.

In the darkness of the sack, Gabriel Townsend prepared to meet his death, praying loudly for God to protect Eve, and for him to forgive his attackers. Then he blacked out.

In a few minutes Gabby regained consciousness and found that he was free and the bag had been taken off of his head. He looked around, preparing to fend off another attack, but the gang was gone. He found a man kneeling by him trying to stop the bleeding of some of his wounds. The big bear tried to get up but fell back to the ground, his head aching badly, and the pain in his back was horrendous.

"Easy friend, easy. Just rest there awhile. You've had a bad time, and I need to get you to a doctor," the man said, smiling down at him with a smile that seemed to make the area brighter.

Gabby glanced at him and found that he seemed to be a man in his middle thirties, average height, wearing his shoulder length dark hair in a queue tied at the back of his head. He had a well-trimmed beard and was wearing a sparkling white shirt and tan slacks. His dark eyes seemed to look deep inside a person, which Gabriel found to be just a little disconcerting.

Gabby was also startled to see that the stranger was wearing well-worn brown leather sandals tied above the ankles. What stood out in Gabby's mind was the fact that, when the man reached down to put some water on his wounds, he could see nasty scars on his wrists.

"Hey man, I really do thank you for saving my life. Those scars say you're no stranger to battles with creeps. If you hadn't come along when you did, I'd be pushing up daisies in the cemetery," Gabriel said with tears beginning to moisten his eyes.

"Abisha," the stranger said, still smiling.

"What?" Gabby asked.

"Abisha, My name is Abisha Davidson. In Hebrew it means God's Gift. Pretty neat, don't you think?"

"Yeah, that is neat. Abisha, I like it. You said Hebrew. I didn't know there were Jewish folks living around here," Gabby said while struggling to his feet. His head was pounding, and he thought he might have a concussion.

"I'm half Jewish, on my mother's side of the family. I don't live around here. I came here to see you."

"Me? Why in the world would you want to see me?" Gabby asked. He motioned Abisha to follow him inside the church. He needed to sit down as the beating was beginning

35

to make him sick to his stomach. They went into his little study, and he collapsed in his chair behind his second-hand desk.

"Have a seat, Abisha. I just need to sit here awhile. I'm not feeling too well."

"I've no doubt but that's true. Here, let me help you a little." He went into the little bathroom, got some wet paper towels and put them on Gabby's forehead. His hands were cool and comforting. To his amazement, his head began to feel better almost immediately. "Lean forwards a little, and I'll massage your lower back. You took a wicked blow to your kidneys."

Gabby did as he was told. Abisha began to gently knead his back. In just a moment, the preacher did not feel any pain. "Boy, Abisha, you sure do know how to work on backs. I don't feel any pain at all. It's almost as if I wasn't in a fight at all," he said in amazement.

"Thanks for the compliment. I've been into healing for many years."

Gabby got up and stretched, then turned his upper body from side to side. Nothing. He was, indeed, healed. The pains in his head and back were gone. He felt so good, he danced a little jig right there in the office and shouted, "Praise the Lord! Thank you, Abisha!"

Abisha laughed, and Gabby joined in. They roared together, pounding each other on the back as men will do. Gabby stopped laughing and became serious. "Hey, how did you stop the beating and get those druggies to take off all by yourself?"

Abisha smiled again, and said, "Let's just say they became confused and started hitting each other. Then they slipped and fell on the wet grass. After a moment, they kind of jumped up and ran away, probably to ponder the evil they had committed and resolve never to do that again. They just needed a little encouragement."

"Well, I'll be doggone if that isn't the strangest story I've ever heard. Anyway, I'm grateful you happened to come by when you did. Thanks again."

"My friend, I didn't just happen by. I was coming to meet you and discuss something very important. Do you have a moment?" Abisha's dark eyes seemed to bore into Gabby's inner being.

"Do I have time? Why, I'm like Lazarus, I've been raised from the dead. Of course, I have time. You want some ice tea?"

"Yes, thank you, that would be very nice," Abisha said.

In a moment, Gabby had two glasses of cold ice tea on the desk. He was perspiring from the exertion of the fight and the fact that the church air conditioner wasn't working. He noticed that Abisha seemed very comfortable in the heat. "Man, this heat is something, isn't it?"

"I am accustomed to warm weather," Abisha commented, then became serious again. "Gabriel, you know how much your Heavenly Father loves you, don't you?"

"I surely do, and that's a fact," Gabby answered proudly, grinning from ear to ear.

"Your Father in Heaven has long watched your struggle to keep this church open and serving its congregation. He knows how you have been discouraged at times, but you kept on working without complaint. Because of your faithfulness, he has a big job for you to do for him. He has chosen you to become one of the last great evangelists of the age. You are going to preach the gospel all over America and the world.

"Your message will be one of the world's last hopes for redemption before God begins the events described in the Book of Revelation. Are you willing to be used by the Father?"

Their eyes locked as they looked at each other. In a moment, Gabriel gathered his wits about him and said, "My friend, I'm not an evangelist. I'm the pastor of a little church that has maybe a hundred souls on a good Sunday. I'm stunned that God would entrust such a responsibility to me. Of course, I will do what he asks, but I'm sure going to need a lot of help," Gabby said. Now there were tears in both of their eyes.

"You will receive all the help you will need. The ruler of this world will try to harm you and Evelyn, but there will always be warrior angels nearby watching over you. You are going to be a centerpiece of the greatest world events of the age."

"I don't know what to say. I feel like I've been kicked in the stomach. Preaching about the last days of earth is breath taking, and I'm no expert. But, I'll do the best I can with God's help. I am honored to be chosen. Wait a minute. You said that God sent you to talk to me. Are you going to be in on this with me? Are you an important person in God's kingdom?"

Just then, he saw the great wounds on Abisha's wrists. "Hey, hold the phone a minute. Those scars on your wrists… are you who I think you might be?"

"Gabriel, I am known by a number of names. The important thing for you to know is that our Father chose you because he knows your character and humility. Now, let's get down to business. We're going to start small then rapidly expand the ministry.

"You need to get to studying the scriptures. Remember to keep the gospel simple so everyone can understand. I'll check back with you from time to time. I'm glad you're on our team," he smiled, turned and sauntered out of the church.

Gabby sat thinking for a few minutes, then he grabbed the phone and started calling members and his wife. Boy, the story he had to tell her.

Chapter Seven

Rabbi Samuel Bernardi was walking toward the port in the lovely city of Haifa, on the coast of the Mediterranean Sea. He loved this ancient city, which has been inhabited since the Bronze Age, around 1500 B.C., when only a few hundred hardy souls lived here as fishermen. On this day, as Bernardi approached the port, the metropolitan area of Haifa boasted a million people.

Part of the city included sections of Mount Carmel, made famous by the many references to the area in the Old Testament. One of the most memorable was the confrontation between Elijah and the false prophets of Baal in the ninth century B.C., as recorded in the eighteenth chapter of First Kings. Elijah's cave was traditionally believed to be on the northwest side of Mount Carmel.

The rabbi was a member of a very religious party in Israel, the Saredim who traced their group's history back to the time of Elijah. He was also a member of a super-secret society dedicated to work toward the coming of the Messiah. He was 60 years of age, and most of his hair was gray.

Bernardi was a slender man with a permanent stoop in his back from a lifetime of studying the Torah, along with other scripture and historical writings. His watery eyes were losing their ability to see clearly, so he had finally given in to wearing wire-rim glasses. He wore the traditional black clothing and was intent on the special duty he had to perform that evening.

A small freighter was anchored off shore waiting for a place to tie up at the docks. Bernardi had no interest in the main cargo aboard this ship, only a small portion. It was his mission to see that the red heifers on board were transported from the dock to a secret location southeast of the city.

A young proselyte named Jonas followed his rabbi closely trying not to get in the way, but anxious to learn what this strange visit to the docks had to do with them. They went to a little café to drink some coffee and pass the time until the ship could dock and unload cargo. A truck would meet them in an hour.

"Rabbi, what is the cargo that is so important, and why do we have to be here to escort it someplace?" Jonas asked while blowing on the hot brew.

"Patience, my young friend. All in good time but not here in this place. Evil men may be lurking here and listening to what we say. We must be careful. Much depends on our success tonight," the rabbi whispered while casually scanning the few men in the room.

In an hour, it was dark, and the ship was alongside the dock already unloading cargo. The truck that had been rented was there. Jonas was surprised to see it was a cattle truck used to move live animals. Its ramps were down and the door opened ready to receive its load. A makeshift pen had been constructed on the dock behind the truck. Jonas could see they were already unloading cattle from the hold by the use of a sling to lift the animals.

One at a time, the frightened creatures were lifted up amid a chorus of bawling and mournful mooing. When they touched the dock, men herded them carefully into the truck. There were no cattle prods or clubs used. The cattle were treated with extreme care.

Finally, the signal was given that the last animal was on the way. Soon the red cow was in the air heading for the wooden dock. But this animal did not struggle or bawl with fright. Her ears were forward; her head was high as she looked with interest where she was being taken. When she reached the dock and the sling was loosened, she walked proudly around the pen looking closely at each man there.

One man stepped into the pen and swatted her on her hind quarters to get her moving toward the truck. It was a bad mistake. Her back leg nearest the man lashed out with a wicked kick that caught the surprised handler just above the left knee. He went down like a sack of sand, grabbing his leg and crying out in pain. The animal looked at him for a moment as if she were trying to decide if she wanted to charge him, but she snorted and walked casually toward the truck.

Now, nearly two years old, Alice had become something special. She was utterly fearless of humans, often eyeing them in disdain. She permitted them to brush her, bring her wonderful tasting grain, and give her clean straw for her bed. She disliked getting dirty and would snort and stamp her front feet if the pen needed cleaning. It was obvious that she was now the boss cow, always eating first and demanding her special spot to rest. Her very demeanor said that she was special, a queen of her kind. She walked up the ramp into the truck without fear and disappeared inside.

The ramp was moved, and the door to the trailer closed and locked. In a few minutes the truck was weaving through the heavy Haifa traffic, unconcerned about the world events beginning to take place that would change history for all time.

Rabbi Bernardi hustled Jonas along the street until they arrived at his beat-up old Volvo parked near the corner. He was like most religious-minded men; he rarely thought about maintenance for a vehicle unless it wouldn't run.

He pulled into traffic, causing a lot of angry horn honking, and got behind the cattle truck. As they were motoring along, Jonas asked, "Rabbi, why is that load of cattle so important? Who cares about a bunch of cows?"

"They are not just a herd of cows, they are very rare animals and must receive very special care until they reach their third year. In your studies in the Torah and the Mishnah, have you come across the 'Parah Adumah?'" the old man asked.

Jonas wrinkled his nose as if that would help him remember. "If I have, I'm afraid I don't remember. Why, is it important?" he asked while holding on to the door handle of the car. The rabbi's driving was causing him real concern.

"Parah Adumah is known as the 'red heifer sacrifice.' The animal had to be perfect in color, red, with no other color or blemish. It could never have been used as a work animal in any phase of its life. The ritual's purpose was to purify people from the defilement caused by contact with the dead. You can read about it in Numbers, chapter 19. It is a great mystery; even the ancient ones did not completely understand its purpose.

Some believe that when a perfect red heifer is is prepared for sacrifice on the Mount of Olives, our Messiah will appear to accomplish the sacrifice," the rabbi said as he cut in front of a car entering the highway, unleashing a new cacophony of horn honking and shouted obscenities.

Jonas looked at his mentor and asked, "Do you believe in this stuff?"

"Yes, my son, I most certainly do. We have purchased perfect red heifers from around the world and brought them to our little farm to care for them until one is chosen. Oh, dear Lord; to gaze upon our Messiah. Israel will be saved from our enemies, and we will become God's people once again."

"Most of the kids I know don't believe in rituals or the Torah. Other guys think it is important to observe the special days, if it's not inconvenient for them," Jonas mused.

"Yes, my son, Israel is far from being a holy nation. Our ancient religious beliefs are followed by few and scorned by many. Ahh, but when the Messiah comes to us, things will be different. I intend to help hurry his return," he said as tears began to flow into his beard.

They arrived at the secret farm. No one could be seen in the area. The cattle were quickly unloaded and herded inside the barn. The one known as "Alice" was first into the building as she considered being first her right. A quick inspection of the barn was done; then they all discovered the grain and hay and began feasting.

Rabbi Bernardi bowed his head and clasped his hands and began to pray quietly. Soon his body was rocking in the familiar manner used by the Orthodox in prayer. Jonas followed his mentor's lead and was soon praying with emotion. Both of the men began thanking God that the time for the Messiah's arrival in Israel was drawing ever closer. He began to weep with joy at the thought of world events that were leading up to the nation of Israel becoming holy once more. Jonas watched him out of the corner of his eye. Public displays made him uncomfortable. He heard a loud "sniff" and turned to see one of the red heifers standing on the other side of the fence watching them. She stood there for a moment and then sauntered casually away.

Chapter Eight

Hiram Meier, the Prime Minister of Israel, hated the secrecy he had to go through to meet with his Director of the Mossad, the famous foreign intelligence gathering arm. Abram Weiss kept trying to impress the prime minister that care was necessary because he was on the hit list of all Palestinian military and intelligence services, as well as the services of almost every Arab nation in the world. Meier would receive a one word message on a slip of paper put in the stack of mail on his desk every morning. He was consumed with trying to find out who put the paper note in his stuff. He was never able to find a single lead, even though he would sneak around the office when he worked late nights and into early morning hours. The note was always there.

This morning's note said "railcar". He knew this meant an abandoned box car on a siding outside of Jerusalem. Weiss would be there before him, and he had to leave his contingent of security agents behind and walk to the railcar. Now he knew why spies were called "spooks," because of their penchant for meeting in spooky places and always at night.

As he trudged along the tracks he heard a sound in an old shed he was passing. The hair stood up on the back of his neck and he picked up the pace. He consoled himself with the thought that it was probably a stray cat after a rat. In a minute he was at the freight car. It took all of his strength to slide the door open enough for him to squeeze inside.

It was completely black. Suddenly, a flash light came on, shinning its beam directly in his face. It startled him, and he stumbled backwards, cursing and making a pitiful attempt to defend himself from the attack that surely was about to engulf him.

"Sorry, Hiram. Take it easy, will you? God, you're so jumpy! I didn't mean to startle you. Come over here and sit down. Do you want some brandy?" The voice belonged to

Abram Weiss. The prime minister knew the spymaster was enjoying himself.

"For heavens sake, Abram, what are you trying to do, give me a heart attack? Did you have to have this clandestine meeting in a rail car in the middle of the night?" Hiram asked disgustedly.

"Be careful how you berate me. Remember, from your lips to God's ear," Abram chuckled.

"What do you know about God? You're a secular minded heathen. You wouldn't recognize God if he punched you in the nose," Meier's attempt at levity fell flat. He found a chair beside a small wooden table that contained some papers and a bottle of brandy with two glasses. An old fashioned kerosene lantern provided the only light, which made the car seem even more sinister.

"Now Abram, I'm in no mood for your games of hide and seek. What news do you have for me?"

"I can tell you that our agents in Iran are positive that Hafez is enriching uranium as fast as he can. They believe he will have a bomb in about six months. The Russians are denying they are helping with the technical aspects of building a nuclear bomb, but don't believe it. They are up to their necks in the research."

"How much time do you think we have?" Meier asked.

"Six months at the outside. We were fortunate enough to get our hands on one of the scientists working in their secret underground lab in the eastern dessert. I think they call it Pudein Mountain.

"Anyway, we were able to 'encourage' the lucky young man to tell us everything he knew. Unfortunately, he did not survive the interview, but we have new intel which leads us to the six month time frame," Weiss said as he poured brandy in the glasses.

"Our military people are not giving us much encouragement. If we send planes to bomb Hafez's secret installations, our planes cannot make the round trip without

45

refueling somewhere either outbound or inbound. We know Syria, Iraq, and Jordan are not going to allow this to take place in their air space.

A year ago we might have been able to fly out over the Mediterranean and then avoid our neighbors by flying over Turkey, but the political winds have all changed. Turkey has advised us they will fire missiles at any war plane flying in their air space. All of these people secretly wish we could be successful and stop the nuclear rush to war, but they all fear angering the entire Arab world if they help us. So, as usual, we must go it alone.

"We can expect no help from America. President Steinmetz has already advised me that all aid will stop immediately, except for a stipend of a few million," the prime minister spoke as if he were making a speech to the Knesset.

"Mr. Prime Minister, it sounds like we have two options. We send the planes and bombs on a suicide mission which may or may not be successful, or we send our own missiles with nuclear warheads first and try to beat them to the punch," Weiss said.

"What's this, the head of the dreaded Mossad giving away state secrets? What makes you think we have nuclear weapons?" he smiled as he sipped his brandy.

Weiss became quiet. After a few minutes of sipping his brandy, he looked up and stared into the eyes of his boss and his friend.

"Hiram, I'm at a loss for an answer that would help us. If we use nuclear weapons, the radiation fallout might cover several counties. The United States and the United Nations would go absolutely berserk and might even attack us. If we don't use the weapons we have, we will be attacked and our cities will be covered in radiation; millions of our people will be killed outright and more will die later from radiation sickness, if they use the bomb, that is. They could elect to use the threat of the bomb to make us careless in defending against a land invasion."

"What about a clandestine operation by the Mossad going into Tehran right away and attempting to assassinate Hafez? With him gone, perhaps the moderates in the country will take it back from the Mullah's," Meier said hopefully.

"Hmm, possibly, but the odds are against such open rebellion. The Revolutionary Guard is too strong and well organized. We have helped to start a few demonstrations of young people in the last few months, but these are quickly stamped out. It's well-known that any student who's arrested in a demonstration against the government, disappears forever," the leader of the Mossad said sadly.

They were both quiet for a few minutes, each knowing what the other was thinking. "It's just like 1949 all over again. Jews came to the homeland hated and alone. No one would help us. The Arabs attacked and tried to drive us into the sea, but we prevailed against all odds and won the war. We'll just have to do it again," Hiram said without conviction.

"Remember, old friend, we had God on our side then. Our people believed in him and prayed to him and he came to our rescue time after time. But now, most of our people do not believe in God. They only believe in money. He may be about to punish us like he did so many times in the past when we turned against him," Abram said as he poured himself another shot of brandy.

"Well now, Abram, when did you get so religious? You're a spy master and send people all over the world to kill our enemies. Are you going to start praying and hope that God forgets what you do for a living?" Meier chided his friend.

"No, I am not a religious man. But I am smart enough to know that we are facing the fight of our nation's life, and it might be a good idea to "have all of our bases covered," to quote the Americans."

"Okay, enough crying in our brandy. You keep getting us the latest intelligence and probe around to find a weakness in their defense that we might be able to use. Grab as many of their lead engineers as you can; see if you can get men into the secret installations and blow them up. Start some more demonstrations. Do anything you can do to slow this process down.

In the meantime, I'll light a fire under the military and get them planning for an invasion from the air, land and sea. You're right, this will be the fight of our nation's life," Meier said, getting up to leave. There was much to do, and time was running out.

"Hiram, have you ever read a Christian Bible?" Weiss asked as he stared at his old friend.

"No, why would I want to commit such an affront to God?" he asked.

"Well, if you get a chance, I would recommend you read one, particularly the last book; it's called Revelation. It contains a prophecy of what we will soon be facing. Hiram… We lose! In chapter seven it states that only 12,000 from each of the 12 tribes of Israel, 144,000, will receive God's seal and survive this coming attack on Jerusalem and our nation. They are the lucky ones. You don't want to know what happens to the rest of us."

The Prime Minster stared at the head of the most feared intelligence agency in the world. He turned and walked away into the darkness without saying a word.

Chapter Nine

Aristotle Tucker, spy, operative, brilliant organizer of spy cells in Tehran, stumbled out of the C-130 Air Force transport plane as it came to a stop at the big base just inside of the Green Zone in Baghdad, Iraq. The 18 hour trip was exhausting, and he felt tired, dirty and not just a little bit grouchy. He was dressed in his "poor street bum" clothing and had already started growing the requisite beard that every man is required to have by the ruling Mullahs.

His plane was met by a young, pimply faced marine, who saluted smartly and asked, "Are you Mr. Tucker, sir?"

"I am, son, and you don't need to salute me. It draws too much attention."

"Yes sir, if you'll come with me, I'll take you to the camp commander, Colonel George Jessup, for your briefing."

"Lead on, son, lead on. Are we riding in this old Toyota pickup?" Tuck asked.

"Yes sir; it attracts less attention from the bad guys."

The ride to the base commander's tent took a full five minutes. The base was like a living organism; vehicles, men, airplanes, and helicopters were all moving at the same time going somewhere on the huge, sprawling military conclave.

The young marine brought the pickup to a gut-wrenching, sliding stop in front of a large tent with men coming and going like mice that had found a wedge of cheese. Inside Tuck was given directions to "park it here until the Colonel has time to see you." Tuck noticed that the men in uniform gave him some pretty unfriendly glances. He decided it was probably the robes that made them nervous.

In fifteen minutes, a corporal motioned him to follow. So Tuck shuffled along, with the right shoe lace untied, to the private room in the tent where Colonel Jessup conducted his part of the war. Tuck was ushered inside where he stood waiting as the colonel finished some paper work. This spy had worked with the Marines many times in the past and knew he was kept waiting to show who was boss.

Finally, Jessup looked up over half glasses and eyed the rather grungy looking man standing before him. Jessup was all marine. He had short, crew cut hair, and a tan, handsome face with deep worry lines on his forehead and a lantern jaw that oozed authority. His gray eyes were alert, missing nothing. His chest had rows of medals on the left side of his uniform shirt. He had been a fighting marine for twenty years and had seen everything war could do to men.

"Well, Mr. Tucker, it seems you need a ride to the Iranian border. Some hotshot bureaucrat in Washington has nothing better to do than send you over here and risk my men's lives getting you into Iran so you can do a little spying?" he asked, his voice hard and condescending.

"No sir. The agency wants me to get in the country to try and learn as much as I can about their missiles," he said, telling only a half truth. He had learned the hard way not to divulge more of his mission than absolutely necessary. History has shown that spies get killed because soldiers giving them a ride talk too much.

"Well, Mr. Tucker, I don't like risking my men's lives to take you into Iran, but orders are orders. I'm giving you four men with black ops experience who know how to kill quickly and silently. One of them is the best sniper on base. Where do you want to go?"

"I need them to get me as close to Ahvaz as possible. I've arranged for transport from there to Tehran," Tuck said.

The colonel stood up and came around the desk. This was obviously the time for the requisite face down with a fighting marine. Too bad Tuck wasn't impressed. Both men were about the same height and each stared into the eyes of the other for a long moment. Then Jessup said, "I'm told you are a pretty tough character and have been in Iran several times and were nearly killed every time you went in. This assignment must be pretty important to get you to go back in," he said.

"Well, sir, the world is getting pretty unpleasant. Hafez is enriching uranium as we speak. He may be able to have a bomb in a few months. But does he have the platforms to deliver one? My job is to find out if he has."

"Okay, Mr. Agency man. You leave at dusk. Get some rest. I'll have your driver take you to a tent where you can sleep. My men will contact you when it's time to go."

Then, surprisingly, he stuck out his right hand. His lipless smile looked like a gash across his face. Tuck was surprised and gratefully shook hands. The colonel went back to his desk and the work piled there. "Good luck, spy man."

"Thank you, sir. I'm going to need a lot more than luck." He walked out of the tent and pimple face was waiting for him by the truck. In a few minutes driving at break neck speed, they arrived at a row of tents. Skidding to a stop, the boy pointed to the nearest one and said, "That's it, sir."

Tuck was grateful to get out of the truck. He grabbed his bundle of gear and went inside. The tent was empty. He found a bunk that was not made, plopped down on the springs and was instantly asleep.

Three hours later someone quietly slipped in under the tent flap and silently approached the sleeping agent. A hand reached out from the shadow and rested on Tuck's shoulder. Tuck exploded in deadly action, grabbing the hand and twisting it away to the side while his other hand grabbed his Browning 9MM automatic with silencer and jammed it under the chin of whoever it was that touched him.

"Hey, take it easy sir," a voice shouted. "I'm a friendly. It's time to leave for the land of the bogey man."

"You stupid idiot," Tuck hissed through clenched teeth. "I could have killed you and that would have messed up my mission. I may just go ahead and kill you anyhow. What are you doing grabbing someone when they're asleep? Haven't you got any manners?"

Tuck was calming down, but he was perspiring from the heat in the tent and how close he had just been to killing one of America's best.

"Sorry, sir, I didn't know you would be so jumpy. I thought you were some stupid desk jockey sent over here to improve his resumé. That's who we usually get to risk our lives for, jerks who push pencils. By your reaction, I'm guessing that you've been across the line before and maybe sent an Arab or two to see Allah. My name is Timothy Waldron. My unit has been assigned to get you across the border to Ahvaz. We'll get you that far, and then you're on your own."

"Okay, Sergeant, I guess I'm in your hands, which doesn't make me feel very secure at the moment. By the way, they're Persians, not Arabs."

"What?"

"Iranians. They're descendants of the ancient Persians. They were once the most powerful nation on earth. I think Hafez wants to be the most powerful on earth again, and he doesn't care how many people he has to kill to achieve his goal," Tuck explained.

"Whatever! My job is to kill 'em. I don't give a tinker's damn about their history. Grab your gear, sir; the other guys are in a truck, and we're ready to go."

Tuck grabbed his bag and followed the tough young sergeant out of the tent where an old beat up Toyota pickup stood waiting. "Why are we taking a pickup and not a Humvee?" he asked.

"Pickup draws less attention. Hop inside and hold on. We have to make time." He wasn't kidding. The truck boiled out of the base, past a check point where Waldron made a guard dive for cover. He loved doing that!

In two hours, they were deep in the desert country when Waldron pulled the pickup over to the side of the road to read a map. He studied it for a few minutes and then pulled back onto the highway.

In a few minutes, a pile of rocks on the east side of the road indicated to him to swing off the road and hit the desert camel trails. The lights were turned off, but he kept the speed high, bouncing all of the passengers around like tennis balls. The guys in the back had a hard time staying in the truck.

They came to a little wadi, paused a moment and then roared across leaving twin rooster tails of sand in the air behind the truck. "Okay, sir, you're in Iran. We have about five miles of desert to cover to get you to that god forsaken Ahvaz. You having someone meeting you there?" he asked casually.

Tuck did not answer. He knew a number of agents who had been killed because a driver got careless and talked too much. "I'll be alright. I've been here before. When we're a mile out let me out, and I'll walk the rest of the way. Don't want to wake up any Revolutionary Guards," Tuck said. He would be happy to get out of the truck. The sergeant was driving way too fast and hitting the bumps at this speed jarred his bad back and rattled his teeth.

"We'll ride a little more, then we all walk. My orders are to see you safely to Ahvaz and try to get back alive," Sgt. Waldron said.

"You seem to know this area pretty well. You been here before?" Tuck asked.

"Yeah, we've brought in a couple of spooks. Can't imagine why they want to go to this dump. There's nothing there but a couple of little houses and a big sheep pen."

"I like to come here because the Revolutionary Guards who are assigned here are a bunch of thugs, and they're pretty stupid. It is really more of a jail sentence to them. Most of them have screwed up in Tehran and are put here for punishment. If I get caught, I might have a chance to bribe 'em into letting me go," Tuck said without much conviction in his voice.

"Your bribe and your Aunt Mattie's dollar will buy you some coffee. I've seen the bodies of people these guards didn't like. They're into torture and mutilation, big time. My advice to you, Mr. Spook, is to forget about the bribe; kill 'em," the Sergeant said while slamming on the brakes which raised a dust cloud that Tuck thought would be seen for miles. The full moon was making the desert nearly as bright as day.

"All right, you hog killers, pile out and get moving. From now on, no talking; we use hand signals. Stay off the trail, probably mined."

The four Marines split up, two on each side of the trail. Tuck followed behind the young Sergeant. The black clothing the men had was perfect camouflage. They were shadows moving over the sand and around the scrub brush. Their movement startled little desert creatures who scuttled out of harm's way, then went back to trying to eat one another.

In half an hour, they stopped at a dried up wadi to rest. Waldron came back to where Tuck was crouched down on one knee. "We should be in that flea-bitten village in another half an hour," he said. "You got someone waiting to move you out?"

"Don't worry, I'll be okay," Tuck mumbled.

The sergeant's feelings were hurt by Tuck being so quiet about his mission. "Okay, spook, have it your way," he said as he got up and signaled the men to move out.

They were a few miles into Iran when they suddenly heard someone coming down the trail. He was talking to himself in Farsi. Tuck spoke Farsi better than he did English, and he heard the man complaining about having to come out here on patrol. He'd been drinking and wanted to lie down and sleep.

The marines waited in silence, now just spots of darkness on the desert sands. When the soldier arrived at their hiding spot, fate played a deadly trick on him. If he had continued down the trail, the marines would have let him pass. But he stopped for some reason. Then he saw that the dark shape was a man.

He started to shout an alarm and bring his AK 47 off his shoulder. A knife ripped his throat out before he could utter a word. They held him down so his death throes would not be heard by anyone nearby. In minutes the silent killers had dug a shallow grave, buried the soldier, and covered the spot with shrubs and rocks.

The young sergeant motioned for the men to move out in a fast trot. The Revolutionary Guard soldier had cost them time that they had to make up.

In a few minutes the shadow of buildings loomed up out of the darkness. There were lights in a couple of windows, otherwise the village was dark. Waldron came back to where Tuck was standing. "This is where we leave ya, spook. Have a safe trip. Give us a call when you need a ride out of this desolation."

"Thanks, sarge. I know you guys have risked your lives for me, and I appreciate it. If my mission is successful, we may avoid another war," he said as he smiled and shook hands with his bodyguard. Waldron smiled and gave the signal for the men to return the way they had come.

"About twenty yards away, he turned and waved at Tuck. He had begun to admire the agent. He wasn't sure he would have wanted to get into the country by himself; too dangerous. Then he trotted off towards the west.

Tuck moved toward the village carrying his colorful tote bag that had all of his belongings, including some super secret stuff from the CIA. In the dark he looked very much like a Bedouin camel driver without the camel. The first shed he came to was full of sheep, which were upset by his arrival. Their braying would bring the shepherd if he couldn't shut them up.

He moved into the shed, sat down, and remained perfectly still. The sheep watched him carefully, ears pointed at him. They were ready to bolt if he moved.

In a minute, they began to lose interest and settle down on the other side of the pen. Tuck removed his special cell phone slowly and sent an encrypted message to a satellite hovering somewhere in space above him. Then he settled down to take a nap. It would take his ride about forty-five minutes to get here. He was a light sleeper and the sheep had grown quiet, so he felt safe enough. Right on time, a man moved out of the shadows and clicked on a little light. Tuck responded with the correct signal and joined the stranger as they jogged around the village and went down a road for half a mile. There, a truck sat waiting for them. Tuck dove into the back, and the driver kicked the engine over and the truck moved away. The truck bumped along the dirt road. Tuck was already asleep. In four hours, he would be in Tehran.

Chapter Ten

It was early morning in Del Rio, but it was already hot. Gabriel Townsend was already at the Jesus Chapel, puttering around the sanctuary. He was cleaning up here and there, but his mind was miles away; one might say a universe away. Tears were streaming down the big man's face. He was filled with anxiety and doubt, the result of a successful attack by demons determined to wreck Gabby's efforts to win souls for Christ. The attack had been so skillful that he failed to recognize that the spiritual war waged against him had begun.

Gabby fled to his office and grabbed his worn, note-filled Bible and turned to Psalm 91. He began reading aloud, furiously moving from verse to verse, while weeping even more. He shook his great head as if trying to clear cobwebs from his brain or scales from his eyes and began reading the psalm again, slowly, meditating on each verse. Now the weeping began to be tears of gratitude, not fear. Verses 9-11 jumped off the page into his love-filled heart.

"If you make the Most High your dwelling - even the Lord, who is my refuge - then no harm will befall you, no disaster will come near your tent. For he will command his angels concerning you to guard you in all your ways."

This big bear of a man let out an animalistic moan as the words from the scriptures sank into his being. Gabby fell to his knees to give thanks. In a few seconds, he sank to a prostrate position, with his face to the floor and began praising God. His fear and anxiety were gone. His mind was clear and working furiously, praying, praising and singing hymns to the Lord. He lost track of time and continued worshipping until nearly noon. He knew he would not be alone as he began his new ministry of evangelism. He read the Psalm again, taking note of the promise of verse 14, "Because he loves me,' says the Lord, "I will rescue him; I will protect him, for he acknowledges my name."

Suddenly, Gabby became alert. He heard something in the sanctuary. Maybe the gang of thugs was coming back in an attempt to finish the job. He was trying to get to his feet when the door opened, and Abisha walked into the room.

"Hello, Gabby, have I interrupted your prayer time?"

"No, I was just finishing. I read Psalm 91 a couple of times and it really gave me wonderful encouragement and the truth that God is going to protect me through the coming months."

"You are so very right, my friend. There will be difficult days but you will never be alone; never!" Abisha smiled at Gabby. His teeth were so white and perfect he would have been an excellent spokesman for a tooth paste company.

"What are you doing here, Abisha?"

"I'm here to work with you on your first assignment. You look tired; did you have trouble sleeping last night?" Abisha asked while standing with his hand on Gabby's shoulder

"You caught me. I prayed a lot about becoming the evangelist the Father wants me to be, but the truth is, I just don't know how to do the job. I'm a pastor, Bible teacher, and the shepherd for a flock of around 100 souls. I've never spoken before a crowd larger than my 100 members, except at Christmas when an extra 50 people show up." Gabby said, looking into Abisha's eyes. "I need someone to teach me what to say and how to say it."

Abisha tried to put an arm around the big man's shoulders, but they were too broad, so he settled for giving his friend a pat on the back.

"Gabby, just relax. You're acting as if the Father just gives an order then walks away, leaving you alone and helpless. He doesn't work that way. I am here to help you, and there will be more help from heaven if the need arises," Abisha said, trying to reassure him.

"Hey, that's great. I'm sorry about worrying, I should have known better."

"Okay then, let's get started. Everything will be simple for you; trust me. Tomorrow I want you to go to the flea market in Del Rio. In the very center of the outdoor market, you will find an old kitchen chair lying on its side. Stand on the chair and start preaching."

"What if no one comes to listen and …"

"Just keep preaching."

"How will I know the best thing to say if no one is listening?"

"A few people will be listening. The Holy Spirit is in you, Gabby, and he will give you the words when you open your mouth to speak. And, should anyone threaten you, I'll have a couple of friends in the audience that will come to your aid. So, fear not my friend, for tomorrow you start on a great journey. Remember, many lost souls are waiting for you to speak the truth so they can be rescued from lives of sin and death," Abisha said.

The enormity of the task set before Gabby made him drop to his knees. But this prayer was different. It was not from a frightened, small-time pastor. This prayer was from a warrior preparing for battle.

That night as he prepared for bed, Gabby prayed, "Holy Spirit, I'm trusting you to put the right words in my mouth tomorrow; I sure would appreciate your keeping the devil and his demons occupied somewhere else. Please show me what you want me to do. I'll see you first thing in the morning and we'll tackle this evangelism thing together. Amen."

Gabby spent time after he and Evelyn were in bed to tell her of the wonderful road God had asked him to follow and the challenges that lay before them.

"Sweetheart, I'm going to need your help and support more than ever before."

"Don't worry darling; I'll be at your side whenever you need me. I love you for agreeing to be used by the Lord. We'll face everything together, and God will be with us. This is going to be the most exciting part of our lives."

Gabby went to sleep with a smile on his face. He slept like a baby.

Early the next morning, Gabby arrived at the flea market. He trudged down the dusty streets of the old bazaar, and low and behold, right in the center of the square was an old kitchen chair lying on its side, just like Abisha had said. He set the chair upright and tried to hold it steady as he climbed up and tried to keep from tumbling back down to the ground.

Feeling almost secure, he glanced toward heaven and began preaching in a loud voice in this very strange environment. "Who wants to go to heaven? Anybody here want to go to heaven?"

The people around were gawking and trying to avoid this massive giant of a man perched atop the discarded old dinette kitchen chair. The old piece of dining room furniture was off balance and wobbled a bit every time Gabby waved his arms, which caught the attention of a few heathen young men who wondered if the preacher might fall from "grace" at any moment. They chuckled at their clever joke.

As Gabby continued to preach, two families stopped and stood in front of this flea market evangelist. He continued to speak as a few other souls gathered, forming a tiny congregation in the dusty square, while the sun dispatched blistering heat upon the scene.

The uninterested crowd of bargain seekers at the Del Rio flea market paid little attention to the big gringo standing on a chair in the middle of the street, probably considering him to be "loco." He struggled to force his first words. After all, why preach if they would not even listen to the gringo in their midst? But he shook his massive head, as if he needed to clear his thinking, and continued to preach from the book of John.

"My friends, this world is an evil place, and there are a lot of people around that want to hurt you and steal from you. But you don't have to face this world alone. The Bible says that God loves each of us with all of his heart. He loves you and me so much that he sent his own dear son to die a horrible death on a cross, to pay the penalty for the things we do that separate us from our Heavenly Father. These things are called sin, and we're all guilty; we're all sinners - you, and you, and you, and me.

"But God's son sacrificed his life and spilled his blood to pay the price for all sin. His name is Jesus, and if you trust him, and ask him into your heart, he will come in and live with you and call you his friend. You will never be alone again. If you believe in him, he promises that you will live with him in heaven forever. It will be beautiful there, no crime, no pain, no suffering, no disease, only beautiful things and beautiful people, people just like you. Won't you trust him and receive eternal life?"

Gabby stopped shouting. He wiped his forehead with his big, red bandana. "This was terrible," he thought out loud. "I've failed Jesus. No one heard me. Oh dear God, I've let you down. Can you ever forgive me?"

Yet he struggled on... "Yes, yes! It is true Jesus loves you, and he died for your sins!"

A tall, handsome, well-dressed gringo was whispering in the ears of some young thugs who had been lounging around, making fun of Gabby. The man gave three of the gang members packs of twenty dollar bills. They spread out among the crowd and started heckling people for listening to the preaching.

They were becoming a real nuisance, and some of the people were backing away from them, not wanting any trouble. Gabby noticed the troublemakers and was getting ready to push through the crowd and try to talk to them or grab them by the nape of the neck and throw them out, whichever came first.

Suddenly, two very big men with bronze faces, wearing bright white clothing made their way to the three jerks. They bent down and said something to each one, while placing a hand on their shoulders. The young men's faces changed from arrogance to fear, and they took off on a dead run to get away. Gabby wondered what the men had said that was so effective. He did not see the handsome gringo's face turn red with anger. He threw his Cuban cigar on the ground and plowed roughly through the crowd and left; his expensive alligator shoes brandishing 24 kt. gold chains were now covered with flea market dust.

Gabby stepped down from the chair not witnessing the flight of his adversary, but he did feel the jab from an elbow in the small of his back. The elbow belonged to Abisha! And despite the brief wincing pain, Gabby was overjoyed.

"Abisha, what are you doing here? I'm glad to see you, I was about to give up," moaned the big preacher.

"Gabby, it's time for the next step to transform you into a powerful witness for the Kingdom," said Abisha. "Do you see that young boy standing there by his mom?"

"Which one? You don't happen to mean the one with the withered and deformed arm do you Abisha?" Gabby asked reluctantly.

"Yes, that's the boy," Abisha responded, "I want you to go over there and put your hand on him."

"You do?" Gabby exclaimed, his heart beginning to pound with doubt. "You mean you want me…to do that?"

"Yes, Gabby, I want you to go to him and put your hand on the boy's throat and speak these words…Boy, in the name of Jesus Christ say 'Mama'."

"Say what?" the preacher questioned. "Why would I say that?"

"Just do it, my friend. Have faith and pray."

Gabriel Townsend was so overwhelmed with the moving of the Spirit in his heart that he would have tried anything Abisha said at that moment. He walked over to the boy, reached out, and put his hand on the boy's throat. He spoke loudly, "Boy, in the name of Jesus Christ say 'Mama'!"

The boy was startled and a little frightened, but he started repeating over and over, "Mama…Mama…Mama."

As the boy spoke, his mother dropped to her knees, sobbing uncontrollably. Her modest blue dress and delicately woven white lace collar testified to her poverty. The little boy ran to his mother and put his only good hand gently on her shoulder repeating over and over, "Mama, it ud... ud be aww..wyte...Mama."

He repeated this several times. But each time he struggled with the words, the little woman sobbed and shook more violently.

"What on earth have I done?" moaned Gabby, looking on the scene in horror. "What's made this woman collapse in such despair?"

The boy's father stepped forward with tears streaming down his face as he told Gabby the whole amazing story in broken English. "My little Pedro, he just three years old when he go outside by himself and climbed a ladder which was leaning against the house. He fell off the ladder. He has bad head injury. He was in the hospital in coma for days, barely alive. We prayed and prayed, and God spared his life. Doctor say it was miracle that he lives, but brain damage caused his arm to be paralyzed and he unable to speak. Doctor say he never speak again. My wife argued with doctor. My precious Maria tell doctor, 'I do not believe you, doctor. The Lord will heal Pedro completely.' She believed the Lord would restore Pedro some day."

"The doctor said these words that pierced our hearts, 'Mrs. Ramirez, I am so sorry to tell you this, but you must not get your hopes up. The speech area of the brain has been totally destroyed. Your child will never say another word, not one word. He won't even be able to say Mama or Dada.' My wife pray for five years, for our God to heal Pedro completely!"

"Mama, it ud...be aww...wyte," little Pedro said again, as his mother sobbed. Suddenly, shouts rang out from the crowd. "The Ramirez boy can speak! The preacher pray for him. He can speak!"

The crowd pressed against the preacher, reaching out to try to touch him. Gabby instinctively jumped back on the chair and began to repeat the message of salvation he had proclaimed only a few minutes earlier, but this time every ear was hanging on every word. Gabby led the crowd in a prayer asking Jesus to come into their hearts and forgive their sins.

As the flea market emptied, Gabby stood by Abisha reflecting on the wonderful events of the day. Just as he was giving Abisha a great big bear hug, he could not help but notice Maria and Pedro walking down the road.

Pedro was tugging at his mother's dress and repeating, "Mama, Mama, love you, Mama," but his withered arm still hung unmoving at his side.

"But Abisha, why not the arm too?"

Abisha put a hand on Gabby's shoulder, "All in good time my friend, all in good time."

Chapter Eleven

It was hot and sunny in Tehran, a perfect day for a student demonstration. Aristotle Tucker had made contact with his small cell of disillusioned university students who were willing to work with him. They never questioned who he worked for. They didn't care; they just wanted to hasten the overthrow of the government before President Hafez took the country down the road of no return and into a war they couldn't hope to win. They knew that his intent was not necessarily to win a war with Israel, but to throw the entire planet into a world war that would fulfill his religious dreams of the Mahdi coming to earth.

Tuck had called a meeting of the group during the demonstration they had helped to organize, because the Revolutionary Guard's thugs would be on the streets to arrest as many demonstrators as they could. Vevak would be there carefully taking videos and digital pictures. The internal security agency would then arrest and question those on the street at their leisure. Often, those taken into custody by the dreaded internal security force were never seen again.

The meeting was held at Tehran University in the secluded section of a beautiful garden. Six of Tuck's young operatives were talking excitedly about the demonstration and how successful it seemed to be as they sat around in a large circle with textbooks, looking like a class meeting out of doors. The four young men used the code names Cougar, Chimp, Lion and Gorilla. The two young women were named Eland and Ghost, the latter name given because of the woman's ability to disappear at will.

No one knew any real names or where they lived. They were careful never to communicate by cell phone or any electronic media, such as email. Notice of meetings was by a slip of paper that simply noted the location of the meeting. The time was never given; it was on a revolving system, where the next meeting was held an hour later than the last.

All were studiously careful to make sure they were not followed; they knew that discovery meant a long, slow, painful round of torture that would end in death. There would be no reprieve or prison sentence. Vevak believed that, when they had the information they wanted, there was no reason to keep the victim alive - too much trouble and expense.

Tuck was dressed in clothes that made him look like a professor in charge of this class of students. His text was Iranian History. He read portions out loud and then opened it up for discussions. These times were when intelligence information was given and plans made for other missions.

After he made his historical remarks, Tuck said in a hushed voice, "Has anyone any information about the possible location of the secret nuclear testing facility where they are enriching uranium?"

The group was silent, casually turning pages in the textbooks while constantly surveying the area for any sign of danger.

Lion whispered, "I'm not sure if this is anything, but I spend some time in a coffee house where government workers hang out. Two guys were whispering, and one said he was going to 'Nari Plain.' His partner told him to shut up, or he would get both of them killed. They kept on talking for awhile, then left. I tried to follow the one who mentioned the place that could get them killed by just saying the name out loud. He lives in a government housing project on the east side of Highway 8. Sorry, couldn't get a name."

"Man, that's wonderful; don't be sorry, you've done a great job. It's the only lead we've gotten so far. I know you guys have to be in class, but Lion can you take me to the project, and if possible, point out the guy to me? I'll try to follow him around. Who knows, he might lead me somewhere!"

"Yeah, he might lead you somewhere alright, right into a prison cell where the Vevak boys will be waiting," Lion said. "If this guy is a worker in the nuke industry, the

Revolutionary Guards will be escorting him to and from the work site."

"I understand, but these are desperate times. If Hafez gets the bomb, war is a sure thing. If Israel thinks the bomb is close to reality, they may make a pre-emptive strike on their own. Then the world's in a barrel of trouble. Let's get out of here."

The group broke up, and everyone went their separate ways. As she was leaving, the spy known as "Ghost" stood close to Tuck.

"This may not be of any help, but I hang out with a guy in the Guard. He's filthy minded and egotistical, but he loves to hear himself talk, and he tries to impress me with information the public doesn't know. I'll see if I can get anything out of him while you learn about the other guy. I'll be by the fountain in front of the palace at dusk tomorrow. Bye!" And she was gone.

"Dear God, please protect these young people. They're risking their lives to help prevent a war and are in danger," Tuck prayed as he walked toward the street.

Unknown to the group, a student had been leaning against a tree reading a textbook. He had watched the group carefully and took pictures with his cell phone when he could. The student taking pictures was spotted by Gorilla as he was walking away. There was no time to lose; he had to catch the guy and get the camera, unless he had already sent the pictures to someone.

Gorilla walked two paces behind the guy, who was dressed in a blue shirt, black trousers, and white walking shoes. Gorilla had been aptly nicknamed. He was a large kid with a heavily muscled upper torso. All of his clothes nearly burst from the strain of his muscles.

The student in blue walked casually to the street and seemed to be looking for someone to pick him up. Gorilla had to think of something quickly. A car was speeding by. Gorilla moved with the speed of a snake. He pushed the student into the side of the vehicle, while yelling "Look out!" in Farsi. The sound of screeching brakes drowned out the loud "clump" the body made when it hit the side of the car. The driver panicked, hit the gas and sped away. Gorilla grabbed the unconscious picture taker and shouted, "I'll get him to a doctor, someone get the license on that car." He picked up the guy as if he didn't weigh anything and started up the stairs to a building that looked like an apartment complex. Inside the door, he dropped the groaning man and searched his pockets until he found the camera. He was going to smash it until the thought crossed his mind that there might be some interesting names on speed-dial. He barreled out the door and down the street where the "accident" had just happened. No one was paying any attention to anything. They acted as if nothing had just taken place in front of them.

The young spy knew he had to get in touch with the cell leader immediately, but the protection for the group was so tight he didn't know how to contact him. Then a thought rammed into his brain. Ghost knew where the guy stayed, and she knew which dorm Ghost lived in. He had to get to her.

Ten minutes later, he was outside the dorm praying that Ghost would come outside. Gorilla was a believer and a vibrant Christian, so praying this prayer did not seem unusual to him. Right on cue, five minutes later, Ghost came out of the building walking with a rather short guy wearing a gray uniform which he didn't recognize. He made himself visible to her and motioned with his head for her to meet him by a huge flowering bush.

Ghost stopped and looked through her purse. "Hasaam, I have forgotten my identification papers. Wait here; I'll be right back." Before he could object, she was gone. She met Gorilla beside the bush, out of sight of Hasaam. "What is it, Gorilla?" she asked.

"Someone was watching us at the meeting. I followed him and knocked him out. I have the cell phone camera he was using. It might have useful numbers. I need to get in touch with our cell leader; I think his name is Tuck."

"You're right, it is. He doesn't know that we know. We don't want to hurt his feelings." She scribbled down an address. "There is a green park bench beside a pool on the south side of this park. The right side arm rest is hollow. Stick a blank piece of paper inside, so that some of it shows under the armrest. That will be a signal that I need to see him quickly. You'll just have to stay in the area and watch for him to show up. Sorry, that's the best I can do."

An hour later Gorilla was in place, but no sign of Tuck. He was just about to give up the whole thing as a waste of time when Tuck came shuffling up to the bench, sat down and began to tie his right shoe. Gorilla wandered over and sat down knowing it was risky for both of them. He whispered what he had found and done, then slid the phone over the bench to Tuck. Tuck didn't say anything. He took the phone and walked away. He needed to be in a safe place where he could uplink the phone with the agency's special equipment where they could download everything.

Tuck was grateful for the work of this little cell of young patriots. They were smart and took action on their own. There was much to do and little time to do it. Tuck prayed to the Lord to help him learn the truth about what was happening in the Iranian government. He felt fairly certain that Nari Plain was the secret nuclear testing site. Getting in there to observe or take pictures was probably impossible. But if he could just find the site, he might be able to learn something of interest.

As Tuck moved around the east side of Tehran, he wandered into a railroad yard with a couple of sidings. He was startled to see a long train on a siding made up entirely of flat cars carrying a cargo of a Russian T-90S and T-80U battle tanks. He could see about thirty in the darkening rail yard. Tuck had spent a good deal of time on the Russian frontier a few winters ago, where he nearly froze to death spying for the agency. He knew that these tanks were the best in the Russian army. But what in the world were they doing clear down here in Iran? It didn't take long to figure out. The Russians were providing tanks for Iran to use in a land invasion of Israel.

Now there was a sense of extreme urgency because Iran was clearly preparing for a land war, which meant Hafez couldn't use his nukes, even if he had them. The whole thing might be a gigantic bluff, and the world was buying into the game, hook, line, and sinker. He took pictures with his special cell and uplinked them to Langley. Then he sprinted to a road where he could hail a cab. In the cab Tuck prayed, "Dear Lord, please help us find out what this wild man is up to. We're running out of time."

Chapter Twelve

Muhammad Hafez was clad in white, chemically treated coveralls and a white cap. This sterile clothing was designed to keep any contamination out of the building where the centrifuges were in operation. His entourage moved slowly through the stark white rooms while engineers worked on their various projects. Hafez was so proud he could hardly contain his enthusiasm. The man in charge of the nuclear project, Sundi Vousef, was walking with him and explaining to him what was taking place at each station.

"This is most impressive, Sundi; most impressive. Tell me, are you on schedule?" the president asked.

"Much closer than we have been. The Russians are cooperating, and testing is moving right along," said Vousef.

"What comes next, a small explosion to see that everything is working properly?"

"If we do a test explosion below ground or in the air, the world will know of it in minutes. Such things cannot be disguised," the engineer replied.

"I don't want to conceal anything. I want the whole world to know that we have entered the nuclear weapons fraternity. This will make the Zionists tremble in their bomb shelters," Hafez proclaimed.

"But sir, what about the United Nations and the Americans? Will they not move against us militarily?"

"The members of the United Nations are interested in only two things: talking and making money. Most of them hate the United States and Israel. But, interestingly enough, our operatives in Washington D.C. tell us that the new president does not like the Zionists either and has cut funding to a trickle. No, Sundi, no one is going to care when we are ready to destroy the pesky Jews."

"Another question, if I may be so bold, what about the Palestinians? They would be destroyed in a nuclear attack.

And Syria and Jordan would certainly be affected by radioactive fallout."

"The Palestinians are a problem. We shall have to have a plan ready, but let's be honest; they are the stepchild of the Arab world. No one wants them, so if a few are destroyed, I doubt that we will hear much complaining. Syria should escape because of the prevailing westerly winds. Jordan may get some, but I am sure they will understand. We'll give them some free oil. That should make them happy."

Hafez's chest was about to burst with pride. He had the control of the world in his hands. It was glorious!

An aide that had been keeping a respectful distance from the president came closer, bowing and scraping like a cheap tailor serving a customer who had cash.

"Sir, may I have a word?"

"You fool; can't you see that I'm busy? What is so important you dare interrupt me?" he screamed.

The aide nearly collapsed but managed to say, "Sir, the president of Russia is on the phone demanding to speak with you immediately. You can take the call in your limousine," he groveled again, bowing and scraping and backing up until he backed into a wall, which gave him the opportunity to slither away.

"Please excuse me, Sundi, I must take this call."

"Of course. I shall wait here if you should need more information."

Hafez entered the limo and motioned the driver to put the privacy window up. He grabbed the phone and forced himself to smile while he said, "Good afternoon, President Propochnik. How wonderful for you to call. What can I help you with?" His smile was more like a sneer.

"Good afternoon, Hafez." The Iranian president noted that the Russian had left his title out of the conversation. "I'm calling to see if things are going better in the testing lab? Are my engineers cooperating with your people?" Propochnik asked.

"Why yes, Andre. Thank you for asking. We are nearly on schedule, and should be able to do a test explosion within weeks."

"We've been thinking, Muhammad. Perhaps a test explosion of a small nuclear bomb might not be such a good thing right now. It would alert the world that you have the capability of producing nuclear bombs, and they would know that we have helped train your engineers. It might cause the Israelis to launch a pre-emptive attack which could set your production back years," Propochnik said.

"No, Andre, I assure you they will not attack. Their planes cannot reach us without refueling in the air, and none of our neighbors will give them permission to do that in their air space," Hafez said with pride.

He wanted to impress the Russian that he was completely in charge and was aware of what the Israelis could and could not do.

"Our people tell me that your neighbors are very nervous about the possibility of a nuclear war with Israel. They don't want any, and I repeat, *any* radiation descending on their people. The Palestinians are particularly adamant, saying they will be killed with the Jews."

Hafez exploded and began screaming into the telephone. "Why those ungrateful wretches! Who's been sending money to keep Hezbollah and Hamas funded? Who's been sending them military supplies? Me, that's who! Israel would have wiped them off of the map if it were not for me. They would be fish food. Now, when we are ready to reach our goal of eliminating the nation of Israel once and for all, they start whining. That's why no Arab state will allow them in their country; they're cowards and whiners!"

If Hafez could have seen the Russian President on the other end of the line, he would have been even more furious. President Propochnik was holding his hand over the receiver and laughing uncontrollably. Reggae Putnovich, his Minister of Defense was in the office with him and had heard the entire conversation. He was laughing as well. Both men tolerated this wild man because he kept things stirred up and the world was watching him and not Russia, who had designs of their own.

One thing they had decided was that there were great riches to be had in Israel, but they would be of no use if they were covered in radiation. That's why they wanted to call Muhammad today and get him to back off. They certainly were not interested in protecting the Israeli people, just their property which must be worth billions.

Propochnik cleared his throat and put on a straight face. "Now Hafez, calm down for a minute and think. If you nuke Israel, the whole world would probably be drawn into the war that would cost billions of lives and billions of rubles. Here is what we are asking you to do. Keep up the public talk about a nuclear bomb being ready in a short time. Heck, tell the press that two or three will be ready soon.

"But we will help you organize a full scale invasion of the Zionists. You can use your troops, and I can guarantee troops from Syria and Jordan, perhaps even some from Egypt and Lebanon. We are going to supply you with the military hardware needed for such an invasion. In fact, we wanted to surprise you…a train load of our T-90S and T-80U tanks are already on a siding outside of Tehran. They arrived last night. Have you seen them?"

Hafez's face was purple. The veins in his forehead stood out like small chords. His neck resembled a rope display in a hardware store.

"Seen them? You ask me if I have seen them? No, I haven't seen your stupid tanks. Why have you waited until now to tell me about an invasion? I'm not going to invade anything. The Jews have too large of an army. It would be suicide. A nuclear attack is what is required, and that's what I'm going to do!"

He sank back into the seat of his limo sweating and spent. He slammed the phone down and motioned for the driver to take him back to his palace. As the limo moved through the heavy afternoon Tehran traffic, Hafez's mind was working furiously. He would have a cabinet meeting immediately, and he would fire the fool that allowed the Russian tanks onto Iranian soil without telling him.

When he got to the palace, he charged into his office and rang for Dannah, his secretary. The beautiful woman ghosted into his office and waited for instructions. Hafez always marveled that her feet never seemed to move. He was captivated by this woman and intended to pursue her romantically. He was staring at her so strongly, that she became embarrassed and lowered her eyes demurely.

"Dannah, call the cabinet members. I want a meeting with them in one hour. No excuses."

"Yes sir," she said and glided out of the room, glad to be away from his staring eyes. She started calling the ministers on her speed dial. In ten minutes, all had been notified of the important meeting.

Muhammad Hafez, the President of the nation of Iran, settled back into his lush desk chair. Impatience with the Russians was evident on his face. *"Those stupid Russians,"* he thought to himself. *"All they can think about is looting the Zionists and getting richer and more powerful."*

He didn't care about invading the Israel and loosing half his army in defeat. He wanted to destroy the Jews. He wanted to start a world war; a holocaust, like Hitler. That was the only way, in his warped extremist mind, that the Mahdi would come to earth. That was his goal, his great dream, to receive the heavenly blessing for making it possible for the Mahdi to return and rule the earth.

Chapter Thirteen

The day was perfect for roaming around the rim of a long extinct volcano like Sharat Kovakab in central Syria. The azure sky seemed close enough to touch. Small wisps of grayish-white clouds moved lazily in an easterly direction. On the rim of the volcano a myriad of plant life flourished with every color represented by a small flower. The hoof prints of sheep or goats could sometimes be seen in the trails cut by their ancestors centuries ago, who, like their cousins, had been in a constant search for grasses to graze.

Dr. Basil Hyde-Newton stood gazing at the horizon. He was a fit and trim 60 year old professor of volcanology at Cambridge University in Great Britain. His grey thinning hair and well-trimmed beard added to his image of being a man of great learning. His blue eyes saw everything, including the fact that one student seemed more interested in his beautiful female classmate than the volcano on which they were standing.

They had been touring the Middle East for several months, visiting active and extinct volcanoes. The students were working on their dissertations while Professor Hyde-Newton was writing what he hoped would become a textbook that would be required reading in universities around the world.

Lydia Hannity was the female volcanologist in the group. She was a serious student of volcanoes, but unfortunately, she was also a real 'stunner,' as the British say. She was tall and lithe with thick red hair that tumbled down to her shoulders. She had emerald eyes that were serious and penetrating, betraying her Irish heritage. Lydia was well aware of the turmoil her appearance caused in the male breast so she purposely dressed in loose fitting clothing that disguised the figure of a model.

Gavin Tennyson was just a guy. Standing about six feet in his stocking feet; his life was and always would be sports and women. He kept his hair cut in the military fashion and his well-tanned face gave the same impression. He was careful to display his well-muscled body whenever he had the chance; his cerulean eyes constantly searching a crowd to locate any woman who had noticed him. He had taken Professor Hyde-Newton's class, not because of his interest in volcanoes, but because he thought it might be easy to get a passing grade. But when he spotted Lydia in the class, Gavin became the playful puppy. He walked in front of her, prancing and preening, hoping for a kind word. And then, when he learned of the jaunt around the Middle East with Lydia and the professor, he knew he would be in heaven for months. Much to his disappointment, Lydia seemed not to notice he was on the trip.

The professor interrupted Gavin's staring at Lydia by beginning to speak about the volcano they had just climbed. Boring!

"You will notice, I'm sure, that the rim of the crater is well-rounded and smooth after eons of erosion from wind and rain, filling the crater with this material. Sharat Kovakab is one of the oldest volcanoes in the region, perhaps one of the oldest on earth. Now, what should we expect to see a little way down the slope?"

The question seemed to startle Gavin who blurted out, "A shepherd and some goats," he ventured.

"Possibly, but I was thinking of something that even remotely pertained to our subject of study," the professor grumbled. He was sorry he had brought Gavin along on the trip, but it would not have looked right to take an extended trip with Lydia being the only student. Tongues would have wagged, and he was not un-nerved by her beauty.

"There should be a parasitic cone around here somewhere," Lydia said seriously.

"Very good. Thank you, Lydia. A careful scrutiny of the eastern slope will reveal to you the very thing you mentioned. It will be our project to trundle down to the cone and do some measurements." He gathered up his pack and gear and moved downhill.

Gavin didn't know what a bug cone was nor why anyone would be interested in the thing, but he dutifully gathered his stuff and followed on down the side of the volcano. He wished they had brought the Land Rover up here. It didn't make sense to have a tough vehicle that could carry everything, and they were walking instead. He would never understand professors.

Unknown to the trio of volcanologists, they were being watched, and not by shepherds, goats, or sheep. They were being watched by two members of the supernatural world, or spirit world, which is just as real as the one we live in but is unseen by mortal residents of the earth. These two denizens of the spirit world were warrior angels on special assignment from the Great Creator God himself.

The angels were around 7 feet in height and very well-muscled. Their faces were bronze, but their eyes were stunning. They shone like many faceted diamonds. They were clothed in sparkling white robes and each had a large sword buckled to a golden sash that was tied around their waist. Their very large wings appeared white in color when still, but they were not made of feathers as ancient artists had tried to depict them. The wings were made of a material known only to heavenly beings. They were graceful and beautiful when they moved. Sunlight shining through them produced a kaleidoscope of breathtaking, fluid colors that moved, increasing and decreasing in brightness.

The appearance of these great heavenly beings would cause anyone to hesitate to confront them, although they did not appear fierce - just powerful, competent, and determined.

Their job was to guard the opening in the parasitic cone, which was shut and sealed by a two inch thick iron door which had no handles, only a keyhole. The door was set back into the mountain about five feet and was covered by dirt, rock, mosses and plants. It was completely invisible to the naked eye, but anyone digging around might be able to discover the secret door. The two warriors were alert, ready to take any action necessary to protect the door from being discovered.

The Cambridge University scientists approached the cone from above. The footing was perilous because of loose gravel and the roots of brush running along the top of the ground. Suddenly, Gavin tripped and took a nose dive, sliding a good ten feet on his stomach. The other two raced carefully to his side to see if he was injured.

"Are you okay?" Lydia asked breathlessly.

"Yeah, I'm okay, just clumsy," he said. "Ouch, I guess my knee took the brunt of the fall," he winced as he looked at the blood and pieces of skin hanging off of his left knee.

Dr. Hyde-Newton arrived on the scene and looked at the damage to Gavin's knee. "I've got a medical kit in my backpack. We'll clean it and put a dressing on, but I can guarantee you that knee is going to stiffen up on you. We need to get you back to the car and to a doctor. We don't want an infection, do we?"

In ten minutes, they had Gavin patched up. He was playing the macho card to the hilt but squealed when the professor put some disinfectant on the wound. Lydia was most sympathetic and carried his backpack for him.

As the trio left, the two angels looked at each other and smiled. All it had taken was to pull gently on one of the roots.

On the other side of the great iron door, events were opposite from what had just taken place in the bright sunlight with the warrior angels. The professor had been right; this was a parasitic cone, and inside it was a tunnel, or conduit, through which molten rock and gases rise to the surface. But that had not happened for centuries.

Heat rose from the reservoir of hot magma still rumbling miles below. Hot gases and ash from the molten lava produced a depressing fog that swirled gently. When it settled, it covered everything with a fine film of blackness that moved again when disturbed. It made vision difficult at best, impossible at other times. The black fog distorted what could be seen.

The ancient ones who lived on the surface called volcanoes "hell," or "Hades," or "Sheol." Whatever the name, it was a place of constant suffering. No human could live in such an atmosphere. None would want to.

But this hostile, ugly, dark place of unbearable heat was not without its tenants. Just a short distance down the tunnel, there was dim light, and rooms had been carved into the walls of the dome. The work must have taken thousands of years.

The first room was very large with an oblong shape that had a centerpiece of solid rock, carved to resemble a conference table. Chairs around this table seemed to have been carved from stalagmites. They would have been quite beautiful if there had been light to shine through the crystal-like material. But the darkness and the fog made them just things.

On the walls were lamps carved from the rock wall. Some ingenious engineering had found a way to bring small amounts of molten lava from deep in the earth to each lamp; there were forty in the room. The lava threw off a yellowish orange glow that brought some light to the colorless cave. A quick survey would show that all of the hundreds of rooms in the area were lighted in the same manner.

And there was always the heat, oppressive and dirty. And there was always the noise, noise made by beings that had inhabited heaven before time began. It sounded like there was continual screaming, fighting, shouting and cursing. For this was the "pit" as described in the book of Revelation. It was reserved for angels who had chosen to rebel against the Lord God. They were locked here until the time was accomplished when they will be loosed for a time.

In the conference room, the great Abaddon holds court over the underworld. In the great Book, he is known as "the beast." His will is law and cannot be challenged. He is a striking being, once beautiful, but now, after an eternity of hatred and anger and being imprisoned in this place, he is ugly and forbidding.

He is tall, like the angels outside the door, 7 feet, perhaps more. He has six wings, like the four seraphim in God's throne room. Abaddon used to be a Holy seraph himself before pride and sin caused his expulsion. His wings are not beautiful like the warrior angels. They are translucent, nearly invisible; but they are powerful, capable of inflicting terrible damage.

He has long dirty hair hanging around his once beautiful face. The striking feature about his face, other than his dead, pitiless eyes, is his square, powerful jaw that gives him the look of a lion.

His tall body is lithe and supple, with rippling muscles like a leopard. His hands and feet are huge, oversized, like the feet of a bear. When he speaks, it is more of a shriek of obscenities, high-pitched and painful to hear.

Abaddon has a second in command, another six-winged seraph that fell in league with Abaddon's thwarted attack on God's throne. This one is nameless but has two great horns of a ram curling back from the front of his head to just below his muscular shoulders. His physique is that of a tall and powerful muscle man. His head and face resembles that of a dragon with deep black eyes, and his voice hisses a reptilian guttural litany of obscenities mixed with belches of smoke and an occasional wisp of flame.

Although he wields the same power as his great comrade, he prefers to take a secondary role, having a black heart that desires to enslave and force underlings to pay homage to King Abaddon. Far below, in the bowels of this dark and foreboding hell, are numberless creatures that make up Abaddon's army, beings that resemble something out of a drunk's worst nightmare. They are part man, vicious and ugly, and part armored horse with the giant tail of a scorpion, full of poison and death. Their six wings resemble those of a giant flying locust, making the thunderous sound of a full brigade of cavalry on the attack. As they fly, long dark hair flows from their scalp trailing far behind their backs. Their sharp teeth gleam and threaten from man-like faces with the ferocity of a charging lion.

The great one rules, screams, profanes and waits for the time of his release. Abaddon has been entombed here since he rebelled, taking for a brief moment a seat on God's throne in the heavenly realm. He knows nothing of how the world has progressed, what humans have accomplished, or the things of beauty on the surface. He dreams and lusts for power and revenge. He will not rest until he can unleash death and destruction on the earth. He plans for war with angels and with God himself, so great is his pride and his hatred.

Abaddon has no concept of time or how long he and his hordes have been imprisoned. He plans and waits and drools with desire.

Chapter Fourteen

Garrison Fong was staring at the pictures of the Russian tanks sitting on a siding on the outskirts of Tehran that Tuck had flashed to the agency. By themselves, the tanks didn't raise any hackles on his neck; Russia sent military hardware to Iran on a fairly regular basis. But something about this string of their biggest and best battle tanks held a sinister connotation that swirled around in his skull like a parakeet in a cage. Tehran's army and the Revolutionary Guard were armed more like a light cavalry geared to defend the homeland, not mount an offensive with heavy armor.

He rang the boss to see if she had time to look at the photos.

"Hello, Garrison, what's on your mind?"

"Director, I have some disturbing photos to show you if you have a minute."

"I'm visiting with the secretary of state right now. We should be finished in a few minutes," she said. Garrison could hear a voice in the background. Charlene spoke again, and said, "Garrison, Secretary Booth would be interested to hear a report from you on what is taking place in Iran. Come on over, and bring the photos."

"Rats," he thought to himself, *"what lousy timing."* He wasn't excited about sharing new intel with anyone from the administration until he knew more about what it might mean. In three minutes, he was ushered into Director Lewis-Sloden's office.

Secretary of State William Booth III remained seated but gave a condescending nod in Fong's direction. His dislike of the spy agency was well-known. He had been given the post by President Steinmetz because they were both graduates of Harvard University and held the extreme left wing view of the world; there was no need for spy agencies and very little for a strong military. Any threat to the country could be negotiated by the nation's super elite. The "intelligencia" would re-direct the leaders of the world's thinking to realize they had all of the answers to all problems or misunderstandings. The elite would call themselves "saviors," but, being atheists, they would not like to use that word.

Garrison took a seat in front of the director's desk and waited.

The secretary did not wait for Charlene to speak; instead he spoke up and asked, "What is your name again?" pursing his full lips. He wore dark rimmed glasses that matched perfectly his salt and pepper hair, which was cut and combed impeccably. His suit, shirt and tie cost more than Garrison had in savings. He glared at Fong, waiting for an answer to his question.

"Fong, sir. Garrison Fong."

"Fong you say? Are you of oriental heritage?" he asked, looking over his glasses. His nose betrayed a small wrinkle, as if he had caught a whiff of something unpleasant.

"I am. Chinese, you know, Chow Mein, laundries, important stuff like that," Fong couldn't help himself. He hated snobs nearly as much as he hated communists.

His comments were met with a withering stare and silence. "I would advise you not to play games with me, young man. The country is full of unemployed people who would love to have your job," he sneered, full of himself.

"Yes, there seems to be a lot more unemployed people in the country since your administration took over. Why do you suppose that is?" At the moment, Garrison didn't care if he was fired; he wasn't going to sit still for this oaf to throw his weight around.

Charlene spoke up, "All right, gentlemen, shall we get down to business? What do you have for us, Garrison?" She was upset that Booth was here. There would be no secrets after he left the room.

Fong slid the photos over to her and away from Booth. He had to get up from his seat to see them. Round two to Fong. "Madam Director, these photos just came in from

Tehran. They show a whole train of heavy Russian tanks parked on a siding. Something about it makes me nervous. The Russkies send lots of military stuff to our friend in Tehran, but it is always light stuff, just enough to make him feel like he is a tough guy. But why heavy tanks, and why now?"

Booth sniffed his disdain for what had just been said. "I suppose you are meaning President Hafez in your snide remarks. Why shouldn't the Russians send him tanks? They have an alliance together, which you might have heard about if you ever read a newspaper." The nose was wrinkled again.

WHAM! The director had slammed a book down on the desk, startling both of the word combatants. She looked like an angry school teacher as she said, "Now listen, children, knock off this crap or get out of this office, both of you. Do you understand me?"

Booth regained his composure and said, "Now see here, don't address me as if I were one of your overpaid staff. You can be replaced too, you know."

"Then do it, blast your eyes. Do it! I'm sick of your patronizing attitude. I'm sure you have much to do, so don't let us keep you from your duties," she snarled while walking to the door and opening it, waiting for him to leave.

"Madam, you have made a very grave mistake," Booth said as he stormed out of the office. She slammed the door behind him.

Charlene went back to her desk and tried to calm down. "Well, this may be my last day in this office, but I can't stand that jerk. You didn't help things, Garrison."

"I am sorry, Director. He makes me wonder why we keep trying to defend this country. If the people want guys like him and his boss running things, let 'em have 'em."

"Okay, forget it. Now what is it about the tanks that bother you?"

"I can't put my finger on it, but the hair on the back of my neck tells me something is wrong with this picture. Heavy battle tanks are not much good in the desert; too much sand; too soft to support the tonnage. So why send them?"

Without thinking, Charlene said, "Maybe they aren't going to use them in Iran." It was so matter of fact, yet brilliant.

"That's it! The Russians are supplying an old style invasion. If they ship these iron monsters on down to Damascus, it's a short hop to Israel. What if they are planning to invade the country and not hit it with nuclear missiles? All of Hafez's rhetoric may have been a ruse to disguise what he is really up to. It makes sense, a nuclear strike kills millions of Palestinians; the Arabs would hate that, maybe even turn on him. And Damascus wouldn't appreciate radiation drifting all over the country either," Garrison said with excitement building in his voice.

The director thought for a moment, gazing at the steel monsters in the pictures. "I wonder if Israel could defend herself against a full blown invasion from a united Arab front like they did in the 60's? She has third generation soldiers who have grown up with Palestinians throwing rocks and launching some mortars from Gaza. But, in this war, they would be facing all of the Arab nations who will be reinforced by Russia and China. They will surely be ignored and abandoned by Europe and the United States. I don't know if she could pull it off."

Garrison was lost in thought. Was this really what was happening? Somehow, he had to get Tuck to get more information about the possibility of a united Arab attack and not using nukes. He got up and tore out of the office, rudely forgetting to say anything to his boss. As he ran down the hallway, he wished he was a believer. He would have asked God to help Tuck get the intel they needed in Iran and then get out of there alive.

Chapter Fifteen

There was a gigantic party at the Ramirez residence in Del Rio, Texas. Word had spread like a grass fire on the plains about how little Pedro had received a miracle at the flea market and could now speak. Friends, neighbors, and relatives from a hundred miles away had come just to listen to the young boy talk.

Quiet for his whole life, Pedro now seemed to want to make up for lost time, talking all the time. As he spoke, the audience would smile and look at each other and nod their heads in agreement with everything he said. None had ever seen a miracle that they knew of, so the novelty of being with Pedro made them feel just a little closer to God. Many thanked God with genuine gratitude and crossed themselves like good Catholics.

After a grand feast had moved outside because of the crowd, a small band began playing, and everyone began dancing. Children were imitating their parents, doing their best to dance. But the boys thought it looked too much like something sissies would do, so girls ended up dancing with each other. The band played wonderful Spanish music and, while the ladies twirled in their beautiful, multi-colored dresses, the men stood around discussing the miracle and giving opinions about how it had taken place. The fact that God had chosen to use a gringo pastor instead of a priest was a curiosity to be debated.

Someone found a piñata and hung it from a limb in an oak tree. The children who had rapidly became bored with listening to Pedro ramble on about things that didn't seem like such a big deal to them, were enlisted to try to break the paper donkey filled with candy. One at a time, they were blindfolded and given a stick and turned loose under the tree, swatting away like minor leaguers at batting practice.

As any boy would, Pedro wanted to try to hit the paper donkey. Some of the adults glanced at each other knowing he would have a hard time swinging with just one arm, but they smiled and cheered him on. When blindfolded, Pedro swung the stick with his good arm in wild circles, always too low to be close to victory. His mother looked at her son trying so hard to hit the donkey hard enough to break it, releasing all of the candy goodies locked inside. She could not hide the tear that made its way down her pretty cheek, just one single tear to mar such a wonderful and amazing evening.

Later as Maria climbed into bed beside her husband, she began to pray for her son Pedro, much as she had every night for the past five years.

"Dear Lord," she began, "how can I ever thank you enough for the wonderful miracle you performed on Pedro so he can speak. I thank you with all of my heart," Maria continued as tears streamed down her face. "You have done such a wonderful thing, and I am so grateful and happy. But Father, I told the doctor that you would make Pedro completely well. That's what I said, 'completely well.' So I am asking you again tonight, please will you make Pedro completely well? Will you heal his arm too?"

Slowly, she drifted off to sleep with her arm across her husband's chest as he snored contentedly.

Later on in the evening, Pedro woke up because the dog was barking in the back yard. Just as Pedro sat up in bed rubbing his eyes, the room became bright with a strange light, and he could see the figure of a man standing in the room.

The little boy recognized the man, "You were at the flea market with the preacher man."

The man smiled a smile that seemed to add even more light in the room. He knelt down beside the bed and gently reached over and took the withered arm and hand. As he did, the little boy glanced at the man's wrists and noticed deep scars. This mysterious stranger looked deeply into Pedro's eyes and whispered, "Be whole, my son. Be whole and completely well." Then the kind man gave Pedro a warm hug.

As the little boy watched with fascination, the man and the soft light gently faded away. Drifting out of sight, he waved his hand at Pedro, and the little boy, not thinking, waved back. The last thing he saw was the smile and the friendly wave.

Suddenly Pedro realized what he had done. He moved the bad arm, but it wasn't hurt anymore. It was strong and healthy. He squeezed his palm over and over and shook his fingers as if he was trying to see if they would fall off. Then he gave a shout that woke the whole house, just like a Christmas morning. He ran to his parent's bedroom and jumped on the bed between them, laughing and shouting.

"The man, the man, the man today!" Pedro exclaimed.

"What man, Pedro? Do you mean the preacher man?" asked Maria.

"No mama, the man beside the preacher. The one who has bad hurts on his arms. He touched me in my room and see, see!" Pedro repeated stretching his once withered arm.

Maria jumped from bed sweeping little Pedro off his feet. Looking to heaven as she wept with gratitude, she said, "The Lord himself has answered our prayer tonight!"

The neighbors heard the shouting and praising, wondering what it was all about, but rolled over and went back to sleep. The next day there was another party, bigger than the one before, as people celebrated another miracle - two in two days. Some were a little frightened by the things that were happening to the Ramirez family.

Another stuffed donkey was placed in the old oak tree. Pedro was given the honor of being the first to try to break the candy loose. You would have never known that one of his arms and hands had once been withered, sickly and useless. When blindfolded, he swung the stick with authority and energy but not much accuracy. After a while, he peeked under the corner of his blindfold, took aim and blasted the critter into a mass of flying candy. The kids cheered and rushed in to gather the loot. Pedro just stood and smiled.

Chapter Sixteen

Rabbi Bernardi was seated on a concrete bench in the gardens near the summit of Mount Carmel. He appeared to be studying because he had a large black book which looked like a Bible but was more likely to be a copy of the Torah. Beside him was a sheaf of papers and a tablet for writing. He was deep in thought and did not notice a young man walk up and seat himself on the end of the bench.

"Hello, Rabbi Bernardi. You picked a very hard bench for your study," the young man said.

The voice startled the rabbi; he jumped a little and dropped the tablet he was writing on. "My goodness, young man, don't you know old rabbi's are timid and easily frightened? What if I had a coronary?" He sized up the fellow as he teased him. This young fellow seemed to be in his thirties. He looked like he was in good shape and was wearing his hair a little long, but he seemed pleasant enough. Then a thought struck him, "How did you know my name?"

"Oh, I have known about you for a very long time, but I don't get to come to Mt. Carmel as much as I would like. I think these gardens are almost beautiful beyond description, don't you?"

"I do indeed. May I inquire as to your name?" the rabbi asked.

"It is Abisha, Abisha Davidson. It means 'God's gift."

"Are you Jewish, my son?"

"Half Jewish on my mother's side of the family." Abisha said.

"Well, half Jewish Abisha. I love to sit here and look at the top of the mountain and imagine it's three thousand years ago, and I am in the crowd watching the great religious confrontation between Elijah and the priests of Baal. Can you picture the drama? The odds were 450 to 1, and there is a great crowd of people watching to see who would win the contest. And that rascal Elijah goading and teasing the priests, telling them to shout louder because their god might be travelling or asleep. It must have been like one of these horror movies young people go to, hoping to be frightened out of their wits. The priests were like wild men. They were dancing and shouting and praying. They cut themselves with knives and swords so that blood covered everything. But no fire! They failed and lay exhausted at the feet of the great prophet of God. Are you familiar with the story, young man?" Bernardi asked, looking over his reading glasses to see what the young man would say.

"I am. Elijah built his own altar and cut up the sacrifice and placed the pieces on it. Then he ordered people to dig around the altar. When that was finished, he told them to pour jars full of water over the sacrifice, the wood and the ground. They did this three times. Then he prayed to the Heavenly Father, and fire came down from heaven and consumed the sacrifice, the wood, the stones of the altar, the ground it stood on, and the water in the ditch. It was very impressive indeed," Abisha said.

"Impressive? Stupendous, you mean. Abisha, can you possibly visualize the drama, the history, the heavens watching this one event in time?" the rabbi asked, a little indignant.

"Oh yes, Rabbi, I can visualize it perfectly; I have a very good memory," Abisha said.

The rabbi missed the last comment. It would come back to haunt him later.

"Then the prophet prayed and the rains came and the drought was over. And what does he get for his reward for this remarkable work of courage and faith? A death sentence; that's what. Jezebel orders his death, and he flees into the desert and prays to die."

"Why do you suppose he ran away, Rabbi?"

"He felt it was all useless and that he was the only one left who did not worship Baal," Bernardi said with great sadness.

"But he had just commanded the power of God to do his bidding and seen miracles done at his request. He had the courage to kill the priests of Baal. Why is he frightened now?"

Bernardi looked at the young man with the very pleasant face and engaging smile, whose eyes seemed to be boring into his heart. "What do you say was the reason for the rapid escape?"

"He had just witnessed miracles but took his eyes off of the miracle maker, and the evil one whispered to him that he was all alone in Israel. He convinced the prophet, who could have been telling the people what God had done, to run away and ask to die."

"Ahh yes, my fine young friend, but can you imagine how he feels as he thinks he is the only one in Israel who believes and that everyone is trying to kill him. Can you just imagine?" the rabbi asked. He liked this man who knew the scriptures.

Abisha's eyes grew moist. "Yes, I can imagine."

Bernardi began to gather his papers and put them in an ancient briefcase, preparing to leave. "I should bring a pillow with me; this concrete gets very hard and my rear end complains," he said smiling.

Abisha got up and stuck out his hand, which Bernardi took and shook heartily. "I would like to visit with you again, Rabbi. Do you come here every day?"

"No, not every day, just when the mood strikes me. Perhaps we will meet again, and I will test your knowledge of the Scriptures with difficult passages," he said and started to walk away.

"Well, next time we meet, I would like to discuss something that took place from ancient times."

"Ahh hah, you are planning to trick an old man with a fading memory. Just what ancient event do you have in mind?" he asked smiling broadly.

"The red heifer sacrifice," Abisha said solemnly while looking deeply into the rabbi's eyes.

Bernardi was stunned. The suddenness of the statement caught him unprepared and surprised. He muttered something in his confusion, and then he gathered himself and asked, "What did you say?"

"I am interested in the ancient red heifer sacrifice. With Israel being mostly secular in their beliefs today, do you believe it might still be performed today?"

"I am sorry, Abisha, but I have become weary in these beautiful surroundings and with our interesting conversation. If we meet again, I may share with you my beliefs about that ancient and seldom used sacrifice," he was nearly whispering.

"Good, I will look forward to another history lesson," Abisha said, smiling his disarming smile. "I have heard there might be a small farm around here that raises red heifers with the intent of finding the perfect one to offer as a sacrifice. Wouldn't that be something? I wonder what our people would think about restarting an Old Testament regulation again. I'll bet the news reporters would be crawling all over the place."

The rabbi was in a huff, and he was upset. "Old Testament, what do you mean, Old Testament? There is only one book of God's laws for his people."

"But Rabbi, a number of Christians live here now, and they believe in another testament. That's all that I meant."

"I'm not interested in what Christians think about anything. I'm disappointed in you, young man. We were having a wonderful conversation, and then you start talking about Christians and red heifers of all things," he mumbled, while thinking about how word had gotten out about the farm. What fool had talked where others could hear? He collected his thoughts and said, "Now, Abisha, don't listen to gossip about such things. I haven't heard about any red heifers, but we raise some prime beef around Haifa. Perhaps you are thinking about one of those farms," he lied.

Abisha's face told the rabbi he could see through the lie making him even more uncomfortable.

Abisha stood before the struggling rabbi, took both of his hands in his and looked into his eyes, perhaps even his heart, and said, "My friend, don't be upset. I think you are one of the wisest men in Israel, and I want to be with you when I am in the country. May I consider you as my good friend?"

Bernardi was smitten. Those eyes were full of kindness and goodness, he was unable to turn away. He smiled back and said, "Yes, I will consider you a good friend, Abisha."

Chapter Seventeen

Diablo was seated in the outer office of the secretary-general of the United Nations located at 760 United Nations Plaza, New York. The office receptionist was dressed in the rich silk brocaded Thai Chakkraphat of her homeland. She had been brought to New York to serve as the personal assistant to Tiero San Rilando who had just begun his term as secretary-general. He was from Thailand and wanted one of his countrymen to serve him in whatever capacity where there was a vacancy.

Diablo was flirting with the receptionist, who was very beautiful and had a generous helping of the Southeast Asian friendly personality. He was dressed in a dark gray pinstripe suit with a light lavender shirt and yellow and orange striped tie. He had unusual, large fire opal cufflinks that blazed when they caught the light. His hair was perfect, and his smile brightened any room he graced with his presence. On his left hand a large diamond pinky ring sparkled in the light. His Oakley sunglasses had a small diamond on each side of the frame. His black loafers reflected light like mirrors while sporting a gold wire around the heels.

The nervous receptionist smiled and tried to continue typing on an HP computer when the intercom buzzed. The voice spoke in the native language of the region she was from. She smiled answering as she turned to Diablo. "The secretary-general will speak to you now. Please follow me." She led him to a pair of large, dark cherry doors, which she opened, announcing him. He went inside, and the doors closed behind him. The secretary-general stood behind a luxurious desk about half the size of Rhode Island. Rilando was standing to one side of the desk with his hand extended to his visitor. Diablo ignored the hand and sat down in one of the plush, gray leather chairs.

Rilando was short in stature, as is common to his people. He had a pleasant face and ready smile and the deference of an Asian gentleman, so he pretended to ignore the snub. He was well-dressed in a dark blue three piece suit with shining brass buttons. He had an unusual addition to his apparel, a pink carnation in his button hole. He seated himself behind the huge desk and looked at Diablo.

"Well, Mr. Diablo, I understand you represent the members of the Arab League. What brings you to the United Nations this fine day?" It was raining outside.

"That is correct, although I am, you might say, an unofficial consultant to the Arab countries of the world. Today I want to visit with you about the rising tension in the Middle East, which is revolving around the nation of Iran pursuing a peaceful use of nuclear energy as a source of clean dependable power. I know you are aware that Israel has threatened to attack the country's research facility," Diablo said.

"I also know that Iran has threatened to push Israel into the sea. 'Wipe them off the map,' I believe is the term their president used," the secretary replied, making it plain he knew the dialogue being bantered around in the world's press.

"Sir, you know that is just rhetoric used to satisfy the Supreme Leader and the Mullahs of Iran. I can tell you he has no plans to attack anyone. He has his hands full taking care of internal problems in his own country," Diablo said while smiling broadly. "They're just a little country trying to get along in the big, bad world."

"Just what is the reason for your visit with me today, Mr. Diablo? I have a very heavy schedule." Tiero San Rilando was uncomfortable around this strange and mysterious man and wanted to be free of him as soon as possible.

Diablo smiled and took out a $60 Cuban cigar and prepared to light up.

"Please, I prefer that you don't smoke," Rilando insisted.

Diablo smiled again and lit up anyway, blowing smoke across the desk in open defiance of the wishes of the secretary. "It is our belief that Israel plans a pre-emptive missile strike against Iran some time in the near future, using the excuse that Iran is developing a nuclear bomb to use against them, which, of course, is absurd. I would like to know what you plan to do to protect a member nation of the United Nations."

"We will, of course, monitor the situation very closely and if any aggressive actions are taken by Israel, we will confront her immediately, in the General Assembly or the Security Council."

Diablo blew a large smoke ring in the air then looked at the secretary-general and said, "And just how does that help Iran if missiles are launched? I want to know how you plan on protecting Iran and the members of the Arab League from the aggressions of Israel and her major ally, the United States."

Rilando smiled a little knowing smile and said, "The United States may not be considered a major ally much longer. There are rumors that the new President does not care for Israel's always crying 'wolf' about the Arabs attacking them. Word has it that most American foreign aide has been cut off."

"Well, that is comforting, but what are you going to do to protect the Arab countries from the warmongering Israelis?" the big stranger asked.

"I have told you we will monitor..." the secretary stopped speaking and sat down. Diablo had taken off his glasses and was glaring at him with big yellow eyes, eyes that inflicted terror.

"Let's understand each other, Mr. Secretary-General. I want you to order preparations be made for the mobilization of United Nations troops and support columns at the first sign of Israeli aggression. Do you understand me?"

"But, but, I can't do that. Votes must be taken and approval given by the Security Council. Then it has to be ratified by the General Assembly. That all takes time, and there has to be some provocation. I can't just decide to do this on my own," Rilando muttered, staring in terror at the yellow eyes.

Diablo replaced the Oakley glasses, and the room darkened considerably. "I know you have rules to follow, but you are used to getting around rules, are you not?"

"What do you mean?" the secretary asked. There was a slight tremor in his right hand.

"Oh, I dunno, maybe I'm thinking about your involvement in the child sex slave racket in your country and the envelopes of cash you receive and deposit in banks in the Cayman Islands. This all started when you were Attorney General of Thailand, didn't it? You've made millions by keeping the big players protected from prosecution. Interpol even has a file on you. You wouldn't want this news to get out just after you have been given this prestigious post at the United Nations, now would you? You want to keep the flow of kidnapped and orphaned babies flowing to your country, don't you? Don't you want to satisfy the lust of the thousands of degenerates who fly to your country and pay fabulous sums to take their pleasure from babies? You want to keep the money coming to you, don't you?"

Diablo was now shouting so loud that the receptionist came running in to see what was wrong.

"Get out and stay out!" The secretary shouted. She rushed from the room and closed the giant doors.

"All right, all right, Mr. Diablo," Rilando was now able to speak, rebounding from the terror of Diablo's presence by virtue of many years of martial arts training and his climb to power in the underworld. For years, he had been studying the occult and the power such practices held over the minds of simple and poor people. He often consulted members of darkness and the underworld, even the dead. He had no idea that Diablo was well-aware of his passion for the powers of darkness.

The secretary now calmly spoke with renewed courage. "All right Diablo, you listen to me. I didn't get to be the highest authority in the United Nations by being intimidated by some fool. You have no evidence against me. Get out of my office before I call security and have you arrested."

"As you wish," Diablo calmly replied while blowing another circle of gray smoke in the secretary's direction, "but I'll be back, and sooner than you think."

Diablo casually walked to the great doors and left the office. Rilando followed him and quickly locked the dead bolt on the huge doors with a distinctive, loud metal bang. He felt ruffled but strangely triumphant as he approached the great mirror hanging on the wall of his office. The ancient mirror was massive, with an ornate frame engraved with numerous symbols of the occult.

Rilando had spent many hours peering into the mirror hoping for a glimpse of the future to gain advantage in his power and authority. He fancied himself to have some skill in this endeavor and attributed this black art to his success in amassing a fortune from racketeering and to his rise to the head position of the United Nations.

As he straightened his tie in the mirror, he could not help but notice a dark figure in the mirror approaching him. He instantly froze in terror as he realized that it was none other than Diablo standing behind him with yellow eyes blazing and icy hands now placed firmly on the secretary's shoulders.

"Listen to me, little man." As Diablo began to speak, the secretary could feel razor-like nails piercing the skin on his shoulders and entering his lungs like frozen ice picks. He could barely breathe, and his face was swelling and turning blue in the mirror.

"Listen to me, little man; you'll have your generals draw up plans for their forces of the United Nations to surround the Jewish nation when I give the order. And when the Jews launch their pre-emptive strike against Iran, you will unleash the armies of all nations to come against Israel and Jerusalem. Oh, it will be sublime, the culmination of my fondest dreams since time began. And I want every Jew dead; do you hear me Rilando? Every last Jew must die!"

"Pay attention, Mr. Secretary General. You like to see the future. Let me show you how you will look in your grave clothes if you don't accomplish this assignment for me."

Rilando felt his feet levitate off the floor, and the flesh on his face began to rot and slide off his skull as he stared with horror into the mirror. Diablo's icy nails were now piercing the secretary's motionless heart.

"Remember, Rilando. Every Jew must die," Diablo's voice faded as the secretary's feet drifted back to the floor, and he staggered almost lifeless to his desk. He ripped open his shirt but could only find small marks on his shoulders. The secretary leaned over the wastebasket and retched up handfuls of his own blood.

Chapter Eighteen

The meeting in the Oval Office in the White House was listed as a scheduled briefing by the director of the Central Intelligence Agency for the benefit of the President and the secretary of state. Outside of the White House, the sky was full of scudding clouds that hurried along to reach a destination unknown to any mere human. The threat of rain made everyone walking on the sidewalks around the government buildings hurry a little faster as they pursued their bureaucratic tasks.

In the Oval Office, President Steinmetz was working on a stack of paperwork. Coffee had been prepared and set on the coffee table that stood between the two white couches in the room. The white and green china was from the administration of Teddy Roosevelt. It was beautiful and inviting, promising warmth and comfort for those coming to the meeting.

The door that was concealed from the inside opened and Secretary William Booth III came in, pushing Director Charlene Lewis-Sloden to the side, so he could be the first to greet the President.

"Hello, Mr. President. Thank you for inviting us to your office for this meeting. It's a beautiful day, isn't it?" Booth gushed. His whole career had been based on his ability to "kiss up" to the appropriate people at the right time.

"Hello, Bill. Come on in and have a seat on the couch. Please, help yourself to the coffee." The President shook hands with his secretary of state and motioned him to the couch.

Charlene stood awkwardly, waiting to be noticed by her boss. When he turned to her, he was not smiling. "Please, madam director, have a seat. Would you pour the coffee for us?" She didn't miss the President's putting her in "her place."

"Of course, sir. It would be my pleasure," she lied. As she poured the coffee, she intentionally spilled some in each of their saucers, which meant they had to use a napkin to soak up the brown liquid before it could stain their ties.

The President ignored the slight and began the meeting. "Madam Director, it seems that some on your staff have a difficult time with protocol, and there seems to have been a shouting match between your deputy and the secretary." His eyes never left hers.

"There were words exchanged by both parties that were unfortunate. Mr. Fong has been reprimanded, and I am sure you have done the same with the secretary," she said, glaring at her boss and the toady sitting across from her. She had come prepared to be fired, and she wasn't about to end a long and distinguished career being humiliated by a President, whose election was a mystery.

Booth puffed up, ready to explode, but the President raised his hand for him to keep his silence.

"Well, Charlene, it appears you have come here wanting to pick a fight. Well, there will be none of that, do you understand me?"

"Yes sir, I do understand. I hope, in fairness, that the understanding goes both ways." She was beginning to enjoy this.

"It does. Now get on with your briefing. What has got the intelligence community so excited?" he asked.

"We believe that the Russian heavy tanks in Iran change the whole game plan for dealing with Iran and Israel. If a nuclear attack was being planned, what purpose do the tanks serve? Just the cost of moving these behemoths is tremendous, and Russia never would have moved them if they were not intended on being used somewhere," she spoke slowly and clearly, ignoring the fact that Booth was even in the room.

"Why can't they be used in some kind of military war games or training exercise?" the President asked, trying to act interested.

"Again, the cost. They have shipped these machines over a thousand miles. You don't do that for war games."

"Then, what do you think is going on?"

"We think the tanks are going to be used in a future invasion of the nation of Israel," she said with some emotion.

"Hah, hah, hah," the secretary hooted. "What are you boys and girls drinking over there? Can I have some? Hah, Hah."

Charlene swallowed hard. She no longer wanted to tell this worthless oaf a thing or two, she wanted to slap his silly mouth shut. "It is not a joke, Mr. Secretary. The invasion of Israel makes much more sense than a nuclear attack that would kill millions of allies of Iran and spoil the land for generations. The Russians and the Iranians know Israel is a wealthy nation. Invasion saves the spoils for the invaders.

"Madam Director, do you really believe the Israelis will just sit there and let these foreigners invade their precious homeland? They'll probably put up a very good fight like they did in the '60s and '70s. The Arabs don't want another set back like that, so who is going to invade, Russia and Iran?" The President was proud of his contributions to the meeting. He was sure she was impressed. He was wrong.

"Sir, I am simply reporting to you our suspicion that our country's position that Iran is producing nuclear weapons against Israel may be wrong. Nuclear weapons development may take another year, but if they are planning a land invasion, that could happen with just a few months of preparation and troop placement.

"Israel is our ally, and we need to share this information with them. We must also be prepared for the fact that an invasion of Israel would invoke our treaties with them, treaties over sixty years old which call for a full military response. These treaties warn our enemies that an attack on Israel will be met with the same military response as an attack on the United States."

She sat back on the couch and looked at the two men. Their faces were blank, expressionless.

Finally, the President spoke. "Charlene, I'm not going to discuss the wisdom of treaties signed in the 1950s and pushed through Congress by the Jewish Delegation. The Jews in the United States have had tremendous political power for a generation, but that may no longer be the case. I am going to have Secretary Booth review all treaties with Israel to see which ones are still relevant and which ones I will ask Congress to repeal.

The Jews in Israel and the Jews in our country are not, I repeat *not*, going to drag this country into a land war with an unknown enemy, which we may or may not win. I will not let the Jewish lobby dictate policy in my administration." He sniffed as he finished.

Then Charlene lost it, and said loudly, "Then whose lobby *is* dictating policy to this government, the Islamic radicals?"

The room was in stunned silence. Booth looked at Steinmetz to see what his response would be. The President glared at Charlene. His face grew dark with splotches of color on his cheeks. He jumped to his feet and stood as tall as he could.

Charlene, believing this was going to be her "you're fired" speech stood and faced her boss with a touch of humor in that she was just a little taller than he. At least he couldn't look down on her. Booth stood up too, but a withering glance from Steinmetz convinced him to sit back down and hold his peace.

"How dare you talk to me like that! Who do you think you are anyhow? Why, you're nothing but a paper pusher at a useless holdover from the Cold War. The agency is an outdated department where lots of people making lots of money do nothing but talk and dream up comical ideas that don't even apply in the twenty-first century. You're a has-been, a throw back with no function in modern diplomacy.

You're trying to start a war against the people of the world with your theories and imaginations. I have my own people in the agency that report directly to me, so there isn't anything you can pull off on your own that I won't know about - nothing! I should fire you, but I'm not going to. In next year's budget, I'm recommending cutting the agency by fifty percent. I want you there to preside over the demise of your beloved CIA. Now get out of here!" he shouted.

"Mr. President, I believe I have heard that you are an atheist. Is that correct?" she asked, looking him directly in the eye.

Startled, it took him a moment to answer. "Yes, I am an atheist, as if it's any of your business. What does that have to do with anything we're discussing?"

"It's just that I think it is a good thing for you because no self-respecting god would want you as a believer; it would hurt his reputation in the cosmos." She turned and walked out, smugly satisfied with the jab she had given him.

The Oval Office was silent. Neither of the men spoke; they were too shocked by what the woman had said. Both felt they had lost the contest of words.

"Why don't you fire her and get it over with?" Booth asked, his hatred for Charlene growing by the minute.

"I want her right where she is for now. My people are watching her and telling me what she is doing, so she can't do anything that would cause a problem. Besides, she has a lot of friends in Congress, and firing her would be a political hot potato right now.

"Forget about her, I have an assignment for you. You set up a secret meeting with the Russian Foreign Minister. Tell him that elements of the United States government believe the Russians are planning a land invasion of Israel. If that is the case, we want detailed information about when and who their allies are. Advise him that my government will do nothing to resist their plans. I consider all old treaties with Israel to be null and void, but that would have to be worked out with the

Congress. This may be difficult because the Jews still have considerable power and must be dealt with carefully."

The President walked to his desk and sat down. Secretary Booth gathered his briefcase and left the room.

Charlene was back in her office in half an hour. She shut the door and sat down at her desk thinking about what had just transpired at the White House. She was now convinced this President and his administration was decidedly pro-Arab and just as decidedly anti-Israel and would not lift a finger to protect Israel in any kind of conflict. The little nation was on its own. The only help they could count on would have to come from their God.

Once, a few months ago when Tuck was in town, he had talked to her about his faith in God and how it had changed his life. He told her to get a Bible and read the book of John when she had a chance, and they would discuss it together later.

Well, Tuck was in Iran, one of the most dangerous places on earth. He might not even make it out alive. But if he did, she was going to have that discussion with him. She determined to stop at a bookstore on her way home and buy a Bible. She would ask a clerk about which one would be the best to buy. She could not know that a man named Abisha was in the bookstore at that very moment, talking to a young lady who was a devout believer in God. Their casual meeting was a sure thing.

Chapter Nineteen

Pastor Gabriel Townsend was frantically trying to get checked into the Crystal Hotel in downtown Fort Worth, Texas. He had to get to his room, change, and get to the new Grand Texas Stadium, located on the edge of town past the old stock yards. This new football arena could seat over 90,000 people. He had no idea how many people might come to his crusade tonight, but indications were that they could expect a big crowd.

This was Gabby's third crusade in a month, since Abisha had informed him of his new responsibilities. His first crusade was held in the Del Rio High School gymnasium. Being a humble man, he had asked God for an audience of several hundred souls that needed to hear about salvation. He prayed and studied and meditated for a solid week prior to the day of the meeting.

His wife Evelyn had been a life saver for him. She was thrilled when Gabby told her how their lives were about to change forever. From the first minute, they would be a team in this journey, and his biggest prayer partner. She took on the duties of planner, contacting city and school officials to work out the details of the event.

Maria Ramirez heard what Pastor Townsend was now doing and volunteered her services. She wanted desperately to do something for God because he had healed her son. She took on the responsibility for publicity, announcing the date, time and place where the crusade would take place. Churches had to be contacted, posters put up, publicity aired on Christian radio. She even landed a couple of spots on secular radio stations as public service announcements.

One of the secretaries at a television station asked, "What is a crusade anyway? Are you going to have a bunch of guys in armor riding around the gym?"

What to call the crusade had been a problem.

"I'm not Billy Graham. Everyone knew what the Billy Graham Crusade was about and what they would hear. They don't know me. We need something else." They all prayed for God to give them something that would reveal the story to the lost. He hoped to make people curious and want to come and see what it was all about.

Late one night after they had gone to bed and Gabby was creating melodious snoring, Evelyn was praying so hard she was trembling, asking God for the answer now because the date had been set, and they were running out of time. Suddenly, she sat up in bed and punched Gabby in the ribs, which produced a loud grunt and smacking of lips as he came partially awake.

"I've got it!" she shouted.

"Got what?" Gabby was having trouble coming out of his deep sleep.

"The name for the crusade! Are you awake? Gabby, wake up, will you listen to me?" Gabby was sitting up in bed, but was beginning to tip over and slip back into a deep sleep. Evelyn poked him hard in the ribs again. He struggled back awake and sat up again.

"Hey, why are you beating me up for crying out loud? Go to sleep, will ya?"

"Gabby, please listen to me, God gave me the name for the crusade."

Now he was fully awake. "He did? Wow, that's wonderful. What did he say it is?"

"The End of the Age Crusade! What do you think?" she waited excitedly.

"The End of the Age Crusade … The End of the Age Crusade! I like it, Sweetheart, I like it a lot. Wow!" They sat and talked for a long time hardly able to control their excitement. They chose Matthew 28:18-20 as their ministry verse, but the backbone of all teaching would be John 3:16. This would be preached from the stage in every meeting, simply and plainly - no exceptions. Now they could really get down to work.

As they were working on details of the crusade, Maria mentioned that Pedro wanted to tell people what Jesus had done for him.

"What do you think, Evelyn? He's so small and still doesn't talk very good, but he wants to help." She was very proud of her son.

"I think it is a grand idea, and Gabby will, too. Hearing personal testimonies from people who have received God's gift of healing are very powerful." It was agreed. Gabby would find the right time for Pedro to come on stage and tell his story.

When Gabby walked into the gym on the night of the crusade, a couple of church choirs were singing praise and worship songs and some familiar older hymns. Evelyn had not told him anything when he was praying and preparing in a locker room. When he walked into the building, he was stupefied. It was full to the rafters. All the seats were taken, and many people were standing in the back and in hallways leading to the arena. There must have been thousands there, waiting expectantly, excitedly to hear what would be said. They were hungry, but they were not sure what it was they were hungry for. They were going to find out.

Gabriel could hardly breathe, and absentmindedly, he loosened his tie. This would become a hallmark of his meetings: this great, smiling bear of a man with his coat off and tie loose, shirt sleeves rolled up while he held up his worn and highlighted Bible, telling crowds about the gospel of Christ.

As he started to speak, tears rolled down his cheeks because he was so overwhelmed. But, as the words began to flow, he gained confidence and strength. After telling the crowd about God's love for them and the power there was in the name of Jesus, he stopped and made an announcement.

"Ladies and gentleman, there is a young man here who wants to tell you about how he met Jesus. Please help me welcome Pedro Ramirez and his mother, Maria."

Maria and Pedro walked onto the platform. Both of them were very nervous.

Maria spoke first. "Pedro fell off a ladder five years ago. The doctor say he never speak again. Not even say 'mama.' Pedro's arm then withered up, useless. My heart breaks for him. For five years I pray and pray that God would heal my son. But, he wants to tell you his story himself."

Pedro stood up as tall as he could, cleared his throat and said, "I now talk. This man put his hand on my throat," he pointed at Gabby. "He say, 'Boy, in the name of Jesus, say Mama!' At first I feel afraid, but then I feel very warm in my heart. I start saying 'Mama' over and over. My talking getting better every day. My teacher even says I talk too much!" The crowd erupted in applause and cheering. When it grew quiet, Pedro continued.

"The next night, a nice man with scars on his wrist came into my bedroom. He smiled at me and touched my bad arm and look!" Pedro shouted and began waving both hands held high toward the crowd. The assembly once again began to clap and cheer but quickly quieted to hear every word as Pedro struggled to finish his testimony.

"Mama says the man was Jesus. I want to tell you, never give up. Have your mama pray, and Jesus will help you like he help me. Thank you."

Using both hands, Pedro enthusiastically waved at people in the crowd, who were laughing, crying, and clasping their hands together, looking on in amazement. The applause began with a few people, and then grew into a crescendo. It was ten minutes before Gabby could continue.

Gathering himself, Gabby expanded on the truths that, not only can you received eternal salvation by believing in Jesus, you can trust him to help you when you need him. There was not a sound in the gym. He began to wonder if

110

anyone was listening or had they fallen asleep because of his preaching. In forty minutes, he gave the invitation for all of those who had asked Jesus to come into their hearts as their savior, to come forward and stand in front of the platform. Hundreds came, many weeping, many with children, some old and infirm.

Gabby thanked God for Evelyn and Maria. They had thought to bring tablets to record names so they could be directed to Bible studies and good churches. But there was one thing he had forgotten: to take an offering. They would have no money to cover their expenses and the rent of the gymnasium.

"Oh dear God, I'm so sorry. It just never occurred to me to ask for money."

Again, God had been working behind the scenes with Evelyn. She had brought a couple of old fashioned metal wash tubs and placed them around the platform. When the people saw the tubs, they began to put money in. The people who had not come forward, did, however, come down and put some money in the old tubs.

It had been a wonderful night. Volunteers helped them clean up, count the money and take care of the lists of people accepting Christ. Gabby decided that the tubs worked so well, that he would never ask for money in a crusade. He would trust that the Holy Spirit would move upon the people, and they would want to give something. Any amount was received with gratitude and thanksgiving.

Pastor Gabriel Townsend became well-known, and his meetings were covered by local television stations. He had hundreds of volunteers, and they needed leadership and guidance, so, after a lot of prayer, Gabby asked his friend, Sonny Wilkerson to take on the day-to-day running of the crusades.

Although a man of prayer and great faith, he was just the opposite of Gabby, rather short and just a tad plump. He had blond hair that was always in his eyes and sparkling sapphire eyes that smiled back at anyone talking to him. Like Gabby, he preferred to be a casual dresser, wearing jeans and cowboy shirts whenever he wasn't meeting somebody important, or in front of a crowd. It soon became the word around the crusade that "Sonny" would handle it. Many did not know his last name; he was just plain "Sonny."

As Gabby was walking to his hotel room, he was completely unaware that the mysterious Mr. Diablo had dispatched a couple of demons to the Ramirez home to inflict harm on little Pedro. They were instructed to paralyze his throat so he could not speak and cause the blood to stop flowing to his arm, so it would wither again; his testimony that was being so effective would be lost, and people would lose faith in what they had seen and heard.

But his hatred for Gabby had grown to such a degree that he was going to see to his fall himself. He had hired a prostitute and a cameraman to lurk in Gabby's room. He had bribed a housekeeper for the key to let them in, having heard which room it would be while lounging around the front desk.

The streetwalker was dressed in black knit lingerie with black stockings held in place by garters. She was blond with a fabulous figure, penetrating green eyes, and full, pouting lips. As they say in England, she was a "stunner!" The cameraman was hidden in the closet by the door with instructions to take as many pictures as possible of the two of them locked in an embrace.

Just as Gabby was about to put the card in his door lock, something bumped him to the side, and he dropped his suitcase. When the two conspirators heard the commotion at the door, they came out of hiding ready to snap pictures of their mark in the arms of the blond lady of the evening.

As Gabriel got to his feet, a bell captain came along the hallway and rushed to help him.

"Sir, are you all right, can I help you?"

"Oh, I'm okay, just born clumsy, I guess." Gabby said, embarrassed.

"Give me your card, and I'll get the door open for you," the bell captain said.

He put the card in, the green light came on and the door unlocked. The helpful bell captain, with the suitcase pushed into the room, only to be engulfed by the gushing blond, undressed lady. Someone was taking pictures while the poor hotel man yelped and fought to escape the clutches of the blond woman. Gabby was standing in the door watching the strange encounter. He didn't know what to do except shout, "Hey, you two, leave that poor man alone!" They didn't hear him so he started to shout, "Mugging, there's a mugging going on in this room. Someone call the desk and get security up here right away."

A crowd began to form and look into the room. Some started to laugh; some were outraged at the conduct of the people in public. The poor bell captain had fought his way free from the blond and was backing out of the room, his face a brilliant red. He smiled stupidly and said, "Gosh, that never happened to me before." He turned to Gabby, and asked, "Do you know that young woman and the guy with the camera?"

"Never seen 'em before in my life." Then he shouted to the people in his room, "Hey you guys get out of there. Security's on their way up, and you're going to be in trouble."

The woman grabbed her clothes, if you call a mini dress clothes, and strode out of the room unashamed. She just figured it would be good advertising. The cameraman took off down the hall.

Gabby went inside, saw that everything seemed to be copasetic. He changed clothes and headed for the arena. He had just learned a valuable lesson. He would never go into a hotel room alone again. This had been a setup and could have ruined his career as an evangelist. "Thank you, dear Lord, for watching over me and protecting me from the wiles of the evil one."

He didn't see the angel who had shoved him aside, standing at his post by the door. The angel was smiling.

The crusade was fabulous. Nearly all of the 90,000 seats were filled. Television cameras from the major networks were there, as were the Christian networks. Everyone wanted to hear this new phenomenon preach. The message was the same. "Jesus loves you and gave his life for you so that you can live with him in heaven forever. He is the answer you have been looking for."

At the end, thousands of people came forward to receive Christ as their personal savior. Gabby stood and prayed as they came. He wept as he watched people so hungry for God that they almost ran down the aisles. Police were there to keep order, but it wasn't necessary and some of them went forward.

After the service Gabby was exhausted. Evelyn was overseeing the counting of the money. A man came up to her and offered the crusade an office building in downtown Dallas for their use as long as they wanted it. There would be no charge; he considered it a gift to Jesus.

During the next week, many churches in cities all over the United States called the new number that was posted on the internet, asking the crusade to come to their city. They were booked until the fall, but a request came in that stunned all of the staff. There was a call from a Bishop in the Church of England. He wanted the crusade to come to London as soon as possible. "Why should America be the only place to receive Jesus?"

Gabby was visiting with Abisha soon after the request came in. "Abisha, this call from London really has grabbed my heart. I would like to make time to go there as soon as possible," he said.

"Gabby, this is the first of many that will come from Europe. The Father is going to open doors that have been closed for nearly a century. I'll help you with the scheduling. It would be good if the crusade had a choir from churches in each city, in addition to praise and worship music. They will be attractive to the older crowd," Abisha said. He was

114

watching Gabby closely. He could see the hint of tears in his eyes. "What is it, old friend?" he asked.

"It's just that people are so hungry for the truth, something that's the real thing, something good and clean in this glitzy world of flashing lights and pornography. I just feel so inadequate, and I have to admit that I'm getting weary, but the need is so great I can't slow down." He held his head in his hands.

"My friend, you must remember that you are not the only crusader the Father has working for him. There are more, one in the Philippines, and one starting off very slowly and quietly in China. A wonderful man in Madagascar is being prepared, and he will be ready soon.

"It's a heart-rending story. He was an underground slave most of his life, until a missionary bought him and freed him last year. When he heard about God's love, there was no holding him back. So take heart. You are part of a great world wide team."

Abisha had his arm around the shoulders of his giant friend, or tried to; he reached as far as he could. He looked closer, and Gabby just drifted off to sleep after hearing of all the crusades around the world. The End of The Age Crusade would be the biggest and needed the "big bear preacher" in the pulpit. Abisha smiled and whispered, "Rest well, my friend. Greater things are yet to come."

Chapter Twenty

What Pastor Big Bear did not know was that the success of the crusades had caught the attention of the mysterious and evil Mr. Diablo. He needed a way to ruin the crusades and stop people from flocking to hear Gabby's simple message about how much God loves them. They were frequently using the 'little Mexican brat' in the meetings to testify about how he had been healed.

"Good grief, the kid's eight years old, and people act like he's a movie star," he thought to himself. Well, he would put a stop to that and show people they could pray all they wanted, but he could hurt someone any time he wished. His plan was simple; he would put a couple of his scaly minions in the kid's room at night and let them do whatever damage struck their fancy.

Demons are denizens of the darkness. They have long, sticky hair and scaly skin, indeed, very similar to rats. They have small, yellow eyes and long, canine teeth, and they drool all the time. These spiritual beasts have long, skinny arms and talons, with sharp nails suitable for tearing. Their legs are kind of short and bowed, but they have big, pigeon-toed feet. They fly haphazardly, like a fly that has been imbibing because their wings are never large enough to support their gluttonous bodies. They smell bad, like sulfur in a garbage dump. All in all, these creatures are ugly beyond belief.

The two uglies that had been assigned to terrorize little Pedro flew to the Ramirez house. One, who was named Grissel, was a clumsy flier, and he flew into the side of the building with a loud bump. He cursed, got up, and tried to smooth his filthy fur, and looked around for the demon in charge of the mission, a gray-tinged beast with worry lines on his forehead. His name was Foomp, a corporal in the ranks of evildoers. To signify his rank, he wore a yellow armband with a skull on it.

"Grissel, you idiot, where are you?" Foomp hissed, his yellow eyes narrowing as he looked at the house for a place of entry. Demons can move through walls and doors, but that requires more energy, and, being naturally lazy and bad tempered, they prefer to use some type of opening.

"I'm right here, corporal, just giving the building a once over," he lied.

"Well, stay close to me. Here's an open window. We'll go in here. Follow me, and be quiet you fool," Foomp growled. He was thinking of what damage he was going to do to the kid that lived here. His Highness had ordered the boy's throat be damaged and one arm made unusable. After they had done the damage ordered, they were free to inflict whatever suffering pleased them. It was going to be a wonderful night.

As they entered the house, they examined it room by room and found everyone asleep, except for a woman kneeling by the side of the bed in her room. She appeared to be talking to somebody.

Seeing no one awake, Grissel snickered, "What a stupid woman," he whispered. "There isn't anyone awake, and she's talking away like she's directing traffic."

They both chuckled and moved on down the hallway. It would have been better for them if they had stayed and listened to what she was saying.

Maria was on her knees praying, as she did every night before going to bed. She didn't pray great theological prayers; she didn't know any. She just prayed what was on her heart, trusting that God not only heard her prayers but answered them in his time and in his way. Tonight, she was uneasy for some reason, and tears welled up in her eyes, tears of concern common to all mothers.

She prayed, "Dear Father, Pastor Gabby told me that Jesus' blood covers us and protects us and that you send angels to watch over us. Dear Father, I have fear for Pedro tonight. I worry the devil wants to stop him from telling people about the miracles you did for him. If you can spare an angel tonight, I'll feel a lot better. Thank you and I hope you have a wonderful night. Amen."

She crawled under the covers just as the hairy vermin scurried down the hall trying to find where the kid was sleeping. They moved to the last door, chuckled, and opened it quietly to look inside. Sure enough, Pedro was asleep in his little bunk bed. Foomp was slobbering all over the floor as he walked to the bed. Grissel slipped on the floor and plopped down like a pile of mud, yowling on the way down.

"Will you shut up, you ugly jerk?" Foomp snarled, hitting Grissel across the mouth.

"Hey, you got no right to hit me," Grissel yelped and took a swipe at his commanding officer. He missed.

With all of the infighting going on in the room, neither of the scaled ones noticed that they were not alone. Suddenly, Foomp saw something and stopped in his tracks. Grissel bumped into him. Both of them froze. Standing before them were two warrior angels, dressed in white with swords hanging from their waists. Their wings pulsed in a multi-colored rhythm as they quietly kept the heavenly beings just off the floor.

"What the hey, you guys can't come in here. We're on a mission from His Highness, and there's nothing you can do to stop us." Foomp puffed up to his full height, but it hurt his back, so he humped over again.

One of the warrior angels looked down at the two repulsive demons. He removed his shining sword from its scabbard and tested its sharpness with his thumb. "Tell you what, you creeps turn around and get out of here, and we will let you go. If you don't, well, things might get unpleasant."

Grissel began to tremble and moved to the door, but Foomp stopped him by grabbing his arm. "Stay where you are soldier! We're not going anywhere until we have accomplished our mission."

The words were just out of his mouth when one of the angels grabbed him by the throat and pushed one arm up behind his back.

"Yeeeoooww! Hey, for crying out loud, cut that out. You want to hurt somebody?" Foomp screamed.

The other angel had Grissel by the neck and threw him against the wall, where he hit with a loud thud and kind of stuck for an instant. The demon shook his head, glared with his yellow eyes at the angel and lunged at him with all of his pitiful strength. The angel caught him in midair by the hair on his head and on his back. Grissel screamed and cursed and kicked but he could not get loose. The angel dumped him in the hall and stood there with his sword at the ready. The little demon knew when he was licked and boiled down the hall to the open window and freedom.

Foomp still felt in charge, and challenged the angels. "You have no authority here. We have been sent by His Highness, and we have the right to complete our mission," he sneered smugly, trying to puff up again.

"Your mission was to harm an innocent little boy, and the evil one sends two of his best, I suppose."

"I happen to be a corporal with a record of great distinction. Now get out of my way, or you'll be in big trouble!"

"This home is protected by the blood of the Lord and cannot be violated." With that, the angel lunged at the demon, catching him off guard. He effortlessly picked the representative from hell up, bopped him on the head with his fist, and carried him to the window and threw him out. Foomp lit in a heap beside Grissel who was standing there not knowing what to do.

"What say, corp, we leav'n?" His yellow eyes were bulging with fear.

Foomp picked himself up, not noticing the dust all over him. "We'll leave for now, but we'll be back just as soon as that woman quits praying for the big guys to be on guard. Come on, and fly in formation will ya?"

"Formation? There's only two of us!"

Pedro slept his innocent sleep, unaware of the small battle that had just taken place in his room. The two angels resumed their position, one at each end of the bed, swords sheathed but ready.

Chapter Twenty One

The disgraced and imprisoned seraph angel Abaddon was sitting in his prison home in the volcano Sharat Kovakab. He and his fallen seraph comrade, known by Christians on the earth as the "False Prophet," were whining about the terrible living conditions in the prison. Needing neither food nor water, they still longed for creature comforts like they enjoyed when they were royal beings in heaven.

"Do you remember how beautiful the throne room of the Most High was?" the prophet asked as he woefully swung his massive ram's horns from side to side. "The huge golden throne with its maroon cushions and how it was outlined in huge diamonds of every hue and different style of faceting. Do you remember the floor was like polished black, transparent crystal with yellow diamonds winking and slowly changing positions, like a miniature universe? The gigantic pillars that alternated in colored marble with cloisonné like gold wire separating the amethyst and topaz colors. They soared skyward for fifty feet, and were capped with gigantic lapis lazuli cap stones.

"Pure white clouds formed the ceiling, which moved and yet did not. I can still see the majestic colors in the walls of the chamber that staggered my imagination because they were made of light pink marble imbedded with countless faceted diamonds, rubies, emeralds and fire opal. You could watch the graceful flowing of the colors, with slow, pulsing changes like a living rainbow. I really loved the huge, white chintz coverings over the openings, and how they wafted in the breeze. The entire room was hypnotic and wonderful."

His mood changed and turned ugly. "Now look at where we live, in the bowels of an extinct volcano! We breathe steam, dust, filth, and hot gases. The heat is so intense that I can't do anything with my hair, and I'm sick to death of dodging the pockets of lava."

"All of this is your fault," he screamed at the top of his voice while pointing a scraggly, misshapen finger at Abaddon. "You had to be the big shot; you had to have The Most High's power and authority. Did you possibly think you could get all that just by sitting on the throne for a couple of seconds?" The prophet spat out his anger with a hissing voice that spewed belches of smoke and wisps of flame.

He made a critical error, thinking Abaddon would accept this criticism with good humor. The fallen seraph leaped at his comrade and throttled him with his talon-like fingers. His nails dug in the putrid flesh. The prophet tried to scream but couldn't. He wriggled to get loose and fell to the floor, where Abaddon flogged him mercilessly with his six wings, with the same power and frightening noise that an irate goose uses to protect her goslings.

The prophet flailed back with six powerful wings of his own and a voice that once shook the doorposts in the temple of heaven with cries of "Holy, Holy, Holy," but all he could do now was curse and flail back at Abaddon.

The intermittent tussling matches of these two shook the depths of the pit and radiated out into the earth causing more and more frequent earthquakes in various places, a sign the Holy Book recorded that would indicate their soon release to bring destruction and domination upon the earth.

The prophet threw back his huge neck which caused one of his massive ram's horns to catch Abaddon under the chin. Abaddon was knocked back but quickly regained his advantage on the prophet, flailing him again with his powerful wings. "Hey, stop it will ya? You're hurting me!" The statement seemed strange for a spiritual being to be issuing, but since the fall from heaven and their imprisonment in this place that the Bible calls "the pit," the seraphim feel pain and can be injured. In battles with warrior angels, a thrust from their sword doesn't kill but gives great pain and the demon is dispatched to this dreadful pit or even worse; the fallen angel could be hurled directly into the eternal lake of fire.

"You dare talk to me that way? I should end your miserable life, but I need you. Someday the door will be opened, and we will be free again to fly and punish our enemies. It will be particularly wonderful to damage and kill humans. They are the cause of all of this misery. Oh, if the Holy One had just never created the things in his own image, more highly favored than the angels, and given them power over us. They were given the right to accomplish things we never could or ever will be able to do. I hate them, I hate them all!"

"You don't hate them, you're jealous of them!" The prophet chided. "They have a body, soul and a spirit. They are made in the image of the Holy One, and he calls them his children. We never will have such things," the prophet said as he strained to get loose from Abaddon's powerful grip.

Abaddon finally loosened his grip on the prophet as he was caught up in a trance of jealousy remembering the words the Holy One had spoken, "Let us make man in our image, in our likeness, and let them *rule*." The fallen seraph was enraged by the words. So much so that Abaddon, this man of lawlessness, took for a moment a seat on the throne in the temple of God in heaven declaring himself to be god. It was a memory his mind had regurgitated repeatedly over many centuries.

Just then, there was a noise that had been heard in the pit only once before. The steel door was opening! Abaddon was filled with fear and apprehension. Was this it? Was this the end? Was he about to be destroyed forever, cast into the lake of fire? His yellow eyes narrowed as he glanced around a corner to where the door had been closed for eons of time. There was sunlight streaming into the tunnel. It blinded him for a second. Demons who had been lounging in this part of the volcano screeched in terror and fled to the lower regions of darkness, where all that could be seen were millions of yellow eyes and rivulets of orange and red lava.

Abaddon regained some of his lost self control and moved with the curious, humped over shuffle of a demon walking. He wafted the air with his wings, and then he stopped. "Air! I'm breathing clean air again, after all of this time." He stopped and relished the feeling of clean air entering his burnt out lungs, but it made him cough.

Then a loud, booming voice caused the walls to shake a little, stirring up more dust as it said, "Abaddon, come to the door!" It was not a request, it was an order.

"Whoever it is who's shouting at me better be prepared to do battle because I am not accustomed to being summoned," he said loudly, with his hand on the handle of his own golden sword.

As he approached the door, he saw a huge warrior angel, clothed in sparkling white robes standing in the doorway, sword drawn, bronze face hard, ready to do battle if necessary.

"Lawless one, the great and Holy God has issued this decree. The time of your release is drawing near. You and your minions will have specific freedoms. You, Abaddon, are hereby granted, upon your release, the power to rule on earth for a period of forty-two months. Your locust army will be given power as the scorpions of the earth have power. They are commanded not to harm the grass, or any green thing, or any tree, but only those men who do not have the seal of the Holy God on their foreheads.

"Your armies are not given authority to kill them, but to torment them for five months with the torment of a scorpion when it strikes a man. For five months under this torment, men will seek death and will not find it; they will desire to die, but death will flee from them.

"You are also commissioned to mark the inhabitants of the earth with your name to demonstrate your possessions.

After the five month period of torment, you may do with them as you wish."

The guardian angel then tossed a black stone at the feet of Abaddon who bent over to pick it up. "The stone contains your name in Hebrew 'Abad' which means "to perish with no hope of escape." Those who are marked with your name are marked for destruction. You will engrave the mark of your name on each one three times as a perfect witness of your domination over them."

Abaddon looked at the stone engraved with his name repeated three times.

אָבַד אָבַד אָבַד

Abaddon had never heard of the mark of the beast nor did he know that there was a number assigned to his name in a reference known on earth as The Strong's Bible Dictionary. Of the 8674 Hebrew words in the Holy Bible, the number assigned to his name, Abad, is 6. The number of his name repeated three times is 666.

Abaddon looked up from the black stone into the bronze face of the huge warrior angel and said, "I accept this challenge. It will be my honor to serve the Most High once again," he lied. His hatred of God was, even now, pulsing greater in his breast. He squinted his yellow eyes, trying to see clearly against the bright sunshine and the bright robes of the angel.

"Say, don't I know you? Are you not one of angels who threw me into this awful place? How long has it been?" Abaddon was edging closer to the door. He was obviously thinking about making a break for it, if he could but lull the angel into being careless.

"Just be ready!" The angel said, slaming the iron door in Abaddon's face. The door banged loudly, which made Abaddon's ears ring, and he squealed in pain.

The prophet, who had been peeking around the corner, listening to what was taking place, was startled by the noise and fell over backward, crimping one of his wings painfully. He crawled to his feet and started to complain, but the evil seraph slapped him across the mouth and said, "Shut your mouth, you fool; we have much planning to do, and we have no idea how much time we have to do it. I'm putting you in charge of training our wonderful friends with the tails like scorpions. I may have an idea on how to identify humans who follow our good friend, Lucifer." He spat out the words.

Lucifer was no friend; Abaddon considered him a loser and the real cause of his imprisonment. He had always been furious that Lucifer had been allowed to reign over the earth, and he was stuck in this hole in a mountain.

But now, with a chance to escape from this place of despair and desperation, he would play the game. And the thought that he was going to be allowed to torture and slay thousands, if not millions, of wretched humans gave him wonderful satisfaction.

Chapter Twenty Two

Agent Aristotle Tucker stood on a street corner in downtown Tehran, nonchalantly watching traffic whisk by on the busy thoroughfare. He was dressed casually; he looked like any Iranian businessman. He walked to a store front and glanced at the items for sale in the window. He wasn't window shopping; he was checking who was close behind and if they were watching him.

He had spent several days trying to link up with any workers assigned to the hidden "Nari Plain" nuclear facility. The security was so tight, he couldn't find a single weak spot. If he could get in touch with a worker who needed money or one he could blackmail because of some moral lapse, he might be able to build a relationship and gain some useful information. But so far, the security surrounding this facility, even its location, remained tight. He was stymied.

Tuck had called a meeting of his little cell for tonight at 10:00 p.m. He had found the location of a "safe" house in a warehouse district located near the giant rail yards. A check of the rail yard revealed that the train load of Russian heavy tanks was still standing on the siding. He could not see where there had been any attempt to unload the tanks, which re-enforced his idea that they were destined for some other location.

The CIA's best operative in Iran was hungry, so he wandered in the direction of the safe house to find a café or sandwich shop. He stopped many times to check if he was being followed. There seemed to be nothing to cause him concern, so he strolled casually along the street until he sighted a little sidewalk café that had a few patrons lounging around and talking about World Cup soccer matches.

He took a seat where he could watch the street, and no one could creep up behind him, the same kind of seat that gunfighters in the Old West always took after Bill Hickok had been shot in the back of the head in a Deadwood saloon.

The waiter came to take his order. He was old, fat, and dirty, with an unkempt beard that covered his mouth. Tuck gave his order in perfect Farsi, and the waiter left with a grunt.

Tuck leaned his chair back on its back legs and rocked gently back and forth while playing with a cup of tea. No one in his sight looked suspicious. He casually looked into a back room when a curtain was pulled aside for the waiter to go in. It was filled with some pretty tough looking characters drinking beer and gambling, although both were discouraged by the government.

Tuck had noticed a lot of men seemed angry all of the time. They were sick of the government spending all of their money trying to become a nuclear power and start a war with Israel. There were shortages of most goods, and getting gasoline could be a real challenge. They produced and sold oil but did not have enough refineries to produce gas in enough quantities to keep everything moving. The young people, in particular, were disgusted, and street demonstrations against the president and the Supreme Leader were common, although put down with harsh police tactics.

The country was nearly desperate in its desire to become a world power, but its citizenry were just as desperate to be allowed to live happy lives as free people. With this much discontent, Tuck should have found it easy to find disgruntled people to work as agents or sell information. But that had not been the case.

When he was here a few years ago, he had a large, well-established spy cell, with dedicated people who kept him supplied with important information. Not now! He was beginning to think he was losing his touch and should retire to the states and buy a farm and raise pansies or something.

His food came. It looked bad and tasted worse. So he just nibbled on it while watching people and trying to see in the back room. He could see that one of the ruffians wore a bright red bandana around his head. He had on a black vest but no shirt. Tuck could see that the man was well-muscled and seemed to have a very bad temper, shouting at the others in the room.

He paid for his food and shuffled down the street in the general direction of the safe house. He had an hour before the meeting but needed to circle the block several times to make sure he was not being followed.

10:00 p.m. came and went. Tuck stood in the shadows for nearly a half an hour. He watched several of the group come and slip in the side door of the old warehouse that looked like it hadn't been used in a long time. It was dark and foreboding.

Finally, Tuck went to the door that had once been painted green. He slid it open and poured inside quickly, shutting the door carefully behind him, making sure there was no noise. The silence in the building was heavy, making it hard to breathe. He smelled dirt and musty cobwebs. The little sounds of night creatures were amplified and frightening. He had a small flashlight that helped him pick his way over debris to a little room where he could see a dim light under the door. He knocked three times, waited, then knocked twice more. The door opened, and Tuck stepped inside to find his entire group there waiting for him.

"Good evening, ladies and gentlemen. I assume you were all careful that you were not followed," he said, half joking

"Yeah, yeah, come on, old man; we know how to sneak around in the dark," they replied. They loved to tease him about how much older he was.

"Okay, be nice now. Anybody have some juicy information for me that will help us find the nuclear works at Nari Plain?" Silence was his answer. He looked more closely at the group and saw one of the girls was missing. "Where's Eland?" he asked.

"Don't know, boss. Haven't seen her since the last meeting." Gorilla said.

Tuck was suddenly alert and jumped at the little noises. "Isn't she in some classes with you guys?"

"She was in stats class this morning." Ghost said. She was the only other female in the group. She and Eland were friends. Tuck was nervous and wanted to get the meeting over and get these kids back on the street and away from here.

"I haven't had any luck finding out how the workers from Tehran are transported to Nari Plain. Maybe they're housed at the site. We need to check for companies that are supplying the place with necessities. Lion, you start checking warehouses and trucking companies that move necessary commodities. We might strike pay dirt."

He started to say, "Hey, you never know," when the whole group chimed in and shouted, "Hey, you never know!" and roared with laughter.

"Okay, okay, you know what I mean. Does anyone have any contacts with construction people? Somebody had to build the fool thing. How about guys in the Revolutionary Guard heavy equipment units?"

"Say, as a matter of fact, I have a cousin in a unit like that. He's a greasy creep and may have some secrets. I'll go talk to him. I think he's a boozer, and if I arrive bearing gifts, maybe he'll like me," Cougar said, sitting up straight with the idea.

"Now we're getting some where. Anybody else have a sleazy relative who seems to have a lot of money and likes the sauce?" Tuck asked. There was no response. He thought he could hear more rustling in the abandoned warehouse.

Suddenly there was a louder noise, and everyone was alert. "Douse that light and get out of here. I smell trouble." Tuck muttered. The group silently melted into the darkness heading in different directions.

Bright lights burst on, blinding them as they ran for safety, but they ended up in the arms of what in America would have been called a SWAT team dressed in black. Cougar made a run for it. Small arms fire nearly cut him in half. He was dead before he hit the concrete. The room was full of shouting and screaming. Occasionally a gun was fired in the air, accompanied by obscenities and cursing in Farsi. Someone had a bull horn which blared orders to lie down.

They may be caught, but Tuck was not finished with the fight yet, not by a long shot. He saw the guy who had done most of the shooting at Cougar standing, straddled legged over the body with his automatic raised over his head like a trophy. Tuck could see his white teeth shining from under the black hood he wore. Tuck forgot living or dying. He just wanted to wipe that grin off of the creep's face.

He palmed his Browning and let off three quick shots at the big man with the white teeth. All three caught him in the head; one took out those bright, grinning teeth. He took head shots at the men close to Chimp who looked like he had a chance to make it into the darkness and perhaps escape. He knew they would be wearing body armor so a head shot was all he had. One man went down screaming for a second, then lay still. The other fired several bursts from his automatic at Tuck, but he dove behind a steel barrel and was not hit. He needed to know how many more men were in the old warehouse and where they were hiding.

Glancing around, he found one guy crawling toward him from behind. This guy was more afraid of being hit by friendly fire from the automatic than from Tuck's pistol. That was a fatal error. Tuck felled him with one shot between his eyes.

There were five more men in black in the room. All of them were now engaged in killing Tuck, forgetting the young men on the floor. They took the opportunity to get up and escape. Tuck paused, smiling as he saw some of his young friends moving into the darkness. He didn't have any hope that he would be able to join them. The bullets whistling past his head told him the end was coming fast. He mouthed, "Dorri, I love you sweetheart. We'll be together again in heaven. Good bye, my love!" Then he prayed, "Dear Jesus, please be with me now and give me the courage to do my best with what I have left."

131

Just then someone shouted, "Hold your fire; stop firing." There was an eerie silence in the room. The smell of cordite was everywhere, and the gray smoke from the guns drifted up past the bright lights, giving the room a surreal feeling of being in a fog.

"Mr. Tucker, lay your gun down, and we will not harm you. There is no escape." Tuck was stunned. How did this creep know his name? The man who was talking stood up very slowly and held his hands in the air so Tuck could see that he didn't have a weapon.

"Mr. Tucker, please, there has been enough bloodshed. Lay down your weapon. I promise; you will be well-treated."

"Yeah, right, like you treated my friend over there?" Tuck growled in Farsi.

The man ignored Tuck's comment and kept talking. His CIA training reminded Tuck that this was a diversionary move to distract him from someone coming up from behind. He turned to check the rear, just as a rifle butt crashed into the back of his head. Bright lights popped in front of his eyes, and mind numbing pain engulfed him.

As he was losing consciousness, he saw Eland standing by the man who had been talking. Eland was smiling at him as he began to slip into darkness. Eland was a double agent! She had sold them out. Then he was on the floor, bleeding badly from the head injury. That was the last thing he remembered.

Hours later, Tuck moaned a little and tried to move. His head felt like a bombshell that had exploded. He couldn't open his eyes because of the pain. He moaned again and whispered, "Jesus, help me!" He lay still for a while, and the pain seemed to lessen. He had been trained to handle pain, and had a high tolerance, but this was more than he had ever experienced. He slipped back into the comfort of the darkness.

Hours later he was back; this time he could open his eyes a little. He turned his head slowly to see where he was, and his heart turned cold. He had been stripped naked. His stark whiteness standing out against the pale, shining gray of the stainless steel table he was on, secured by leather straps around his arms and legs, forcing him into a spread-eagle position. The room was dark except for a large fluorescent light over the table, but he could see that the walls were grey, concrete blocks. The room was without windows. His heart sank. He must be in a Vevak prison. Vevak! It was the name of the Iranian Secret Police. The very word caused people instant terror and dread. The super secret organization deserved its reputation. Being in their custody would mean certain, cruel tortures and a slow, agonizing death.

Tuck was sure of his fate. He could barely see two men dressed in gray jump suits, wearing black rubber aprons. One was wearing a red bandana on his head. They were putting on big, industrial rubber gloves; the kind used by electric line men working with high voltage. He caught sight of what looked like a dark colored electric prod, about three feet in length. The men were engrossed in their work. In the dim light they moved like specters drifting among tables of tools.

Tuck was not a fool. There would be no gentleness here. With the way he was positioned on the table he knew how they intended to use the prod. These psychos would receive great pleasure from the disgusting, inhumanity of the torture.

He tried to think of something else. He pictured the beautiful Dorri, his Iranian wife. He cherished her with all the passions burning in his life. They had married late in life, after she had a career with these same people as a renowned chemist. Her talent had been used by a former president to invent a bacterium that would destroy the great grain reserves in the United States. Tuck had been assigned the case and finally tracked her down, saving American people from starvation and a wrecked economy.

Dorri had changed her career to teaching and became a citizen and his wife. She was also a believer in Christ after the terrible scars had been healed by his touch. Her father had cut these horrible wounds into her face when she was a child.

Tears came into Tuck's eyes when he thought of the pain his death would cause Dorri. Then he heard the awful "Zap" as the death mongers tested the prod. He began to tremble uncontrollably. He was ashamed of the fear that enveloped him and tried to will it to stop. It didn't work. He wanted to scream, "What do you want to know, I'll tell you, just don't come near me with that thing!"

The two pain scientists discovered something and started to argue. The shouting grew louder, and Tuck could hear that one was calling the other a fool and an oaf for forgetting to bring in a special pair of scissors designed to "skin" people alive. One swore some more, then both men tore out of the room together, presumably to find the instrument of torture. The thought of it made Tuck turn his head and vomit on the table.

Suddenly, the room was filled with a bright light. Tuck turned his head and was taken aback. Abisha was standing by the table. Tuck was sure he was hallucinating but looked closer, and there was that wonderful smile of the man Tuck knew was his savior.

"Abisha, dear God, Abisha. Run, get out of this place. They'll kill you if they find you here. It's too late for me. Save yourself, please, run!

"Aristotle, I am not going anywhere. Our Heavenly Father sent me here to rescue you. I don't have time to tell you what I have planned, just trust me." Abisha said.

"Trust you? Are you kidding? But, please hurry. I'm terrified of what they have planned for me, and I don't have the strength to be courageous," Tuck whispered.

"Tuck, I am going to put you into a deep sleep, close to death. But remember, I am with you always."

With that, Abisha touched Tuck behind his right ear. The CIA agent was immediately unconscious, and Abisha was gone. The bright light was also gone, so when the two arguing human demons returned, everything seemed as it was before. They tinkered with their instruments for another minute or so, and then approached the table. Their eyes betrayed the pleasure and anticipation they were enjoying as they looked down at their victim. "Hey, there's something wrong here. Get the stethoscope and check this guy's heart. He doesn't look right," the first torturer said, peering down at the white body on the table.

The second fiend returned with the needed instrument and checked for a heart beat. He moved the rubber tip all over Tuck's chest. "This guy's dead. You idiot, what did you do to him? He couldn't die just like that," he said as he waved his gloved hand over the body.

"I didn't do anything but put the straps on him. He was fine the last time I checked him. Now what do we do? The boss isn't going to like this. He wanted all the information the guy had, and we got nothing," the first killer said, fear creeping into his voice as he thought of what might happen to them for killing the spy. Then he began to tremble; he knew he might end up on the very same table and expect the same torture he was planning to inflict on this American.

"We've got to get him out of here and get him buried. Then nobody will think to check on him any further. We tell everyone he died of cardiac arrest. Got it, dummy?"

"Ya, I've got it, and don't call me dummy."

The two men took off their aprons, unstopped the table wheels, threw a grungy sheet over the body, and moved the table down the corridor to a set of doors that led outside. They wheeled the evidence down a ramp and up to the back of a pickup. They unceremoniously dragged Tuck onto the bed of the truck, closed the tailgate, and went back inside the prison building. As soon as they were gone, Abisha appeared with two large men with very bronzed faces. They lifted Tuck carefully from the truck and carried him away into the gloom of the coming darkness.

Chapter Twenty Three

President Hafez was at his desk, listening to a harangue from the Supreme Leader about his inability to stop student riots. He held the phone away from his ear as the screaming became louder and louder. He had to be very careful when speaking with Tieman Koumani, the Supreme Leader of Iran. This man was the true leader of the country. Hafez served as president only as long as Koumani wished it.

Hafez stared at the ceiling until his eyes were drawn to the beautiful figure of Dannah, his secretary. She was dressed in a light blue gown that was as sheer as gossamer, revealing her breathtaking figure. The Iranian President found himself staring at this beautiful woman.

She looked up suddenly, and caught him looking at her. Dannah turned slightly red in the face, with a classic feminine blush, that made her even more appealing to the president. If Koumani could have known what he was thinking as he spouted his religious hatred, he would have had a stroke. Hafez began to dream of a closer relationship with his secretary as he watched her glide out of the room.

Finally the call was over. It was nearly 9 p.m., and he was scheduled to meet with Danush, his brother, whom he had appointed to be the head of Vevak, the secret police. The phone purred, and Dannah told him that Danush was waiting to see him. He entered. Most found it startling to see how different the two brothers were. Muhammad was short and somewhat frail looking; his brother was taller with a stocky build.

"Tell me, brother, do you have leads as to who is behind these blasted riots? The Supreme Leader is crawling all over my back. I told him you would have the problems solved shortly, and the culprits in prison. Did I tell him the truth?"

Danush looked at his brother with genuine irritation. "You did not tell the truth. We have been unable to track down any kind of leadership. The riots just seem to spring up without planning. The young people hate you, brother. They don't like your boss either."

"I could care less what they like or don't like. Round 'em up and put 'em in prison. It must be the Christians. They have always been trouble makers."

"As you wish. We know which classes some of them take at the university. We'll arrest them there, in front of the other students. It will be a good deterrent, taking them out in handcuffs. The Americans call it a 'perp walk.'" Danush said.

"Speaking of the Americans, I understand you captured an American spy and some of the people working with him. What information has he given you when you 'encouraged' him to talk?" The president asked, anxious to hear the kinds of torture that had been used.

Danush was silent for a minute. His eyes were downcast, and he played with the handle of his briefcase.

"Ah, I'm afraid I have nothing to report. He died before we had a chance to apply any of our methods that encourage telling the truth."

Hafez glared at his brother and pounded the desk with his right fist.

"What do you mean, 'He died?' I thought you had professionals over there who could keep people alive almost indefinitely. What happened? We needed to know what he had learned and what he has told the CIA."

"I am well aware we needed the information he undoubtedly had in his head. I'm telling you what happened. He just died before we got started," Danush reported. He was getting a little tired of his brother pressuring him like he was a landscape worker or something.

"Well, at least we know a CIA operative is now dead and buried, and we don't have to worry about him from now on." Hafez looked at his brother who was now silent again.

He got up and walked around the desk so that he was standing directly in front of his seated brother. "I said I'm glad we don't have to worry about him now do we."

Danush cleared his throat and said, "There is a little problem."

"What problem?"

"We put him in the back of a pickup outside of the prison. The men went back inside to clean things up. When they went back outside, the body was gone."

"Gone! You have to be kidding. The great and terrible Vevak lost the body of an American spy, outside of your own prison! This is terrible."

"Sorry. Things sometimes happen," Danush said simply.

"Things just happen, do they? Well, I'll tell you what is going to happen to you, dear brother. You're fired! You're incompetent and a fool. Get out of here before I have you shot," the president raged.

"Easy, brother, easy. I don't think you want to fire me. I have been keeping a little diary. In it, I have recorded every, ah, shall we say illicit job you have asked us to do for you so you could be re-elected. Without our help, you would be just another street sweeper," Danush said with a crooked grin on his face.

"Why, you miserable snake! Do you think you can blackmail me?"

"Yes, I do. Now shut up and let's get down to business on getting the Christians arrested, shall we?"

Hafez was stunned. No one talked to him that way, but he played along for the time being.

"The Christians, yes, we have to arrest the Christians. Take care of that right away. Now get out. I have others waiting."

Danush got up, smiled at his brother and walked out of the room. When he was gone, Hafez punched the intercom. "Dannah, get Sasheen in here right away."

In five minutes the giant man, dressed all in black with a massive black beard and black eyes, came in and stood waiting. He had been the black ops inside man for three

Iranian presidents. All had used his skills, and all feared him above all others.

"My friend, I have a job for you. Do you know my brother, Danush, the Director of Vevak?"

The black robbed giant nodded. Few had ever heard him speak. For many, it had been the last words they heard on this earth.

"Good. He has become a liability. It is necessary that he disappear, without speaking to anyone, if possible. He just left the office."

Sasheen nodded and glided out of the room, his black robes ballooning out behind him.

"Well, brother, very soon you'll learn not to try to blackmail me. I'll tell our mother you are overseas on assignment."

Around midnight, an old Toyota pickup was bouncing over the camel track in the Eastern Iranian desert. Its headlights cast a beam of light, sometimes on the sand, sometimes in the air; making driving treacherous at best.

Finally, the journey was finished. The giant Sasheen got out of the truck and went to the back where he let the tailgate down. In the back of the pickup was a bundle tied with ropes. Sasheen reached in and dragged the package to the back and let it fall to the ground. It emitted a loud grunt followed by a string of obscenities.

The giant took out a huge knife and cut the cords holding the thing together. He grabbed the edge of the covering and yanked it roughly, and a body fell out onto the sand. It was Danush Hafez, the president's brother and the head of Vevak, the most feared governmental agency in Iran. Hafez was furious. He started to get up, but Sasheen's right boot caught him under the chin, and he sank to the desert floor with a moan.

"Listen, whoever you are, this is a terrible mistake. Do you know who I am?"

Sasheen just stood and looked at him. He had a huge, machete in his waistband. Danush saw it, and the bluster disappeared from his voice.

"My friend, listen to me. I can make you rich beyond your wildest dreams. Just name it, and it's yours. What's your price?"

The boot lashed out again. Danush was on his knees looking up at the giant, and the boot caught him in the stomach, lifting him an inch into the air and knocking the wind out of him. The director of Vevak lay on his side gasping for air. The pain was terrible.

Suddenly, as if there was justice in the world, visions of torture inflicted on people in the name of the state came to his mind. He had always enjoyed going to the prison and watching the new techniques invented for the sole purpose of causing maximum pain without killing the prisoner. He had watched with pleasure and excitement when women were the victims. Oh, how they had screamed until their voices were gone, and they eagerly awaited death.

"Your clothes. Take them off." The giant ordered. His voice interrupted the silence of the desert night.

"What?"

The boot struck again, catching him in the throat. He gagged and coughed and rolled on the ground. Finally, he was able to begin to undress. He stopped when he was down to his shoes and underwear.

"All off, now!" The moonlight was bright enough for Danush to see the leg draw back for another blow.

"Okay, okay. Please don't kick me again."

In seconds his naked body was painted a ghostly white by the moon and stars. The desert was silent, as if it were watching the drama playing out between the two men.

"Walk!" Sasheen demanded.

"Walk, where?" The boot started again, and Danush walked gingerly in the direction the giant pointed. Cactus spines, dried twigs, and sharp rocks made walking barefoot extremely painful. He hobbled and stumbled and cursed. They came to the edge of what looked like a deep ravine.

"The desert adder waits for you. It will give you comfort and rest, after the pain of the bite. There is a nest down there with hundreds of snakes. Good night director."

With that he took the giant knife and stabbed Danush in the side, which made him fall down on all fours. A kick pushed the unfortunate man over the side. He screamed all the way to the bottom: then there was silence.

"Aiee!" Silence. "Aiee," again silence. It appeared the adders were welcoming him to their home.

The giant took out a shovel and pushed rocks and sand over the edge, enough to cover the body, which might not ever be discovered. When he finished he got into the truck and began the long drive back to Tehran. He drove in silence. He was not aware of the strange irony of what he had just done. An American spy had been freed by divine intervention, and the head of the agency that wanted to torture him was now dead!

Chapter Twenty Four

Rabbi Samuel Bernardi was enjoying the sunshine early in the morning, lounging around the fenced in pasture, watching the red heifers enjoying real grass. Their diet of special hay, grains, and salt, mixed with vitamins, was the most balanced diet any cow had ever eaten. But a cow is a cow, and they love to graze and chew grass even if they are not really hungry. The one known as Alice had just passed her third birthday. She was exploring the field and the fences. Like all cattle, the grass really does look better on the other side of the fence, even though she was standing in grass that rose to her knees.

The rabbi looked up and was startled to see his friend Abisha walking toward him. This was supposed to be a secret place; how had the young man discovered it? It made Bernardi a little angry, and his greeting to Abisha was a little gruff.

"Well, hello, young man. What are you doing here?"

"Hello, Rabbi. I learned there was a herd of Red Angus around Haifa, so I thought I would see if I could find it and see the animals."

As Abisha spoke, Alice, who was exploring the far side of the field, stopped in her tracks. She swung her head around, facing Abisha. Her ears came forward and were rigid. Then, the most amazing thing happened. Alice broke into the comical, awkward trot that afflicts bovine beasts and headed directly toward the two men. She slid to a stop in front of Abisha, reached her nose toward his hand and sniffed loudly. She then gave a lovely "Moo" that was such a soft sound, meant for only the two of them.

Cattle are incurably curious and when the other cows saw Alice running to greet Abisha, they all joined in a happy romp, some running, some walking fast. Many running had their tails straight up in the air, a sign of great excitement. Alice paid no attention, for now Abisha was rubbing behind her ears in a most delicious manner. He was laughing, and scratching and petting her with genuine affection. She pushed against his hand, gently imploring him not to stop. It was a wonderful, happy, idyllic scene.

Rabbi Bernardi was amazed at the scene he was witnessing: animals behaving in a most unusual manner, trying to be touched by Abisha, ignoring him.

Abisha laughed, and in a playful manner said, "All right, ladies, go back to what you were doing. The rabbi and I are trying to have a conversation." Immediately, the young cows turned and wandered away, obeying this friendly human. Alice started to leave but stopped, came back and licked Abisha's hand one last time, staring into his face. Abisha smiled and said, "Don't worry little one. We will meet again soon." She seemed satisfied and strolled casually away, turning once to look again. She felt so good that she gave one of the other cows a head butt in her ribs, causing her victim to give out a loud grunt as she jumped to get out of the way.

Both men roared with laughter as they wandered away to take a seat on a bench under a gigantic orange tree, which was in blossom, the fragrance permeated the area. The shade was cool and refreshing. Neither spoke for a few minutes as they enjoyed the beauty of the place.

"Praise God for making such a beautiful place," the rabbi said as he stroked his beard with his left hand.

"Yes, indeed," Abisha said. "The Father is the Great Creator."

The rabbi looked again at the red heifers peacefully grazing in the tall green grass, but then fixed his eyes on Abisha. The rabbi was nervously wondering if revealing any information of the planned sacrifice would be safe. "Tell me, Abisha, why a young man like you would have such interest in the ancient red heifer sacrifice, the Parah Adumah?"

Abisha pondered for a moment as if thinking while he casually picked an orange blossom and was examining it closely. "Yes Rabbi, but first you must tell me, why it is of such interest to you to the degree that you would be raising these special animals."

"Perhaps Abisha, you have read the great Rabbi Maimonides? He wrote in the Middle Ages that, at the coming tenth red heifer the Messiah himself would accomplish the completion of the sacrifice? Have you heard of such things?"

"So is that why you have interest, Rabbi? You want to see the Messiah?"

"Yes, Abisha," Bernardi responded slowly shaking his head from side to side. "I fear in these dangerous times with all our enemies surrounding us that the coming Messiah will be our only hope."

"I quite agree, and I am very familiar with the event accomplishing the completion of sacrifice." Abisha glanced down at the deep scars on his own wrists as he continued, "My memory is quite good."

The remark did not catch the attention of the rabbi.

"Abisha, you are a unique and learned fellow, but these things are beginning to make an old man weary."

"Yes, Rabbi, I must be leaving and thank you indeed for letting me see these wonderful animals. But before I go, would you permit me one more question?"

"Very well." The rabbi remained nervous about the young man's presence at this very sensitive facility but found himself drawn to Abisha, most especially to his inquisitive yet seemingly all knowing eyes. "Yes, yes, very well Abisha."

"Have you perhaps read of the late Rabbi Louis Jacobs who wrote of the great paradox of the red heifer sacrifice? To him, the great paradox of the red heifer sacrifice was that the priests who performed the purification became themselves defiled. This mystery - that the Parah Adumah purified the defiled and yet defiled the pure - even the wise King Solomon was unable to explain its true significance. So what do you think, Rabbi?"

Bernardi was stunned. "You are asking me what I think? When not even the great Solomon could explain it, how could I? But tell me then Abisha, how would you explain such a thing yourself?"

"If you can hear it, this is the answer written many years ago by a rabbi, a Pharisee of Pharisees whom we refer to simply as Paul. In his second letter to the Corinthians he wrote this, '*God made him who had no sin to be sin for us, so that in him we might become the righteousness of God.*' Is this not the type of paradox to which Rabbi Jacobs was referring?"

"I do not understand these things," the rabbi responded gruffly, but then softened as he looked into Abisha's caring eyes. "All I know is that I long to see the Messiah of Israel." The rabbi felt that he had never met anyone with such knowledge and wisdom. As they shared a warm handshake, the rabbi happened to notice the deep scars on Abisha's wrist and for a fleeting moment he wondered deep in his heart, 'Could such a thing be possible? Possible that he could be shaking the very hand of the one he longed to see?" He quickly shook off the thought, and yet his heart held a desire to see more of the young man. "I hope to see you again, Abisha."

"Yes, Rabbi. You can count on it."

Chapter Twenty Five

The Prime Minister of Israel, Hiram Meier was riding in his bullet-proof limo to the army headquarters building on the north side of Jerusalem. He had just left a meeting of the Knesset. It had been a tumultuous affair, with the Labor Party charging the other as being weak on defense, and the Social Democratic Party charging the Labor people of trying to foment trouble with the Palestinians by building more settlements in the Gaza Strip area.

The Social Dems, as they were called, wanted peace at any price. They were willing to meet and discuss any point Hamas or Hezbollah brought up against Israel, believing the purely illogical idea that talk will prevent war, and all that Hamas or Hezbollah wanted was peace and more land; never mind that both were receiving money and military hardware from the sworn enemy of Israel, Iran!

Meier was exhausted. This constant wrangling and arguing, with no decisions being made because of obstructions from the Social Dems, drove him to wish for a civil war to eliminate the socialist faction from the country. Iran was pushing ahead in every area to prepare for war. Israel's intelligence department reported that the making of nuclear warheads could happen this year. Iranian production of medium range missiles was increasing at an alarming rate. They would have several hundred ready to fly in months. Then, where would Israel be? Alone and in terrible danger was the only answer he could arrive at; when, at the same time, the socialists were throwing flowers at the enemy in Palestinian border areas. The Israel that God had chosen to be his representatives on earth had turned their back even on the Holy One. So, in his mind, the nation was truly alone and close to death.

The limo pulled up at the headquarters building, and heavily armed guards rushed to the vehicle, to provide an escort for him. Inside the fortress-like building he was met by

General Ezra Korach, head of the Israeli Army. He stood at attention and saluted the prime minister, who awkwardly returned the salute and stepped forward to shake hands.

"Mr. Prime Minister, how very nice to see you. Please come with me to my office; we can have some tea," the general said. A career Army officer, he was not tall, perhaps 5 feet 10 inches. However, he stood and walked ramrod straight. He kept his receding blond hair cut short.

A vain man, he felt it necessary to have his uniform pressed daily, and he often changed shirts many times due to the heat of summer. One chink in his vanity, he had given in to the need for glasses. But the war was only half won as he wore silver rimmed half-glasses and continually looked over the top of them.

General Korach was a secular Jew. He didn't put any stock in the people in black wearing side curls. He was a man of action, believing God was not necessary as long as one had tanks that were well-maintained. He tolerated the Orthodox Jews but had little use for them. The general was a man of action and left the reading of the Torah to others. He had an even harsher view of politicians, ranking them somewhere between pond scum and horse dung. But he knew where his funding came from, so he was very adept at 'kissing up' to those he privately despised.

His office was comfortable but stark. The walls were covered with war scenes of battles fought in the Six Day War, which he considered to have been the greatest days of his life.

The two men sat across from each other on small leather couches.

"Well, Mr. Prime Minister, what is the purpose of your visit today?"

The prime minister wasn't listening. He was looking outside through small windows. It was a beautiful day, and he longed to be on the beach at Haifa.

"Mr. Prime Minister?" The general raised his voice one octave.

"What, oh yes, excuse me. I momentarily moved to the beach. General, I am here at the request of the Knesset. Intelligence tells us that Iran is well on its way to producing a nuclear warhead, perhaps as many as three. If they get more accuracy in their medium range missiles, you can guess as well as I what their targets will be. What steps have you taken to intercept those missiles when the time comes?" Meier asked, knowing the answer. He had heard it many times before.

"We are prepared to launch the American anti-missile weapons. They have a high accuracy rate. We should be able to knock a few of their best out of the sky, when the time comes," the general said.

"You mean, if it comes, don't you general?" Meier asked. He could feel an argument coming on, and he wasn't up to it.

"No, I mean exactly what I said; when the attack comes, as we both know it will."

"I have been instructed to contact the United States and the United Nations to ask them for assistance in defending Israel from that madman. It's foolish. They are not going to give us any kind of help. Neither the American President nor the secretary general of the United Nations wants to believe that Iran will attack us. They keep warning us not to try and defend ourselves with a pre-emptive strike, warning us they would consider it an act of war against the United Nations, and they would react accordingly. If that isn't a threat, I don't know one," he said wearily.

The general sat quietly for several minutes. His brow was furrowed, his lips pursed, his head was down near his chest. He was deep in thought and seemed troubled by what he was thinking. Finally, he broke the silence.

"Sir, we both know that the world in which we find ourselves in today is predominately anti-Israel. Never, since the Second World War have so many nations turned their back on us. We are a speck of dust in the world's eye. We must face reality. The next war may and probably will be our last. Because we are so outnumbered by other nation's armies and navies and air forces, are we to roll over and fall calmly into our graves? Sir, this will not happen as long as I am in command of our armed forces. Invaders are going to pay a heavy price in blood." The general was up and moving around the room as he became more and more agitated.

"Why do you think the world hates us so badly, Ezra?" asked the prime minister.

"That's easy, it's because our enemies are Arabs or Arab apologists. You have to give the Arabs credit for using their oil as a weapon against us and, at the same time, spreading their beliefs around the world."

"But Ezra, it's not just the Arabs. Every nation on earth is turning against us. I wonder if the Orthodox believers might be right. This is not going to be a war against us as a people. It will be a war between good and evil."

The general stopped pacing and eyed the prime minister. "Don't tell me you are falling for that bunch of ancient clap-trap?"

Meier got up and looked out of the small window. How he wished he was on the beach.

"We need something to believe in Ezra, something bigger and outside of ourselves, because I believe it is going to take something supernatural to save us. It's not going to be our Prego Missiles, or the Cruise Missiles, or the Jericho or our Arrow Missile Defense System. Don't look so surprised. I read the reports you send me. But, we both know that a couple of well-placed nukes, and we're out of business and pushing up daisies."

General Korach did not like what he was hearing. Such defeatist attitude from the top of the government could spread like the desert wind, filtering down into the military and the people. He made up his mind to try another time asking for a pre-emptive strike against Iran. He believed the psychological effect on the Iranians and their neighbors would be devastating. Then, and only then, would they come to the bargaining table with their tails between their legs. They respected power and nothing else. If the Arabs were happy to die for their religion, he wanted to make a bunch of Arabs very happy indeed!

Ezra cleared his throat. He was uncomfortable. He needed a change of uniform. "Sir, we must discuss a strategy for our defense if we are to survive the attack we both believe will come in the not too distant future." He waited for just a second, and then he slammed his hand down on the desk. In his austere office, it sounded like a hand grenade had exploded.

"You must give me the green light for a pre-emptive strike against Iran. It doesn't matter if we hit their nuclear sites; what matters is that it will terrify the citizens, and they will riot against the government. Hafez knows that, if he fires back, we can wipe him off of the face of the earth. We must do this to survive! He is going to use the same strategy on us, can't you see that?"

"No! Do you hear me? We will not be guilty of starting a war. We must continue to try to sway world opinion to our side. The United Nations is our only hope," Meier said.

His hands were shaking, and his voice wavered. He knew he was hoping for a lost cause but couldn't bring himself to defend Israel with a missile strike against the maniac in Iran.

"Do you hear yourself? Do you hear what you're saying? The United Nations? What kind of horse dung is that anyway? You know they are not going to help us. You're the prime minister. It's your job to protect our country, and you've become the greatest appeaser since Chamberlain."

Meier stood up. "General Korach, I am ordering you to do nothing to start hostilities with any of our Arab or Persian neighbors. For your sake, I hope you understand me."

Korach stood to full attention. His uniform shirt was splotched with sweat marks. It was a strange sight. The prime minister returned the half-hearted salute and left the office. He had made up his mind, he was going to Haifa and roll around in the surf, and he didn't care what emergency came up.

Korach stabbed his intercom. "Get Lt. Colonel Cohen in here, ASAP." He sat down to think. He had a plan, a plan that might save the country, but he was going to need help to pull it off, and it would almost certainly mean a court martial and time in prison. Not the way to end a distinguished military career, but he felt there was no choice.

Lt. Colonel Levi Cohen stood before his desk five minutes later. He stood ramrod straight, but he had the loose, "ready for action" look of a career military man who kept in shape. Muscles bulged all over his body. He had a sincere face, but his dark eyes were what grabbed attention. They were piercing, no nonsense, I-know-you're-lying eyes.

"Levi, I'm going to ask you something that may lead to your court martial or worse. You can decline to answer if you wish, and I will understand. How can I launch a pre-emptive missile attack on Iran?" Korach waited. He knew that he had just put his career in the colonel's hands.

Cohen stood absolutely still. Only a small tic above his left eye betrayed the strain he was under.

"Well, General, the truth is you can't! To launch would require that you recruit the men who have access to the control keys and launch codes. If you talked to all of them, there would certainly be a leak, and the government would send in troops to arrest everyone they thought might be involved. Which, by the way, would be the perfect time for Iran to launch an attack on us. I'm sure they have spies in our midst so the word would go out very quickly. Anyway, it can't be done. There are so many 'fail safe' provisions in place that no one man could effect a launch." He paused to judge what effect he was having on the general.

Korach stood for a moment, lost in thought. Finally he looked up and gazed at his Lt. Colonel. "Well, Levi, I'm going to do it anyway. I'm going to hit those animals before they hit us. I think we are in a count down right now. They are just getting all of the details worked out; then they attack."

"But how? How can you launch anything? The launch signal takes two keys being turned at the same time, and they're ten feet apart. You would have to have that guy on your side. Before launch, you would have to have the programmers on board to get the missiles to a target. How could you ever pull all that off in this lifetime?" Cohen asked, but his eyes betrayed him. He was thinking of the possibility of making it happen.

General Korach smiled as he looked at his colonel. He could see the ideas whirling around in his head. "Can't do it, eh? Is that what you really believe? You have an idea, don't you. I wonder if it is the same as mine."

"Sir, there might be a way. I'm not sure how you make it happen, but I think there might just be a way."

"How?"

"It's simple really. All you have to do is get the launch codes from the prime minister. But that would mean a very long time to get them by using a spy. There is iris eye identification before any files will open. We need somebody from the Mossad to advise us. Heck, they may have designed the security service in the first place." Cohen said. He was now excited, and his mind was racing ahead of him.

"You sure you want in on this, Levi? Your career will be over when we are discovered."

"No problem, we'll probably be dead anyhow."

Korach laughed and got out a bottle of smuggled Scotch whiskey and two glasses. He poured both of them two fingers of the smooth beverage. Then he held up his glass for a toast. "To Israel!"

"To Israel, God help us!"

Chapter Twenty Six

In the Kremlin a meeting was taking place that could lead to dire consequences for the nation of Israel. The President of this northern nation, Andre Propochnik had called for a secret meeting with top members of his staff, to be held in a secret bunker deep in the bowels of the building.

This room had a history of housing meetings that changed the world's balance of powers on many occasions. Attending today would be Boris Chukin, Director of the FSB; Reggae Putnovich, Minister of Defense and General Nicolas Solkov, Supreme Commander of the Russian Army.

When Propochnik arrived at the bunker, he questioned the two army sergeants guarding the door. "Has the room been swept for bugs today?"

"Yes sir, it was done an hour ago. It was clean. Nothing was found."

The President did not respond, just pushed past the guards and went into the room, which was dark and gloomy because of the lack of windows. Two kinds of lighting were used: fluorescent for brightness and incandesant for the soft yellowish glow to make the room seem more comfortable. The dark green walls were covered with huge oil paintings of past historic figures in Russian history. All of them seemed to have been painted when they were angry. The large conference table was surrounded by oversized leather chairs.

There were no electrical devices of any kind in the room; no video recorders, tape recorders, radios or televisions. No record of the meetings were ever kept. A tablet and pencil lay in front of each chair, the only method of assisting someone's memory. Any decision made in this room would have a cover story written and published through normal channels.

Propochnik made his way to a well-stocked bar located at one end of the room. He poured himself a generous shot of Crown Royal, then took his seat at the head of the table.

The minister of defense arrived next, greeted the president then moved directly to the bar. Vodka was his libation of choice. He filled a glass half full then took a seat and slouched down somewhat. He had terrible posture, which made his protruding stomach more pronounced.

Next to the meeting was Boris Chukin, the director of the FSB, which was the new name for the old KGB. Chukin was unpleasant at all times. He stared at people, not saying anything. This was his way of making people fear him, which was exactly what he wanted. He chose a generous glass of sherry and seated himself opposite Putnovich, offering no greeting.

General Solkov arrived last. He hurried to sit down, taking no liquor to prepare him for the meeting. The light in the room played off his chest of medals that extended from his shoulder to the bottom of his ribs. He placed his hat on the table beside him, folded his hands and waited, as he had waited through thousands of meetings in his career.

"All right, gentlemen, let's get down to business. Our intelligence people tell us that Iran is on track to be able to produce nuclear weapons within months. If Hafez puts these warheads on a few missiles and send them to Israel, there will certainly be a war in the Middle East. Israel will counter attack with everything they have in their arsenal, which, by the way is substantial. We could have nuclear clouds in Israel, Syria, Jordan and Lebanon. Certainly the same fate will be faced by Iran. That fool, Hafez doesn't care if he starts a world war; in fact, that is just what he wants to do. He is a religious idiot and believes his god will reward him in heaven. It is impossible to reason with religious fanatics!" The men in the room nodded their agreement. All good atheists, religion was a mystery to them, and they couldn't understand why people believed in something they could not see.

"We have a wonderful opportunity here gentlemen. If we play our cards right, we can get others to do the fighting, and

154

we walk in and pick up the pieces. Israel is fabulously wealthy. We must come up with a plan to cause that wealth to flow to Moscow, not Tehran."

Chukin spoke up, "Our people in Jerusalem, Haifa and Tel Aviv have been unable to turn up any credible evidence that Israel is planning a pre-emptive strike. They are kept in check by the United States, whose new President has made it clear his country will no longer bail them out of trouble. As you know, he has cut off almost the entire financial aide they were supplying the country. Whatever happens, Israel will face the world alone if war does start."

The head of the nation's spy network sat quietly for a minute, eyeing each person at the table to gauge how his comments had been received.

Propochnik cleared his throat and said, "Gentlemen, this is good news. With the United States out of the picture as an ally, we should be able to do just about anything we want when the time is right. General, if there is a, shall we say, *skirmish*, what can we expect in the way of resistance?"

Solkov sat up straighter in his chair, if that were possible and said, "Sir, the Israeli army is well-trained and well-equipped. Marching into the country would be met with stiff resistance, exactly because they know no one is going to help them. Their Air Force is the best in the Middle East. They have a number of missile systems that are top of the line, like the Prego and the Jericho systems. Israel also has the American Lance missile, which has nuclear capability. Their submarines are equipped with American cruise missiles, and they are really good at hitting their targets. For missile defense they have the Arrow defense system. My belief is that they will be tough to invade without very heavy losses."

"My goodness, General, that was not a very positive report. Surely, with the most of the world's armies gathered against them, they will sue for peace and hope for the best," the president said, looking over his glasses at the general, who was now becoming uncomfortable.

"Sir, I consider that to be unlikely. Many still believe they are God's chosen people, and he will come to their rescue."

"Who will come to their rescue?" asked the president.

"God!" the general added reluctantly. This meeting was putting him on the spot more than he liked to be.

"But General, there is no god. That is all religious poppycock to keep the masses quiet," the president said, pounding the table lightly with his right hand.

"That's not what a Jew believes. And, please remember, Mr. President, that the Christians around the world see them as the chosen people and are to be respected as such. The Christians and Jews believe in the same God. Who knows how they will react if Israel is attacked. They may unite and come to their aide."

"How do you know all of this religious stuff?" the president asked suspiciously.

"My people did a lot of research when we were preparing war games a few years ago, and one of the targets was Israel. We read a lot of literature about the Jews and the Christians. There is something that is very interesting. The Christians believe that there will be a great battle in Israel, with armies of the North invading the country. Their Bible calls this the battle of 'Gog and Magog', and it's supposed to be the last great battle; then the world comes to an end."

President Propochnik had a crafty smile on his face. "Tell me Solkov, who wins?"

Solkov was now extremely uncomfortable. He hadn't intended for the conversation to come to this; he was only trying to impress the president with his knowledge of a potential enemy. He needed a drink. The room was thick with the drama taking place. All eyes were on him as he made his way quickly to the liquor cabinet and poured himself a stiff jigger of whiskey.

"Well, Solkov, we're waiting. Who wins this biblical war?"

The general cleared his throat and mumbled, "God does!"

"What was that, I couldn't hear you?"

"I said, God wins."

"Har, har, har, that's a good one." The president laughed so hard tears streamed down his cheeks. He pounded the table and coughed and laughed some more. "You mean to tell me that the armies of the world are defeated by something that doesn't exist?"

"I'm just quoting what I can remember being told. I'm sure it is nothing more than a fable." He seemed to shrink as he made his way back to his seat.

"Ahem! Whew! I haven't had that much fun for a long time. Now, Chukin, what kind of espionage setup do you have in Jerusalem?"

"Not much, I'm afraid. The people are amazingly loyal to their country. They fight and argue over politics but are loyal to Israel. You may not be aware of it, but there is a huge contingent of Russian Jews in Israel. They have been migrating there since the end of the Second World War," Chukin reported.

"I should think you would have some good possibilities there."

"Not really. They are Jews first, Israeli second, and they trace their history to Russia."

"Well, whatever you need to do, do it. I want a good system of intelligence up and working within a month. Understand?" the president asked.

"Yes sir. I will do my best."

"Now, gentlemen, this is the plan I have been working on," the president said as he slid to the front edge of his chair. "We are going after Israel in a big way, if we can keep that idiot, Hafez, from contaminating the whole area with radiation.

"Putnovich, get those tanks sitting in Tehran moved to Syria, as close to the Israeli border as you can. Talk to the Syrian president; he has always been agreeable to work with.

Try to get the tanks on station within a month, and at the same time move as many troops as you can to southern Russia. Get war games going in Syria, Iran, Jordan, Lebanon, anyplace that will take a few of our troops on their soil without having a hernia. I'm going to get our ambassador to the United Nations to work the room and see how much support there might be for a confrontation with Israel if she launches an unprovoked missile attack against Tehran. My guess is most nations will agree to punish her.

"And gentlemen, when the time comes, Mother Russia will be the first ones to cross the border and take possession of the nation in the name of the United Nations."

He sat back in his chair and wiped the perspiration from his forehead and face.

"I applaud you, Mr. President, for a well-conceived plan. Who knows, this may be the first step in reviving the old Soviet Union!" Chukin said. He applauded, and the others joined in. This was an exciting, historic time, and they all felt privileged to be a part of it. What they did not consider was the fact that the God they did not believe existed might have a plan of his own, which would mean defeat and death to the Russian Army.

Chapter Twenty Seven

Garrison Fong was frantic. No word from Tuck had come in for several days, and he had missed his scheduled contact times. He must have lost his special cell phone because they knew someone who did not know the codes was playing with it and trying to make a call.

Then, a few minutes ago, they had received a call from one of the people Tuck was working with in Tehran. It was a young women's voice. She said she was known as 'Ghost,' and their meeting had been broken up by Vevak agents.

"One of our people was a double agent and told Vevak where we were meeting. They came and shot up the place. Several of our people were killed, and Tuck was hit over the head real hard and was taken away," she reported and started to cry. "If he is in the Vevak prison he will never come out alive, and his death will be too terrible to describe." She kept on crying. One of the agents took over talking to her to make arrangements to try and get her out of the country.

Fong just sat there, stunned into disbelief. "Not Tuck, please not Tuck," he found himself saying to no one in particular. What could he possibly do for his friend? He absent-mindedly wondered if his friend had one of those old fashioned poison pills that he could take to kill himself.

The director burst into the room, looked at Fong and knew that the news she had just received was true: Tuck had probably been tortured to death in a Vevak prison. She looked at Garrison, and her heart went out to him. His face was gray, and there were great bags under his eyes. His shoulders were rounded, and he sank deeply into his chair, not hearing or seeing anything in the room.

Charlene walked out to the desk where the people were still working with Ghost to get her out of that God awful, despicable country. She asked the man on the desk if anything had come in. He looked at her through tear-flooded eyes and said, "No, director. There is no news."

"How am I going to tell Dorri?" she whispered to herself. What could she say to that sweet, gracious young woman who had seen so much pain and suffering in Iran, from her own father, and the former Iranian president? Now this!

Then pangs of guilt descended on her as she recalled how Tuck was talking about getting out of the espionage game, but she had always had just one more assignment that no one else could do as well as he could.

She couldn't take any more news; she collapsed in a chair in the hallway. The dam holding back her tears broke. She sobbed and moaned and mourned the loss of her dear friend and colleague. Tuck was just about the bravest man she had ever known. She remembered that he was going to talk to her about his faith in God when he got back from Iran. She had planned to listen to him more as a courtesy rather than a genuine interest, but that was immaterial now; he wasn't coming back.

As she sat in the hallway grieving the loss of Aristotle Tucker, a voice demanded attention and brought her back to the present.

She looked up through her tears and found to her disgust the Secretary of State William Booth III was standing in front of her. He glared down at her like some pompous Greek god. "Well, what is going on here? Why are you sitting out here in public blubbering like some school girl who just broke up with her first boyfriend? Get control of yourself woman, public persona and all that!"

She tried to get a hold of herself. "I'm sorry. We have just had the worst news. Aristotle Tucker, one of our best agents has been captured by the Vevak in Iran. They are infamous for the ingenious ways they have of torturing people while keeping them alive for a long, terrible time."

"So, what's the big deal? Just get another agent. With unemployment what it is, you should be able to find someone who wants a cushy job like you have here." His snarling sarcasm cut her to the quick, and she was immediately enraged. But, before she could speak, she saw Fong moving toward the obnoxious bureaucrat.

Neither Charlene nor the secretary of state had seen Fong standing just inside the door listening to them. His hands were balled into fists. The look in his eyes would have warned anyone with some brains to shut up. Booth did not have that much intelligence.

"You incompetent piece of trash, you're talking about a friend of mine who may have just given his life so a worthless creep like you can live in peace," Fong snarled.

Booth was enraged and started to speak, "Why you Chinese..." Fong's hands closed around the secretary's throat, and they tumbled to the floor in a writhing, cursing heap. Booth tried to scream for help, but Fong's grip was too tight and getting tighter. There was no doubt that Garrison was going to kill this man he considered to be a worthless piece of humanity.

Charlene was so surprised by the attack, it took her a second to realize she was about to be a witness to murder. She came to her senses and started shouting, "Security. Someone get security here now!" She tried to grab Garrison's hands, but she was surprised to feel the strength he had in his arms and hands. Booth's eyes were bulging out of his head as he fought and struggled against his attacker.

Just before it was too late, security agents arrived and grabbed Garrison and peeled his hands off of Booth's throat. He lay there coughing and struggling to breathe and began to vomit all over himself. It was soon evident that another of his bodily functions had failed him.

Garrison Fong suddenly became quiet: somber. He was fully aware that he would be charged with assault and sent to prison, but he couldn't have cared less. He was saddened that he had been unable to complete the kill before security arrived to pull him from the body of his victim. Never had he felt such satisfaction as he had when his hands closed around

Booth's neck. He now resigned himself to what was bound to come.

William Booth III, Secretary of State for the United States of America, sat on the floor of the Central Intelligence Agency, cursing and choking and flopping around like a beached sea lion. A crowd of agency workers had formed, and when they heard about what happened, they broke out in applause and cheering, pounding Garrison on the back in approval of his attack. A number of people took pictures of the secretary as he rolled around on the floor. Some people were recording his tirade against Garrison.

"I demand that this Chinese thug be arrested for attempted murder." He turned to Charlene and continued, "You were here, and you saw how he attacked me without provocation. I am holding you personally responsible for this heinous attack on an official of the United States. I'll see to it that every person in this agency is fired and put out on the street. I'll put all of you rats back in the gutter where you belong.

"Now help me get up," he demanded. He was rumpled, disheveled, and covered with vomit and other fluids. None of these things missed the attention of those taking pictures.

Charlene motioned for the security agents to help him to his feet. As he got up, he reached for his briefcase, which was lying nearby. Apparently, when he dropped it, the locks gave way.

When he picked it up, it flew open, and its contents fell to the floor. Charlene gasped when she saw the document sliding across the floor. She bent over and picked it up. The title on the cover read…

OPERATION ELAND

Booth got to his knees as he grabbed for the document, trying to snatch it from Charlene's hands. His grasp fell short as the CIA director side-stepped his attempt and started flipping through the pages. He tried again to grab at the document but this time Fong, who had escaped the grasp of

162

the security guards, placed a round house kick on the side of Booth's head causing him to collapse onto the marble floor. Fong and Charlene both recognized the name, Eland, as a member of Tuck's spy cell in Iran. The document contained directions and authority from the secretary of state setting up Eland as a double agent for the purposes of exposing and endangering Agent Aristotle Tucker of the CIA. Booth had arranged the whole disaster.

"I wish I had kicked him harder," breathed Fong as he stared at the document. "This piece of scum may have got Tuck killed."

Booth groaned and struggled to stand up. Charlene instructed a police officer who had arrived on the scene to put cuffs on Booth as she stared into his eyes.

"William Booth, as Director of the Central Intelligence Agency of the United States of America, it is my duty to inform you that you have the right to remain silent. Anything you say can and will be used against you in a court of law. You are under arrest for the crimes of treason against the government of the United States and conspiracy to commit the murder of Aristotle Tucker, an agent of the Central Intelligence Agency. Take him away, boys."

"But why Charlene? What would be the motivation to do such a thing?" asked Fong, "And why would he be carrying sensitive and incriminating evidence like that around in his briefcase?"

"Pride leads to sloppiness; he must have felt invincible. Either that or he was obsessed with keeping the evidence in his possession where he knew at all times that no one else was looking at it. And as for the motivation, it is probably the usual," Charlene spoke, as she continued to search the briefcase. "Ah, here it is. Banking records. I see here a deposit of $7 million into a bank in the Cayman Islands three months ago."

"What a jerk," Fong said, "Arab oil money can travel long distances. Heh?"

"Evidently. There has been a price on Tuck's head for some time so I'm not surprised. I just hope he somehow survived."

"Charlene, if anybody could make it out alive it would be Tuck. There may still be hope. We've heard nothing definitive yet."

Charlene became somber, "Back to work, guys. Remember, we still have a missing agent to try and bring home. Garrison, come with me."

They both moved to her office; she slammed the door and turned on him like a mother tiger protecting her cubs.

"Garrison, what's the matter with you? Have you lost your mind? Attacking the secretary of state in the hallowed halls of the agency, what were you thinking?" she scolded.

"If you want the truth, I was thinking I wanted to kill him. I'm still kind of sad that I didn't. I will never understand how slime like that makes it into the government. But I did assault him. What will happen to me now?" he asked.

"I don't know yet, but if you ask me, your attack on Booth was all in the line of duty. If you hadn't lost control, we would never have apprehended him," she said. Then she couldn't contain herself any longer. She grabbed Garrison and gave him a bear hug that took his breath away. He was so surprised that at first he thought she was attacking him. She hugged and cried and looked into his eyes. "Garrison, I've never been so proud of anyone in my life."

"Thank you, it just sort of happened."

Just then, the director's phone purred. She answered it and stood as still as a statue for a minute. Then she motioned him to come to the desk. She switched the phone to speaker and said, "Someone from Iraq wants to talk to us."

The phone crackled for a second, then a familiar voice came on the line. "Hey, guys, this is Tuck. Have I got a story to tell you when I get back!"

Charlene and Garrison whooped, cheered and danced around the room. Finally, Charlene got her wits about her and

164

asked, "Tuck, we heard Vevak had you, we had given you up for lost."

"It's true, and I gave up, too. But just as the goons were going to go to work on me, guess who shows up in the Vevak prison in downtown Tehran? Abisha! Don't ask me how he got in there or how he found me, but there he was wearing a white robe. He looked down at me and said that he was going to make me sleep. And that's all I remember, until I woke up in the green zone in Baghdad. The guards say three men in white robes carried me into the hospital, and said to watch me, that I had a bad concussion. But, my head feels fine now. I'm praising the Lord for rescuing me and saving my life.

"I'm taking the next plane home. I should see you tomorrow evening. Oh, and I'm more certain than ever. Iran isn't going to use a nuke on Israel. They want part of the spoils if they can get the rest of the world to join in the fight."

Garrison couldn't wait any longer, "My friend, you gave us a terrible scare. When you get back, bring Abisha in so I can shake his hand."

"I will if I can, but he's not here. A guard overheard him tell the guys in the white robes that they needed to get to Israel. I'll bet he's there now, helping people like me. I tell you, I love that guy!"

Chapter Twenty Eight

In the penthouse suite at the top of the newest hotel and casino in Las Vegas, the sinister Mr. Diablo was watching the action on the casino floor. He loved watching people gamble; it was one of the most profitable businesses he had designed and made a reality. All through history, greedy men had loved to gamble, hoping to win fortunes with little money to bet. For the heavy gamblers, they willingly gambled and lost their pay checks, food money, rent money, everything - putting their families out on the street.

Las Vegas was one of his greatest accomplishments of the century. As he sat in an overstuffed chair watching the many color monitors that displayed every area of the floor, he thought back to the start of gambling in the city. The legalizing of casino style gambling had been easy back in 1931. People were out of work and gambling promised jobs.

He smiled as he thought about how successful he had been in getting the poor to take their last dollar and gamble it away in hopes of gaining fast and easy wealth. Then in the '60s, he used the mob to build and start the first hotel and casino. Why not, the Mafia had unlimited amounts of cash of their own, plus control over union pension funds, which provided them millions of dollars to use.

Now, the famous strip was lined with scores of hotels and casinos, each one bigger and more beautiful than the others. Each hotel had its own theme, special attractions and millions of lights. Each hotel cost more and more, until the latest ones were not costing millions, they were costing billions as they sought to be bigger and better than all the rest. And what a success this street of millions of flashing lights had been. The hotels and Las Vegas itself spent millions of dollars on advertising, promising people all over the world wealth and happiness.

Diablo was taking a few days off. He was lounging around in a pink shirt with open collar and sleeves rolled up.

He wore casual slacks and maroon loafers with gold chains. His trademark Oakley sunglasses were on the bar. His yellow eyes scanned the television screens restlessly. He was smoking a huge Havana cigar and sipping from a snifter holding the most expensive brandy money could buy, although it hadn't cost him anything. The suite, food, and drinks were free. He was a valued guest, just like the biggest losers who loved to be treated like royalty and thought nothing of dropping millions of dollars in a few nights.

Diablo was extremely proud of the theme the city of Las Vegas had come up with, "What happens in Vegas stays in Vegas." He also loved the nickname, "Sin City." He took great pride in that one.

He switched his monitors over to the airport and watched people arriving on commercial flights that landed about every five minutes, 24 hours a day. Then there were the private jets, owned by the wealthiest of the wealthy. They came from around the world to enjoy the gambling, booze, drugs and sex they had been promised. Diablo occasionally would stroll down the sidewalks past the pawn shops. He chuckled when he saw all of the wedding rings that had been sold to get money enough to get home, wherever that was. Ruined marriages, drug and alcohol addiction, sexual diseases were the real products of this great, wicked city. One of the casino owners had once pronounced a great truth, "Gambling is for losers."

Diablo was in a great mood. Everything around the world was going his way. If he was right about the world's political climate, the hated Israel might just cease to exist in a few months. What a coup that would be! Surely the One he hated so desperately would be consumed in the war when it came.

There was a light knock on the door.

"Come in," he said with the immense cigar clenched in his perfect white teeth.

The door opened and a large, ugly creature slid into the room. He was hairy, like the fur of a rat, with bare patches of scaly skin. He had a big crooked nose and large yellow eyes that had vertical slits and he appeared to be near-sighted. On his back he had a pair of dirty wings. He wore a type of breastplate and a sword hung from a red sash around his waist. He walked with a clumsy gait toward Diablo. When he got near his master, he bowed and saluted with his short, hairy arms. He was a demon and apparently a demon of some rank.

"Well, Agrippa, where have you come from this fine day? I hope you have been tormenting Christians," Diablo said.

"Highness, I have just come from the barracks in Syria. Two of our men on patrol were coasting around the Sharat Kovakab volcano a couple of days ago and swore they saw some warrior angels on the side of the mountain. They flew as close as they dared when they heard what sounded like a large metal door being unlocked and opened." He waited to see how his information was being received.

"So what? It's probably on old mine shaft that's been closed for who knows what reason." Diablo was distracted by the sight of an old man putting his last dollar on the black three on the roulette wheel. The croupier started the wheel and rolled the little ball in the opposite direction. The old man must have been praying, his lips were moving silently. The ball dropped into the red slot. The old man seemed to sag as he turned and shuffled away. Later that night the news would casually report the finding of an elderly man who had hung himself in a cheap hotel room.

"Now, Agrippa, what were you saying?" The cigar was sending blue gray smoke drifting toward the ceiling.

"Highness, I was reporting two of our troops seeing what they thought to be warrior angels on the side of the old volcano in Syria. They swear they heard the angels call out, 'Abaddon, come here.'"

Diablo leapt out of his chair and grabbed the demon by the throat and started shaking him. "What did you say?" he demanded.

Agrippa was struggling to breathe. Diablo was lifting him off of the floor, and his large, crooked feet were thrashing around as if he was trying to swim. "They said they heard the angels say, 'Abaddon, come here.'"

"Is that all they heard? Did they hear anything else?"

"There was some talk, but they could not hear what was said. In a minute the big iron door was slammed shut, but the angels stayed around. It looked like they were on guard."

Diablo dropped the demon who stumbled back to his feet awaiting orders. "Can you believe it? After all of these centuries, I hear that name again. This must be the pit the Holy One cast him into after Abaddon sat on the Holy Throne. What could this mean? What is God up to? I am the ruler of this world, why would he want to release Abaddon?"

The thought of Abaddon's release from the pit immediately opened a shaft of fear deep inside Diablo's black heart. Abaddon once held the high position of angelic beast, a six winged seraph, and his voice had the power to shake the doorposts of the temple of heaven. Diablo held little true power himself, other than his great deceptive abilities. But the massive power of Abaddon was pure destruction, just as described by the meaning of his name. Diablo was also not so sure that the two of them were on friendly terms. As a matter of fact Diablo thought he may have faintly heard, in the vast distance, the voice of Abaddon screaming curses toward Lucifer the deceiver as he was being incarcerated in the pit.

Agrippa was eyeing the brandy and hoped his boss would offer him some. Diablo turned to him, his yellow eyes blazing with intensity. "Get back to those barracks and assign men to watch that door from now on, day and night. Put at least four men on the job. Oh, would you like some brandy as a reward for bringing me this important news?"

The demon smiled a crooked smile and nodded his head, agreeing some brandy would be a suitable reward for a job well done. "Yes, your highness, that would be very agreeable with me."

"Well, forget about it! Get out of here, and get on the job. Keep me informed, got it?" He swatted the demon like an oversized house fly, knocking him toward the door. Agrippa gathered himself together and scuttled out of the door. When he was outside, he mumbled, "Someday, big shot, I'll see you get yours!" He unfolded his wings and walked to the outside staircase, where he took flight on an unsteady course.

Diablo was thinking a mile a minute. As the former angel of light and one of the greatest of the angels, he still had permission to visit heaven and accuse the faithful to the Heavenly Father, as he had done with the ancient Job. So, now he had to get to heaven and poke around and see if he could pick up any information. If the Holy One would allow him, he would ask clever questions and something of importance might slip out. His evil mind was also hatching a scheme that he believed could influence and manipulate the opinion of the Holy One. Such was his arrogance!

He went to the bedroom to change clothes. He never returned to heaven dressed like a rich and successful businessman. He put on a simple dark blue pin stripe, with a white shirt and a pale blue tie. Black shoes finished the wardrobe change, and he was ready for the journey that would take him most of the day. He shook his wings loose, walked to a big window and went out to the balcony where he took off skyward.

The expanse between heaven and earth is incalculable, but angels, even fallen angels, are able to cover this vastness in just a few hours. Humans are unable to grasp how this transportation works. Perhaps it is the same principle in which light travels through space. Their wings, of course, are of no use in the vacuum of space but work well in the atmospheres of heaven and the earth.

Upon arrival in heaven, he moved with immense arrogance toward the vast throne room where he anticipated the Most High God might be found. He was recognized by angels immediately. There were no greetings; just stares as his presence brought back painful memories of his attempt to become god and how he and a third of the angels who had supported him were cast out of the heavenly realm.

He used the name Mr. Diablo on earth to mask his real identity, which made working with people much easier. It was especially useful in deceiving Christians. They let their guard down when they did not recognize the name as being someone who was dangerous.

There were, of course, Satan worshipers scattered around the globe. He cherished their worship services and sacrifices and the full display of evil unleashed made him swell with pride. His name in heaven was formerly Lucifer, a title he much preferred to the name Satan which means "the accuser."

He actually would prefer to be addressed as 'the Great Lucifer' or even 'the Great Satan', whose kingdom is the earth. He would prefer those titles but wasn't prepared to squabble about it now; he had important business on his mind.

So, when he presented himself to the doorkeeper of the Great Throne Room, he simply said, "Lucifer requests an audience with the Holy God."

"Where did you come from, Satan? Never mind, wait here," the doorkeeper said with disdain, leaving Lucifer to stand alone. The beauty of the vast room flooded him with emotions. The immense size caused everyone seeing it for the first time to question if, indeed, it was real. He saw the clear crystal floor, the jewel encrusted walls that were constantly changing like a moving rainbow. No mortal could ever have envisioned such a majestic place, let alone constructed it. Its size and beauty boggled the mind of the beholder.

The doorkeeper angel returned. His face was solemn as he came close to the fallen angel. "Have you been smoking?"

"What are you talking about? I had a cigar, but that was hours ago," he replied angrily.

"There is a washroom just over there, across the street. You will find mouthwash there. Use it! You will be standing before the Creator God of the Universe, and you don't insult him by smelling like a tobacco factory." He turned and walked away.

Lucifer was livid. *"No one treats me this way,"* he thought. *"He may be the Creator God, but I am the god of the world."*

After a minute, his pride allowed him to go to the room where he was directed. Inside he found the mouthwash, used a little, and went back to the throne room. A knock produced the same angel doorkeeper. His nose twitched with displeasure, and he said, "You cannot enter the Holy Room with shoes on your feet. Take them off!" When the evil one complied with the order, the angel motioned for Lucifer to follow him.

Inside, Lucifer settled down and gazed at the wondrous room and remembered how desperately he had wanted to be God and rule the universe from this immense and holy place. The beautiful seraphim, each with six wings and clothed in fine white linen were still flying around the throne saying, "Holy, Holy, Holy is the Lord." They did not speak with the power and volume usually heard but spoke in more hushed tones so those speaking could be heard. Lucifer glared at them, and he was filled with jealousy and hatred. His demons who served him could never compare with these fabulous creatures' beauty and power.

The doorkeeper reached out and touched his elbow in an attempt to get him to move toward the throne. Lucifer jerked his arm away and glared at the angel, who was unimpressed. "Don't touch me. No one touches Lucifer the Great."

He had not noticed six warrior angels standing along the hallway. They quickly surrounded him, swords half drawn, and the one in charge said, "You do as you're told, or you'll be touched all right. Now get moving, Evil One." As he began walking, a warrior escort fell in beside him.

"You can't talk to me like I'm some simpleton! Do you know who I am?" Lucifer raged. He had momentarily forgotten that, in heaven, he was known as Satan, not Lucifer.

"I know who you are, and if you don't shut up, the interview is over. Got it?"

Satan realized he was on the brink of being thrown out, so he gulped and shut his mouth. Soon he was in the throne room. The angels forced him to stop about twenty feet away and kneel. He started to protest but did as he was instructed. He did refuse to bow his head before The Great and Holy God, who was seated on his majestic throne, surrounded by a rainbow of green that slowly changed colors. He was too magnificent to look upon!

His great head shone with blinding brightness, like white rays from the sun, or bolts of sheet lightning. The train of his robe spread to the crystal floor and glowed with a lesser light. His eyes defied description! They seemed to meld colors together, making hues unknown to man. Lightning flashed and there were peals of thunder that left no doubt about his power and majesty.

His voice was powerful, full of energy and strength. It filled the room and was felt by all there. Warrior angels were standing a respectful distance away but ready should their Lord need them. The twenty-four elders stood in their white robes with their hands raised in worship. Four seraphim flew around the throne, using only two of their six wings saying, "Holy, Holy, Holy is the Lord."

Defying human description, these powerful angelic beasts had faces of a lion, an ox, an eagle and a man. They were covered with eyes, seeing everything at once. The archangels were not present.

The Lord spoke to Satan, "Where did you come from?"

Satan answered, "Oh, the usual, roaming about on the earth and walking around on it. I've been considering the rebellious Abaddon and how your righteous and holy judgment confined him to the pit forever. Surely one who took a seat on your throne could never be set free from the pit."

The Lord said, "Are you not aware that it is written that the beast was, and is not, and shall ascend out of the bottomless pit and go to perdition? And those who dwell on the earth will marvel, whose names were not written in the Book of Life from the foundation of the world, when they behold the beast that was, and is not, and yet is?"

"Is Abaddon to be set free? How could you do this, Righteous One? This lawless rebel took a seat on your Holy Throne!" Satan pleaded with panic in his eyes as he accused Abaddon.

"It is written that you shall not tempt the Lord your God," the Lord said as he motioned to an angel bearing a small chest that looked like a miniature treasure chest. The angel stepped toward Satan and placed the small chest in his hands and commanded, "Open it!"

Satan opened the chest and carefully looked inside. "What is this? A key?"

The angel spoke to Satan, "This is the key to the bottomless pit. You are the one who is to put the key in the lock and turn it. Your judgment awaits you, and you Satan shall now, by decree of the Most High God, never enter this court again."

A great voice was heard in the throne room, "Now is come salvation, and strength, and the kingdom of our God, and the power of his Christ, for the accuser of our brethren is cast down, who accused them before our God day and night."

There was a great rumbling and shaking as Michael and his battalion of warrior angels entered the throne room. They grabbed Satan and flung him down, hurtling and spiraling to the earth as the great voice continued in the throne room, "Woe to the inhabitants of the earth and of the sea! For the devil is come down to you, having great wrath, because he knows that he has a short time."

As Satan spiraled headlong towards the earth, he could hear the seraphim circling the throne singing, "Holy, holy, holy is the Lord." It was melodious and beautiful.

Lucifer, (aka Mr. Diablo) fell back to earth as his evil mind was planning how he and his demons could even yet thwart God's plans. He still had one more ace up his sleeve. Perhaps this could be his time! If he could just somehow persuade Abaddon to join him; they could rid the earth of the Jews once and for all. After all, a Messiah of the dead would in reality be no Messiah at all. If he could defeat Jesus by killing every last Jew, he would surely be the ruler of the universe. What a delicious thought!

Chapter Twenty Nine

Dark clouds heavily laden with rain moved slowly over the city of London. The darkness in the middle of the day covered human endeavors with gloom and melancholy. Mr. Diablo was attending the meeting of the London chapter of Atheists United. He had asked them if they would object if he invited the London branch of the environmentalists organization, which was, in reality, a new religion patterned after the ancient pagan "Mother Earth" beliefs.

The atheists were a little taken back by the large number of people attending from this organization. They, however, considered themselves liberal pragmatists who had a big enough tent to welcome anyone, except Christians, who they labeled as "intolerant Bible thumpers."

Diablo mounted the platform and took the pulpit and microphone away from the one who had been assigned to give the opening remarks. He started speaking with a happy, sweet cadence. His suit was a bright light blue, and he was wearing white shoes.

"Ladies and gentlemen, this weekend our great city will be faced with the most dangerous meeting since before the second world war," he said, no longer smiling. His Oakley sunglasses reflected the lights on the chandelier hanging from the hotel ceiling. He had the full attention of the people in the room.

"This Saturday, an American evangelist will be holding a meeting in the soccer stadium. Estimates range as high as a million people will be attending one of the four meeting days. This man has said that the only way anyone can get to heaven is by putting his faith in an ancient prophet. This means that all my good friends here are just plain out of luck! He also proposes that the Americans do more off shore drilling for oil and open new coal fields in West Virginia.

If that isn't enough, he blasts all environmentalists as just being part of an ancient pagan religion that worships our wonderful Mother Earth." Diablo rested for a second. He could hear murmurings coming from the crowd. He was right on track with the responses exactly what he wanted.

"This intolerant evangelist will be trying to convince the audience that you are evil people and have no rights in his world." The crowd was growing restless and the murmurings were turning to shouts of "No," and "We have to stop him."

"I am proposing that we make a concerted effort to disrupt these meetings and keep him from spreading his lies and intolerance. If we plan things right, we can have people scattered all over around the stadium. Then we start shouting and waving flags from our various groups.

It would be good if a few people got pushed around. This will accomplish two things: it will frighten the audience and get us on television. If the police are dispatched, our results will be even more positive. The goal is to stop him from preaching his lies and show the people there that we are a force to be reckoned with. Are you with me?" he shouted.

They came to their feet in unison, shouting and screaming and vowing to put an end to this guy, Gabby Townsend. Diablo stood on the platform with both arms raised in the air accepting the applause and comradeship of the strange gathering of the fringe element, who, in years past, would have been considered "freaks" but who were now a potent political power. Every cowardly politician would now kneel at their altar.

As Diablo walked off the platform, he stopped to talk to some of the men he knew to have any unsavory, violent past along with the muscle to go with it.

"Gentlemen, it might be a good idea if some of the people get roughed up pretty good. A little riot here and there would be very helpful.

"Anybody who has the opportunity to work the evangelist over will receive £1,000 in cash. If he happens to be killed, the reward will go up to £100,000!" There were evil grins in the group. It was obvious that most of them would be trying for the bigger number.

Diablo shouted to the group to be quiet as he jumped back up on the platform. "Ladies and gentlemen, we have already organized a sizable group ready to do battle with this congregation of creepy wimps! I will be in the audience to guide events as they unfold. Look for me; I will be wearing a white suit, white shoes, and a white straw hat. I'll signal where there are weak areas that can be overcome easily. Okay guys, lets go get 'em!"

The room exploded in cheers and threats. "Let's kill 'em," they raged. The mob left to get liquored up, wishing it was already Saturday.

Unseen by the blood-thirsty crowd, was a tall, handsome man with a very tan face standing in the back saying nothing. When the meeting was over, he left hurriedly.

Gabby was now a marked man with a price on his head. A small army of villains would be in the crowd waiting their chance.

The man who was in the meeting was soon visiting with none other than Abisha, who was visiting little children in a cancer hospital. Wherever he went, his wide smile brightened up everything. After he had visited with every child, he met with the man, who was, in reality, a disguised warrior angel.

"Tell me, Tennyson, what was the meeting like?" Abisha asked.

"The Evil One did a good job of bringing a bunch of groups together who are always looking for a chance to start trouble. He put a price on Gabby's head of £100,000 that had some hotheads foaming at the mouth. He said he was going to be in the stadium Saturday wearing a white suit so they can see him and follow his directions of where they should terrorize people.

"Sir, this could be a real mess with lots of people getting hurt, which is what the Evil One wants, along with as much television coverage as he can get," the angel said seriously.

"Well my friend, we've been in difficult places before, this will be no different. We need to beat our yellow-eyed friend at his own game. I want you to get a hundred warriors in the stadium Saturday and every night of the crusade. Have them all dressed in white suits. This should confuse the trouble makers, who will, no doubt, be drunk to begin with.

"If there is any trouble, they are to infiltrate the group when they try and disrupt the meeting. You are authorized to use as much force as necessary to remove the most dangerous protesters. But, remember, I want as many of these lost souls as possible to stay and hear the message that God loves them with a love that never ceases."

"It shall be done as you wish." The angel and his master walked side by side out of the clinic.

Saturday afternoon came, and Gabby was leaving the details of getting the crusade ready to his staff, led by his beloved Evelyn. He shut himself in his hotel room after it had been checked by hotel staff. Now, he was lying on his face on the floor praying and weeping.

"Holy Father, there may be a quarter of a million souls here tonight and millions watching on television. I am too weak to face them. Please give me the courage and strength to tell them the simple gospel of how much you love them and how they just need to trust you and believe in your son."

He pushed himself up on his elbows and took his worn Bible and turned to John 4:23, "Yet a time is coming and has now come when the true worshipers will worship the Father in spirit and truth…"

"Please, dear Lord, give me the words to show the people how to worship in spirit and truth."

There was a knock on the door, and a staff member said it was time to go to the stadium. He got up, washed, and put on a light suit because it was very warm for London. He took nothing but his Bible. A car drove him to the stadium. He couldn't get over how huge it looked. He was overwhelmed and felt the urge to turn around and run away. But that only lasted for a moment. He was anxious to tell the people about his friend Jesus, who had died so they could have their sins forgiven and live with him forever.

An elevator took him to the field level. The platform had been built about a third of the way down the field. A choir was singing wonderful hymns. The praise and worship bands had just finished. People were in a receptive mood.

He walked to the platform and took his seat to the right of the pulpit. He was still praying in his heart, when he heard his name called and applause welled up from the crown. He looked for the first time and saw the stadium was filled, with standing room only. The butterflies raged in his stomach and he was afraid for a moment that he might throw up. He stood at the pulpit, waiting for the crowd to become quiet. Then he began.

"Good evening, ladies and gentlemen. What a beautiful city you have here, what's it called?" he teased.

"London!" the crowd roared.

"Okay, well I want to assure you that, as beautiful as London is, there's another city that is hundreds of times more beautiful. It's called heaven, and you can live there with God forever, if you do something very simple."

He read John 3:16 to the crowd, and as he was reading, he thought he heard some shouting in the audience. Gabby felt that this must mean there would be a good response tonight. He kept on preaching his simple message.

"God loves you so much that he sent his only son, whose name is Jesus, to come to earth, live a sinless life, and die on a terrible cross to pay for the sins you and I have committed or will ever commit. Three days later, he arose from the grave and is alive today, sitting at the right hand of God the Father. All you have to do to get to this beautiful city, and to never be alone again, is to tell Jesus you have sinned, ask him to forgive you, and invite him into your heart. That's it. He will come in and live with you forever. The church term for it is called 'salvation,' and Jesus is known as our 'savior.'"

Now there seemed to be a commotion on the right side of the stadium. He thought he saw a number of men in white suits. Gabby glanced around, and saw men in white all over the place. In a couple of places, he thought he saw a little scuffle, but it didn't last.

The message was over, and the invitation given. The aisles filled with people coming forward. He saw some of the men in white helping elderly people come forward. Some carried little children for their mothers, as both wanted to know this wonderful Jesus. And some of the men in white had their arms around some pretty grubby looking goons, who were weeping as they were helped to the front for prayer. None were turned away, even though they had come to cause trouble and disrupt the meeting. By the end of the crusade, hundreds from the unsavory groups were saved.

Gabby wept, as he always did when people gave their lives to his friend. The crusade was a tremendous success that Saturday, and for the rest of the week. Hundreds of thousands of people became believers.

Diablo was furious and cursed many of the pagan religions for not doing more to disrupt the meetings. As he calmed down, he decided there would always be another chance. He was surprised, however, by the unusual number of men wearing white suits.

Chapter Thirty

Barrack Huessen, the Iranian Minister of the Interior was meeting with a secretive looking little man in a seedy hotel which was located in the south side of Tehran. The denizens of the street knew it was better not to notice anyone as they walked by the hotel in which the Minister of the Interior was sitting in the lobby talking to a little weasel known only as "Jergus." The overstuffed chairs they were seated in were dirty and smelly. Huessen was certain that crawly things were making their way into his clothing as he sat there. He wanted out of this place...now!

"Jergus, what happened to the American spy that Vevak had in custody?"

Jergus was not a good double agent. He trembled slightly and continually wiped his forehead with a dirty handkerchief. Perhaps in a shower, he might weigh one hundred pounds, but that didn't happen very often. His chinless face was thin, and his rat-like eyes darted back and forth.

"I dunno," he stammered. "The boss said they were just starting to work on the guy, and he died. What a wimp!" the coward said. Even thinking of the Vevak torture room made him want to pass out.

"Well, where's the body?" Huessen asked.

"Dunno that either. The guys left him in a pickup. When they went to get him, he was gone ... just disappeared." He glanced around the empty lobby.

"I have another assignment for you. This one is worth a thousand American dollars. You interested?"

"Sure, I'm always interested in easy money. Who do I have to kill?" He snickered at his little joke. His rodent nose twitched above a little mouse of a mustache.

"I want to know who Vevak is working for. Somebody's paying them to plan for the assassination of our president when we get our first nuclear bomb," Huessen said, watching the little man closely.

"Are you out of your mind?" he shouted without thinking. "I can't get information like that. What do you think this is, a movie? If there is a plan, it will be so secret that no more than three or four people will know about it. And they sure as the world are not going to tell me. Are you trying to get me killed?"

"Oh, shut up, Jergus. I happen to know you have contacts at the highest level of the organization. I need this information in a week."

"A week! You are out of your mind. That kind of work will take months, if not years." He got up to leave. He looked at the minister and was horrified to see a small automatic pistol aimed right at his gut. Huessen waved the gun, signaling him to sit back down. His eyes said he was prepared to kill him.

"Now, my little friend, let's get down to business. Whoever is financing this unpatriotic act will be in contact with someone high up, probably the Supreme Leader Tieman Koumani. If they do, Vevak will know about it," the minister said quietly.

"But sir, the head of Vevak is the president's brother. Surely he would warn him if he were in any danger. This whole thing must be the result of eating bad food before bed," Jergus whined.

The minister reached in his pocket and pulled out a sack and handed it to the weasel-like creep who would gladly sell his mother into slavery for $100. Inside was $500 in old bills, impossible to trace. Jergus handled the money and licked his lips.

"Tell you what, my friend. Get me the information in a week, and I'll raise the ante to five thousand dollars. How's that for a good deal? And I don't think there is any love lost between brothers. The president has him at Vevak where he can keep an eye on him. If there's enough money, Danush would turn on his brother in a second."

Jergus hadn't been listening; he was fondling the dollar bills. "Five thousand dollars! Man, that's great. I don't know how I'm going to get you anything, but I'll give it a try." He gave a grimace, which passed for a smile. He got up and was gone out the back door. The minister looked around, saw no one, and left by a side door, where his limo and its very nervous driver were parked. He got in, and the limo whispered quietly into the empty street. Huessen knew that if this meeting ever got back to Hafez, the president would have him tortured and killed. He was taking a big risk, but he felt it was worth it. He had big political plans of his own, and if he could just get in with the right people, he might be able to achieve his secret goal … to be the president of Iran, and stop this nuclear nonsense before Israel decided enough was enough and bombed them into cement dust.

As the black limo raced down the street to take the minister home, another car pulled away from a side street and fell in behind them with its lights off. It stayed a careful block away, until some early morning traffic made it possible to move closer without being seen.

At 7:00 a.m. the following day, Jergus was working on his new assignment. In reality, he was a very creative detective, working in his own way and with his own methods. He saw a secretary, who worked in the office of the Supreme Leader in a coffee shop, having a roll and sweet coffee. He couldn't be seen talking with her, so he slipped her a folded note that said, 'It's worth $100 for you to tell me anything of interest happening with Koumani. I'm interested in calls, visitors, and letters, anything unusual.' He saw her look his way and give a little nod of her head as she got up to leave.

Later that night, he was at the same coffee shop sipping iced coffee. It was a very hot evening. He saw the woman sitting in nearly the same spot as she had been that morning. She glanced his way, got up, paid her bill and left. She did not take the paper she had been reading with her. He waited for a minute. The other patrons were paying no attention to anything but their coffee and sweet rolls. He got up and walked casually to the table where the paper was, stopped and glanced at it, acting as if a story had caught his interest. He picked up the paper and sat down and began reading. When he was sure he was not being watched he opened the paper to the center. Written at the top of the page was a message, "Russians call often." That was it. He took the paper with him as he left.

The next night he was in the old flea bag hotel at the same late hour. The minister came in, looked around and sat down opposite the little conspirator.

"What do you have for me?"

"More importantly, what do you have for me?" Jergus asked.

"If your information is of interest, you will have your money," Huessen said. He didn't like negotiating with this piece of trash like they were equals.

"I can tell you the Russians call the Supreme Leader often. Is that of interest?"

"It is indeed. What do they talk about?" he asked.

"Hee, haw, hee!" he snorted. "You're a funny man. You know I can't get that kind of information. Ask the Supreme Leader, he's the only one who knows that answer. Give me my money!" Jergus demanded. It was the last sentence of his life. Huessen tossed him a paper sack. As the little man reached up to catch the sack, a .22 long nose tore into his heart. He dropped like a sack of hammers, still grasping the paper sack, which was full of cut newspaper. He had trusted a man who trusted no one and was not about to have this little man holding such information over his head to be used later as blackmail.

Huessen put the still-smoking automatic back in his pocket. He looked around the lobby and saw they were alone. He hurried out to the alley and climbed into his black limo. It pulled into the street and whispered into the darkness. A block behind them, a car pulled out into the late night traffic and followed the limo from a safe distance. The late night intrigue continued just as a drunk found the body of the unfortunate Jergus. He searched the body for anything of value, found a dollar in change. The drunk took the money and left.

Chapter Thirty One

On the slopes of Sharat Kovakab, wild grasses and flowers were flourishing since a gentle rain that lasted three days brought much needed moisture. It was a peaceful and serene scene. Further down the mountain, shepherds were watching their sheep graze peacefully. The air was fresh and clean after being scrubbed by the rain. Soon, it would be dark, and the stars in the crystal clear sky would shine and twinkle in their proper places in constellations that have danced the skies since the beginning of creation. Scientists say the universe is expanding at the speed of light and has been for billions of years. They love to hide in their immense numbers, which are incomprehensible to man. How then are the constellations in the same place in the sky where they have been located since man first started charting them in the days of the Babylonians?

These questions were of no interest to the two warrior angels guarding the great iron door. What was of interest was the noise coming out of the pit. They wondered if they should warn their supervisors of increased activity.

Behind the massive door, it was anything but peaceful and serene. There was a great deal of activity way down deep in the bowels of the pit. Abaddon and the other fallen angelic beast, the False Prophet, certainly did not like each other very much, but for now, they were cooperating in organizing the millions of barbaric locusts and impish demons into some kind of order.

Abaddon was barely visible in the orange light from rivulets of lava that was trying to shine through the steam and dust. The dust was a problem. The great demonic locusts with huge tails like scorpions were restless and quarrelsome. They were stomping around, causing the black dust to swirl into the air, choking everything and making it more difficult to see.

The great seraph was engrossed in the problem of numbering the dreadful locusts and getting them into some kind of groups for ease of movement when the time came. Abaddon screamed for quiet. The walls shook, triggering yet another earthquake, this time north of Borneo. The great locusts and impish demons suddenly were silent.

"Now keep it quiet while we get you organized!" It was quiet except for the occasional cough and stamping of huge feet.

The prophet was looking over some clay charts. "Why don't we use a military system of organizing the locust troops for marching and for fighting?"

Abaddon thought for a minute. "Yes, that's an excellent idea. Let's see, a legion will contain 6,000 of the hideous locusts at full strength," he said.

"That's right. A phalanx would have 128; a cohort would have 480 led by eight centurions. We can use this system to bring order and direction in our assault to torture and dominate man. How many locusts do you think are in this hell hole with us?"

"I'm not really sure, millions at least. We can divide 6,000 into a million and we get 166 legions. If we put a hundred of our ugly friends in charge to relay our orders, we should have pretty good control and discipline. Write that down so we can remember it when the time comes. Wait a minute; we need to get these big fellows into legions now to start training. They have a huge task ahead of them, marking my wonderful name on all of those humans. Won't that be fun to watch?"

The Prophet just snorted. He didn't want to start a fight. "We'd better figure out a way to apply your wonderful name so that it sticks to 'em no matter what they do to get it off. Any ideas?"

"Call down there and have them send us one of the locusts with the longest scorpion tails so we can experiment on applying the mark. Make sure they send up one that has the extra large poison stinger, all black with a little red tip. We'll probably have to teach them how to spell my name.

They're not very bright, just very angry and very strong," Abaddon said.

In a few minutes one of the demonic locusts, destined to torment mankind, was ushered into Abaddon's presence. Abaddon shivered then grinned. These guys were really ugly and powerful. They had the heads of demonic, angry men with long, scraggly hair. Their fearful mouths gleamed with the razor sharp teeth of lions. Their upper bodies were well-muscled and covered in armor. The body was that of a large horse with six wings and the gigantic tail of a scorpion. Just for a minute, the great seraph doubted anyone would be able to control such a creature. Much to his surprise, when he snarled, "Come here," the monster obeyed immediately.

"Let's see how we can get him to burn my name on a human." He drew the Hebrew symbol for his name on a clay tile. "Engrave my name three times with your poisonous tail! This will be a perfect witness of my authority over the humans."

אָבַד אָבַד אָבַד

The locust was clumsy but obeyed. It took him just twenty seconds. He did it again and was much faster. The third time Abaddon's name was finished as fast as the beast Abaddon could write it himself.

"But, my dear friend, Abaddon," the Prophet chimed in, "you have put me in charge of the training, but this is one of the brightest of the creatures. Some of the other locusts, though just as ferocious, are too stupid to inscribe your name."

"Arrg!" grumbled Abaddon with the disdain of a disgruntled pirate. "Well, surely they can do this," as he grabbed a blank clay tile and carved as he spoke. "This symbol "6" is the number of man."

Abaddon, being one of the most powerful of created angels, knew many things intuitively, and he had witnessed history first hand, flying near the throne of heaven until the sixth day of creation.

Abaddon reminisced, "For eons, including the first five days of earth's creation, I, the great Abaddon, was in a position of holy authority and favor. I knew in my heart that, when the Holy One had completed the creation of the earth, he would appoint me as a supreme ruler over it. But on that dreadful sixth day, the day of man, God created man and said those awful words, 'Let us make man in our image, and let him *rule!*'

Six is the number of man, and the number six shall be his mark. Mark it deep into man's flesh three times! It shall be a perfect witness of my sublime rule over him, 666 burning painfully deep into man's flesh. But only those locusts who are too stupid to engrave my name shall engrave the number 666, the rest shall engrave my full magnificent name!"

Abaddon then commanded the barbaric locust, "Engrave the symbol '666' on the clay tile."

6 6 6

"Wonderful, well done! Now we need to try it on something alive and wriggling. He reached into a pack of demons that were squabbling about something and grabbed one unlucky fellow by the throat. Abaddon gave the screeching and struggling imp into the powerful hands of the barbaric locust and said, "Inscribe the mark on his forehead or the back of his hand. Mark it deep into his putrid flesh! No, I'll tell you what, put it both places. Use your tail, and don't spare the poison, but don't kill him! These things must be done delicately to relish the torture!" Abaddon screamed as he ascended into a euphoric frenzy with the thought of soon burning his mark, the mark of the beast, deep into the flesh of hated mankind.

The imp struggled and yelped and screamed. The creature held him in his powerful arms while the scorpion tail came over his back and repeatedly stung the demon above his eyes, engraving the mark. The hairy thing bellowed and screamed in pain. His yellow eyes were bulging from his head as the poison went into his system. In seconds, it was over, and the mark went deep into the forehead and the back of his hand. The victim couldn't stop screaming and writhing in pain. His eyes watered and clouded in the heat.

Abaddon looked closely at his mark with great pleasure. Abaddon, the beast, would soon be released to ascend out of the bottomless pit. The beast would force, without mercy, his symbol of torture and domination on millions, if not billions, of hated humans. The mark of the beast was plain, easily read, but the sores ran with puss and blood into the poor demons eyes, causing another source of dreadful pain.

The great Abaddon was ecstatic. They had the answer on how to put the mark on billions of human beings. It thrilled him to think of the screams from thousands upon thousands of people receiving the mark at the same time. It would be wonderful to see the hated humans suffer in a way they have never faced before.

"But you have forgotten an important detail, oh Great One," the prophet chided sarcastically, ducking his head to escape a swipe from Abaddon's fist. With no time for another earth shaking tussle, the Prophet continued, "How to track down billions of humans is the question. There are a lot of places to hide on this earth, my comrade."

"Yes," responded Abaddon, scratching his lion-like chin in deep thought. "You must dispatch 100 of the legions to track down hiding humans. But position the other 66 legions at locations where food and essential goods are stored. If someone shows up starving, they will get the mark. None will be able to buy anything without either my name or the number of my name engraved in their hand or forehead.

"You are also to begin training the demon imps to force the humans to build a great image of me for mankind to worship. The weakly imps are not much good for anything, but they should be able to handle that task. Threaten them that if they fail or give up, they will get the mark themselves!"

He turned to the prophet. "Okay, we've got the plans ready. You get the legions organized. Give them a standard that they can see and follow in the heat of battle. The demon centurions must be the largest you can find, smart and able to give orders, and deal out punishment if anyone gets out of line."

Now it was just a matter of time, although Abaddon had no way of measuring the passage of time. All he knew was that he wanted out of this place. His features furrowed with hatred as he thought about the trouble humans had caused him. Humans, and that low life Satan!

Chapter Thirty Two

Charlene Lewis-Sloden was the director of the Central Intelligence Agency, she felt as if she were working for a foreign power. What information her agency garnered from the network against Iran was turned around and used against Israel.

She had been called to the Oval Office by President Steinmetz who demanded a review of the intelligence she had gathered about a possible pre-emptive strike by Israel.

When she stepped out of her limo into the gray light of a rainy day with blustery winds, she felt cold, as if she had walked over a grave. She showed her credentials to the smart looking Marine guard. She smiled at him, and he returned her smile even though it was against regulations.

Charlene was shown into the Oval Office and found that the President was there, with his feet on the desk as he smoked a cigar. Her nose automatically twitched in disdain. The secretary of state was also present. Steinmetz had pulled strings with a judge who owed him a favor to get Booth off the hook in the Operation Eland affair. His arrogance permeated the room, and his lips curled in a humorless grin that resembled the snout of a Doberman protecting his property. Charlene was incensed and vowed to get Booth one way or another, but this was neither the time nor place. She took a seat on one of the couches and waited.

"Thank you, Madam Director, for coming over to give us a briefing on our friends the Israelis. What news do you have for us?" the President glowered at her. He hated her and didn't care if she knew it or not.

"Mr. President, our intel tells us that the Israeli government feels isolated from the rest of the world, and they are just waiting for an attack from Iran. Their intel is much better than ours, so I am sure they are working on their own time table. We think Iran will have a nuclear weapon soon, although we are getting rumblings that the Russians are telling Hafez such a nuclear strike will do too much damage to neighboring nations, who might, in turn, attack him." She stopped and waited for a response.

"Hafez is an idiot. He wants to wipe out Israel, but heck, who doesn't?" he laughed. Charlene was horrified by what she had just heard but kept her peace. She knew that Steinmetz was trying to irritate her.

The Secretary of State, William Booth III, burst out laughing. "Hafez doesn't care if he wipes out Israel. He wants a world war, so some religious guy can come back to earth. You can't tell what a nut like that will do."

"Tell me, Charlene, what are the odds that the Israelis will launch a pre-emptive strike against Iran?" Steinmetz asked. He had turned his back on them and was looking out of the windows at the drizzle coming down. He dropped cigar ashes on the blue carpet, but he didn't notice this affront to the historic room.

"Will she be acting alone or with allies?" Charlene asked.

"As far as I know, she doesn't have any allies. The people of the United States are tired of bailing this trouble maker out of jams. If she attacks Iran, it will be the policy of this country to treat her as a hostile nation, and we will react accordingly."

"That certainly is a change in policy from what we have had for sixty years. It will cause a firestorm among American Jews and Christians who support Israel."

"I am not concerned about the feelings of religious extremists. They're the same as the fanatic Hafez."

"Well, to answer your question, we think the odds are fifty-fifty at best. If the Iranians launch missiles, nuclear tipped or just plain warheads, Israel will respond with everything they have. They know they will be fighting to the death, so anyone standing against them had better be prepared for the worst," she said.

She wanted out of this room made horrid by the two classless humans sitting here.

William Booth spoke up, "I'm sure we have your assurance that you will pass on any intel you receive from the region. We particularly want to know what Israel is planning to do and when. If they become the aggressor, we will stop any aid, and we will take the position that their militarist stance will force us to work to foil their plans. You can read whatever you like into that. You are a Jew lover, aren't you?"

Charlene lost it. She grabbed an antique book standing on a small table and threw it with all of her might at the sneering face of the secretary of state. She missed!

"How dare you say such a thing? I have served my country for longer than you have been in office stealing from this great nation." She turned on her heel and stormed out of the office. It galled her to hear the two men laughing at her.

When she got back to her office, she was still trembling from her encounter with the two men she now felt were doing their best to see Israel destroyed. As she sat at her desk, Garrison Fong rushed in, then stopped as he saw her face. "Good grief, Madam Director, you look terrible. What is wrong?"

Charlene unloaded on him. She was so embarrassed that she couldn't help crying. "Those two creeps are up to no good. Do you know what I think they are up to? I think they are planning on going to war against Israel! Israel, for God's sake, our only real ally in the region. I wish we could get the Jewish press involved to put some pressure on Steinmetz. He crumbles under pressure."

Garrison was lost in thought for a moment and then remembered why he had charged in the room. "We have just heard from our deep cover agent in Tehran. Her code name is 'Angel', and she is in so deep no one knows about her but Tuck and myself."

"Well, for heavens sake, what did she say?"

"She says the Russians are putting pressure on Hafez to give up the idea of a nuclear strike. The radiation would affect too many friends in the area. They are pushing for a conventional military invasion, which may include the United Nations."

"How in blazes does she know that?"

"Now, now, secrets and the need to know, and all of that stuff. I am going to tell her to get out of there now, while leaving the country is still possible. She has served us well for several years, but it is getting too dangerous to leave her in country. Oh well, you are the director; I guess you can be trusted. Her name is Summer Montabon. She's an Iranian, but her home is in New Orleans. She is Hafez's secretary," Garrison said.

"What a coup! You guys are great. For heavens sake, get her out of there as soon as you can get a message to her." Charlene was feeling better already.

"Done, Madam Director, but this doesn't help us with the two 'choir boys'!"

"I think my time here is over. I expect a visit from the President's hatchet man tomorrow with the news. I don't care for this administration and shouldn't be serving it."

"I understand completely. I may be right behind you."

The director's phone purred, and her secretary told her someone outside wanted to see her.

"Send him in," she said. "This may be the ax man now."

The door opened, and both of them dropped their jaws to the floor in surprise. It was Tuck, alive and well and standing there grinning at them.

"Tuck, dear God, it's Tuck!" Charlene shouted. Garrison just stormed over to their favorite spy and nearly knocked him down as he gave him a smothering hug.

"Easy guys, I'm on your side," Tuck said laughing.

"My gosh, Tuck, how did you get home? Are you all right? Have you been to see Dorri yet? Will you speak up and say something?" Garrison gushed.

"Well, great scot, would you guys give me a chance to speak? The Air Force flew me home today from a remote Army base in Iraq," Tuck said.

"But, how did you get there? We heard you were captured by Vevak and sent to their torture prison!" Garrison asked.

"You're right, they did, and they were getting ready to use the most barbaric tool on my body that has ever been made by the mind of man. I was terrified of what they were going to do to me. My friends, I prayed to my Lord Jesus with all of my heart.

Just before the goons were going to start working on me, Abisha, of all people, appeared standing next to me. He whispered to me that he was going to put me to sleep, and that he would not leave me - ever! The next thing I knew, I was in Iraq. The guys in the medical tent said I had a bad bump on the head but that was all. They said a man in his thirties with long hair, wearing sandals, brought me in, with two big men with bronze faces. They guessed the men had been in the desert sun a lot. They were wearing white robes.

That's the story, folks. Now, is that a miracle or what? I know it sounds bizarre, but that's what happened to me and how Abisha saved me from a terrible death."

Tuck wiped back tears from recounting the story he had just lived through.

Charlene said, "This Abisha fellow is quite a guy. I would love to meet him."

"He would love to meet you, too. He is sent to us by our Heavenly Father on personal missions for individual people," Tuck said, and looked at Garrison. "Would you like to meet my friend, Garrison?"

"Your story is so amazing, I would be a fool not to want to meet such an incredible man. Tell me more!"

And Tuck did, he told them about how God's love for them was so great that he allowed his only Son to die a terrible death to pay for all of the sins of mankind - past, present and future. He told them that his Son was named Jesus, and he lived a perfect life, was brutalized by the Romans, and hung on a cross.

Tuck told them that the Son died, was in the grave for three days, and then arose, alive, having conquered death. "He is alive today, still working in people's lives. He is the key to having eternal life with the Father in heaven. All you have to do is believe on his name, and that he is who he says he is, the only Son of God."

Tuck looked his two friends in the eye and said, "Time is running out on this old world. Do what I did, and what my dear Dorri did, invite him into your life, and we will all live together forever in heaven." Tuck stopped, embarrassed that he had been talking so much.

Charlene spoke first. Her eyes were moist with emotion. "Tuck, I want what you have. I want to ask God's son into my life." Tuck was crying now, and he knelt quietly with her, taught her how to pray and receive Christ. And it was done.

Garrison watch the whole thing fascinated. Suddenly he made up his mind and dropped to the floor and prayed the same prayer. Then there was laughing and hugging and pounding each other on the back as joy swept over all of them.

Then Tuck stood up and, laughing said, "I can't crawl around on the floor with you people. I've got to get home and see Dorri. I'm sure she is worried."

Charlene and Garrison laughed and waved good-bye to their friend who was now their spiritual brother.

In Jerusalem, Abisha stopped walking down the street, smiled and whispered, "Yes, my friends, we will all be together forever!"

Chapter Thirty Three

It had been a scorching day in Israel. Rabbi Bernardi had waited until the cool of the evening to make a pilgrimage to the Mount of Olives, just outside of the city of Jerusalem. He was carrying an old and much worn copy of the Tanakh. It was peaceful here and shaded from the sun. It pleased him to sit and read from the Holy Book and try and imagine in his mind's eye the great and holy things which had taken place here down through the ages. These rocky slopes that had been trod by men for thousands of years were steeped in history and mystery. Sitting here, he was almost able to imagine what it must have been like when he read any particular book.

He loved this remarkable city, this great Jerusalem which has been conquered so many times by so many different peoples. But the Lord God had always restored the city and forgiven her people - always before.

The rabbi's reading took him to the prophet Zechariah. As he scanned the familiar pages, something led him to read chapter 14. He must have read this hundreds of time in his life, but this time the words flew off the page and burned into his brain. A war was coming, a terrible war with death, plunder and slavery.

Bernardi was Italian by birth, but Jerusalem was his home. He felt he loved the magnificent city nearly as much as God did. Now, a prophecy too terrible to imagine predicted half of the population would be taken into slavery, and there would be much violence and killing.

"Dear God above, please, not again!" he prayed out loud and began to weep silently, betrayed only by the shaking of his shoulders.

He heard footsteps coming up the path. He tried to wipe the glistening tears out of his black beard, but he was unsuccessful to the discerning eye. He looked up and was pleased and surprised to see his young friend Abisha walking toward him.

Abisha smiled and waved a greeting to his friend, Rabbi Bernardi. "Hello, my good friend. Doesn't this ancient tree give wonderful shade? One wonders what famous people recorded in the Tanakh have sat where you are sitting. I am sure there were many. It gives such a grand view of the city."

"Hello, Abisha. I suppose you are going to tell me you just happened to be wandering around outside the city in the heat of the day and came up here to rest in the shade of the same tree where I have sought refuge."

Abisha's laughter rang out over the valley. He didn't snicker, he roared with mirth, the kind of laughter that is so contagious. He raised his arms in surrender and seated himself on a rock across from the rabbi.

"You've caught me, my friend. I was looking for you, hoping to have another wonderful conversation. You are very stimulating to converse with, and I was hoping you might have time for us to have another discussion."

As he sat down, Bernardi could not help but notice the kindness in this man's face and particularly his penetrating eyes. His ready smile put one at ease, and as he sat across from him, the rabbi felt like a college professor about to give an oral exam. This rather handsome young "student" was dressed in his usual white shirt and tan slacks. The ever present worn sandals gave the feeling of comfort and stability. He did not have his long hair in a queue. It was loose, and the light breeze wafted dark curls playfully around his face.

"Well, Abisha, what is on your mind? Do you want to talk about the weather, or the price of diamonds on the Amsterdam market?"

"No, I noticed you were reading from the Tanakh. May I ask what book you were reading?" Abisha's eyes never left Bernardi's. "Were you praying for peace for Jerusalem?"

Rabbi Bernardi was aghast. How could he possibly know that? "You are more observant than is comfortable. One might feel like you are prying into private matters. But, you are exactly right, I was praying for peace for Jerusalem. These are perilous times. We are surrounded by enemies who are committed to wiping us out as a nation. The newspapers say that our old ally the United States has begun turning their back on us, howling for us to give up more land to the Palestinians."

The rabbi was becoming more incensed with every word he spoke. "More land! It is well-known by our military that Hezbollah has received shipments of Scud missiles from Iran. They are right on our borders, for the love of heaven!"

"Would it be all right if I were to call you Samuel? 'Rabbi' seems so formal and intimidating," Abisha asked.

He had pulled up a tall grass stem to twirl in his hands. The act exposed the horrendous scars. Bernardi noticed them again.

"Of course, you may call me Samuel. You have become a good friend, but wait a minute, how did you know my name?" he inquired.

"Let's just say we have some mutual friends." Once again, that disarming smile.

"Well, you are most mysterious and turn up at the strangest times."

"I noticed your tears as you were reading. Was it one of the prophets?"

"Yes, I was reading the prophet Zechariah, and the most troubling chapter 14. I will share a truth with you. It seems that, ever since I have met you, I am seeing things in the prophets that I have never before experienced. I can't give a good reason; it just happens."

"Let's just say that is a good thing."

"Well, chapter 14 is not a good thing. Jerusalem is going to be surrounded by powerful enemies once again. The city will be conquered, and there will be great suffering of our people." His eyes moistened again as he looked at the buildings just across the valley and imagined the terror of war.

Abisha was also moved by the suffering of his friend. "What else does it say?"

Bernardi pointed at the portion of scripture with his long, boney finger.

"Look Abisha," he began reading, "Zechariah explains that the Day of the Lord is coming. On that day, all nations shall be gathered against Jerusalem to do battle. The city shall be taken, the houses ransacked, and our women raped. Many will be slaughtered, and even half the city shall be taken as captives."

Abisha reached over and touched the rabbi's hand. "Yes, what you read is true, but it is important that you read the rest. A remnant will escape and not be cut off. My friend, there will be survivors."

"Oh! But the suffering, Abisha. The coming death and torture of so many of our people! Thus, my tears."

A tear found its way into Abisha's beard as they both gazed at the city. "Yes, Samuel, I have wept over Jerusalem in the past, and I continue to do so."

"But how can anyone survive such an attack, Abisha? What must we do for our nation to survive on the earth? I believe only the arrival of our Messiah can save us."

"Precisely, my friend. Look at what this says." Abisha pointed at the book. "Read it aloud to me please."

"It says the feet of Messiah shall stand on that day upon the Mount of Olives which shall split, forming a deep long valley through which the survivors shall flee and escape. They shall be protected from their enemies as they flee through the valley formed in the mountain."

Bernardi's face lightened, and the corners of his mouth twitched as a smile tried to escape. "Yes, I see that now, but how will the survivors get to this dear mountain after the attack has begun, and how do we know that this will be the day that Messiah will come?"

"May I ask you a question? What event are you planning on the Mount of Olives?"

Bernardi was shocked at the question. He knew exactly what Abisha was getting at, and he was angry that someone let the secret slip out. "How did you know about this? "he asked angrily. But Abisha's eyes captured his and bored deeply into his inner being.

"Oh, well, I might as well tell you," he began to be excited but whispered to his friend like they were two conspirators. "We now have the perfect red heifer at the precise age for the sacrifice, the Parah Adumah! The altar of cedar wood must be placed near the summit of the Mount of Olives and the heifer tied and placed upon the altar at that site. Hyssop and scarlet will be added to the offering."

Abisha was listening intently. He leaned forward, his eyes boring into the rabbi's. "Ahh, now we are at the heart of the matter. Samuel; who is it that will have accomplished this sacrifice?"

Bernardi was taken aback by the question. He regained his composure and said, "Why, Abisha, you must remember that Messiah himself will come and stand at the altar of the red heifer sacrifice right here on this mountain. Messiah himself shall accomplish the sacrifice."

The debate took on the aspects of a great fencing match: thrust, parry, regain balance. Abisha was now intense. His brow was furrowed, and his eyes seemed half closed. He asked the next leading question, "Won't the mount of Olives split when Messiah is standing there? Isn't that what Zechariah wrote?"

Bernardi was silent, pondering what Abisha had just said. He imagined that the angels in heaven were listening to this conversation. He had never felt so alive and his brain so acute. He almost forgot to breathe. Nothing in his life compared to this discussion on the top of a historic mountain. He looked again at the book, and exclaimed, "Why yes! Yes, my young friend. That is exactly what he wrote." He stabbed the verse with the same boney finger and read, "And those in attendance at the Parah Adumah will be the ones who escape through the valley." He paused and looked toward the sky. "Yes, Abisha, I see the answer!"

Abisha leaned over and grasped Bernardi's hands in his. His eyes said clearly that he loved this great student of the scriptures. Then he spoke, but this time with unmistakable authority. "You must be prepared and ready to rush the altar and the red heifer to the mountain site and gather the people the moment the attack on Israel begins."

Bernardi was trembling with excitement and anticipation. "You can depend on it; I will be ready because, at that point in history, Messiah will come! He will accomplish the sacrifice, the mountain will split and the people will make their escape through the valley! The Messiah shall be present, and many will be saved as they flee through the valley of escape!"

Abisha was no longer the attentive student; he was the instructor demanding attention to what he was saying.

"Samuel, you must appoint and organize leaders of each of the twelve tribes of Israel. They must recruit and instruct 12,000 from each tribe. These all must be assembled, and the moment the war begins they must rush to this site where we now stand on the Mount of Olives."

The rabbi and Abisha both looked out upon the city of Jerusalem. Tears were streaming down both of their faces as they wept about the coming attack on the city they both loved dearly.

"When Abisha? When will Jerusalem finally be restored after this attack?"

"It is written in the Bible, the Book of Revelation, that the Gentiles will tread the holy city underfoot for forty-two months."

Bernardi glanced slyly around over his shoulders, smiling like a diamond thief in a jewelry store. "I have read this book!"

Abisha grinned like a fellow conspirator and said, "I know you have!"

They laughed and walked together down the path back to their beloved city.

That night, as Bernardi was saying his prayers, he was consumed with the task Abisha had given him. How would he go about locating 12,000 descendants from each of the twelve tribes of Israel? He didn't have a clue about how to start or where to begin. He became overwhelmed and begged God to show him what to do and give him help to do it.

"Oh God," he prayed, "I'm not as good a record keeper as you are. Please show me how to accomplish this monumental task. Amen."

Chapter Thirty Four

The giant war room in heaven was dominated by two massive pieces of furniture. One was the colossal conference table located in the center of the room. It was made by the most skilled old world craftsmen. The table had no seam; it was one board, a huge, round, cross grain slab made from a massive redwood tree that had grown in Northern California since before the days of Rome. It had been sanded and polished by hand for uncounted hours by these skilled artisans until the finish was as smooth as water. Then several coats of a gloss lacquer finish were applied, leaving a gleaming red table seating twenty-four.

The second was a ten-foot high transparent globe with each country highlighted in a different color and outlined in polished gold. This magnificent sphere revolved slowly from its position in the middle of the conference table. Whoever entered the room was struck with awe when they saw these wondrous pieces of craftsmanship. The Creator God sometimes strolled into the room to admire their beauty.

The room was twenty feet in height with a light blue ceiling supported by twenty-four columns made from light pink and beige marble. The capstones were brushed copper. The walls were white granite with gold sconces providing some of the light along with windows four feet high that went the full perimeter of the room.

In addition to the twenty-two silver chairs with maroon cushions, there were over one hundred hand carved wooden chairs for warrior angels of lower rank. Directly opposite of one another stood two golden chairs for the use of the archangels.

The archangel uniform was a white, knee length robe fastened around the waist with a golden sash. From the sash, hung a gleaming silver sheath, encasing a brilliant golden sword with emeralds imbedded in the hilt. They wore polished gold breastplates, and their long white hair was tied back by woven gold bands.

Centurions were also dressed in knee-length white robes, held in place by a woven silver sash supporting a bronze sheath and sword. They wore polished bronze breastplates and helmets with a bright blue plume.

Warrior angels wore white robes with a silver breastplate and sword. A strap over the back supported a great golden shield that could be swung into action at a moments notice.

Battles in the supernatural realm are very different from the bloody conflicts mankind uses to inflict his will on others. In angelic warfare between the heavenly hosts and the forces of the evil one, there are no guns or bombs or grenades. Battles are a one-on-one mysterious affair with drawn swords being used, similar to the combat of the Arthurian fables.

A gavel struck a wooden plate on the great table, and the Archangel Gabriel stood to address the massive room full of the centurions and captains of the heavenly host. Lower ranked angels, who had been scurrying around trying to get organized, rushed to take a seat. On the great table, battle plans were spread out, along with the scrolls of the Holy Scripture. The room became silent. Gabriel looked around the room at the leaders of the forces of the Creator God. They stared at him with what could only be described as awe. The archangels are the best of the best, and they would do the Lord's bidding without question or hesitation.

"Servants of the Most High God, we are here today in preparation for the greatest evacuation plan in all of history. The Creator God has decreed that this urgent evacuation will take place under your precise field leadership. This massive departure must be executed with lightning speed. No one eligible for evacuation can be left behind. The historic Day of the Lord is coming, and each of you will have specific assignments which I am certain you will carry out with honor and distinction."

He stopped for a moment and looked intently at the leadership of the protectors of the Holy God, all the heavenly realms, and those whose assignments included protection of many human beings.

"Warriors, I am at liberty to announce to you that very soon the Lord Jesus will be returning to earth!" A great roar rose from the warriors; chairs were shoved back as they stood and cheered. Each angel held his sword high over his head, ready to do battle. They chanted, "Glory to King Jesus!" as they shook hands and punched one another on the shoulder in the manner of soldiers everywhere.

Gabriel reached over the table and opened a scroll to First Thessalonians. He pointed to chapters 4 and 5. His long pointer stick rested at the beginning of the verse, and he spoke with a loud, rumbling, baritone voice.

"Here we see that the Day of the Lord will come upon planet earth like a thief in the night. You and your legions are assigned to accompany the Lord as he descends from heaven with the sound of my shout, which will encompass the entire earth and with the sounding of the trumpet of God.

"Now pay attention, this is how it will be organized. The dead in Christ will rise first, being resurrected out of their graves. The two transport legions, 8 and 9, are in charge of accompanying these resurrected souls upward. You centurions, make sure your legion standard is held high so we can keep everyone together. This is going to happen very fast, so rehearse with your warriors what they are expected to do and when."

Gabriel looked around the room. Every eye was on him. "Okay, let's continue. After those who are in their graves are raised, the ones who are alive remaining on the earth and who are calling on the name of the Lord Jesus must be immediately evacuated. You will take them to meet the Lord Jesus in the air."

A messenger slipped quietly to his side and gave him a message. The great angel nodded his head and continued.

"Legion 7 this is your commission. Make absolutely certain that no one who calls on the name of Jesus is left behind. Every eye will see the Lord Jesus in the air but realize that there will be many who will refuse to call on the name of the Lord. Waste no time on these people; they have chosen their fate.

"These instructions are found in the scroll of Revelation 6:15, and this is how they will act. These will be hiding from the Lord, cowering in fear in caves and behind rocks, crying out to be hidden from the face of the Lord. They are not to be evacuated!"

Gabriel spoke quietly to an aide and then continued pointing to Revelation 14:6.

"During these events, Legion 5 will closely follow my lead as I shout out a final gospel call over every nation, people, and language, giving everyone on earth a last chance at salvation."

The archangel tapped the pointer on the scroll at Acts 2:20. "Do not forget your assignment. Listen carefully to the people on earth and observe their lips. Whoever calls on the name of the Lord Jesus must be immediately evacuated by you. Got it?"

"Yes, sir!" the throng shouted.

"Carry them to meet the Lord in the air. None can be left behind. Complete evacuation is of utmost importance.

You are all well aware of the rebellious seraph Abaddon, who lies incarcerated in the pit," Gabriel spoke as he placed his pointer on Second Thessalonians 2:3.

"This man of lawlessness is to be revealed and released upon planet earth on the day of this great evacuation. Do not forget the great power he displayed as he took a seat on the throne of God declaring himself to be god.

"Especially remember our comrades who fell in battle as we overcame this lawless one and cast him into the pit. You know about his destructive powers. I need not remind you that, should anyone be missed and left behind, they would have no hope.

"Then, when all are gathered in the air, the assigned legions will escort this great saved multitude of all nations up to the throne room of heaven as seen here."

Gabriel continued tapping his pointer on the scroll of Revelation 7:9.

"At this point, Michael and his legions will take over the campaign."

Gabriel handed the pointer across the table to the archangel Michael and took a seat. Michael stood and began his briefing.

"I'm going to be speaking primarily to the First and Second legions, but I want all of you to pay close attention in case something happens to a centurion. You must be ready to take over any position that may fall in battle. I have complete confidence in each of you. You will meet the Lord Jesus and his two witnesses in the air and accompany them as they descend to stand on the Mount of Olives on the Day of the Lord, as seen here."

Michael reached across the table and tapped the scroll of Zechariah Chapter 14.

"This will be the time that I stand up in protection of the remnant of Israel who will escape from Jerusalem on the Day of the Lord. Our primary defensive focus will be here, the Mount of Olives. Your mission is to provide protection for the 12,000 of each of the twelve tribes of Israel who shall be gathered at the Mount of Olives at the location where the Lord Jesus shall descend and stand.

"Jerusalem will be taken by the forces of all nations. Many will be killed by the enemy. Their houses will be ransacked and the women brutalized and violated. Many will be taken into captivity. But you must hold your position at the Mount of Olives. The survivors of the Jerusalem attack, the 144,000, must not be cut off. They will escape to the Mount of Olives.

"The absolute protection of these people is your mission. No stray shells, mortars, or bombs can be allowed near this site. All of the survivors must be protected at all cost. We do not want any casualties.

"These 144,000 will behold the Lord Jesus as he stands on the Mount of Olives. They shall look upon him whom they have pierced and weep as one who weeps for his only son. The mountain will split, forming a long, narrow, and deep valley. The remnant of Israel will flee through the valley and escape the destruction taking place in Jerusalem.

"Legion 2 will lead air defenses and guard the forward progress and provide protection as the people flee eastward. Legion 3 will stay behind and provide protection and support to the two witnesses who will guard the entrance to the valley from the west. It is from this location that these two witnesses will begin their prophetic pronouncements of the plagues of tribulation upon the earth. Your legion will stand with them for 1,260 days and in accordance with further orders, which shall proceed from the throne room of the Most High from time to time."

Gabriel and Michael both rose, as did the whole assembly. "Servants of the Most High, you are dismissed. We trust that you shall be ready and that you shall lead your troops with honor and distinction."

The two archangels sat down together, not only as great leaders but as great friends.

"This will be the biggest event since God made man. It is my honor to be working with you to make sure it happens just as the Lord has directed," Gabriel said to Michael.

"Those are my feelings as well. For this, we were created. It is our purpose for being!" Michael said. "Just think what a thrill it will be to be present when Jesus returns to earth as king. The cosmos will stop and cheer!"

The two giants of heaven stood, shook hands and left the war room. The earth was about to change forever.

Chapter Thirty Five

Rabbi Bernardi was working in the barn on the carefully guarded Red Angus cattle farm near Haifa. There were other men doing general farm work but none were helping him, which was exactly what he wanted. He had been working on his project for most of the morning, so he took a break and wandered out to the meadow where the cattle were grazing. He loved looking at them; they were beautiful beasts, and Bernardi considered one of them to be priceless in terms of importance to the nation of Israel.

He was hanging his arms over the top plank of the wooden fence, enjoying the sunshine and the wanderings of the animals. As grazers, cattle take a few bites of grass and chew it while they take a few steps, always looking for better, greener, tastier grass. Few things in life have the aura of contentment that rival these bovine beasts casually wandering and eating and whisking their tails over their backs to brush off pesky flies.

Bernardi took in the picture. He smiled while looking through half closed eyes at the perfect pastoral scene and praised God for the privilege of observing his creation.

He heard footsteps coming through the grass and was about to turn to see who it was when an arm went across his shoulders and the pleasant voice of Abisha said, "Hello, Samuel. Isn't this a beautiful day?"

"Hello, my friend. Yes, indeed. I was becoming so contented that I thought of taking a nap."

"Forgive me for disturbing you. I can come back another time," Abisha said.

"Nonsense. You stay right here. I need to get back to work in a few minutes. Some friend you are; you could help me, but you show up when the hard work is already finished." They both laughed heartily.

The cow named Alice was lying down sleepily chewing her cud when she spotted Abisha. She got to her feet as fast as the awkward rocking motion cows must use would let her. She took a long, comfortable stretch then walked rapidly right up to Abisha. He laughed and stuck out his hands to rub behind her ears, which made her grunt with pleasure. She tried to lick his hands, but he knew about her rough tongue, so he moved his hands to rub her face.

"Hello, little one," he said with genuine pleasure. "I'm afraid we are going to have to put you on a diet, you beautiful rascal. You're getting fat!" She snorted, feigning being insulted, and stood as if she were part of the conversation.

"You're spoiling that animal," Bernardi scolded. Abisha just laughed and kept petting her.

All of a sudden there was a downpour of rain. "Hey, where did that come from? Come on, let's get to the barn."

"Why, Samuel, you act like you're going to melt in a little water. It's wonderful and refreshing," Abisha said as he jogged along with the old rabbi.

In the barn, they wiped the rain from their faces and sat down on some bales of hay. Standing before them was the project Bernardi had been working on. It was a stack of cedar, pine, and fig wood in the shape of a rectangle, but with one end open. It stood about four feet high and was built on pallets nailed together to form a strong platform that could be lifted onto the bed of a truck by a forklift. The pleasant fragrance of the newly cut wood filled the barn.

"What are you making, Samuel?" Abisha asked.

"I think you know what this is. It is the altar for the red heifer sacrifice, known in scripture as the Miphkad Altar. With the dangerous climate in our world today, I have made this so that it can be rushed to the Mount of Olives.

Abisha studied the altar closely but said nothing.

Bernardi looked at him, hoping for encouraging words about his handiwork. "Ahh, Abisha, when we have the ashes of the red heifer, progress can begin to rebuild the Holy Temple. What a wonderful day that will be!"

"Samuel, haven't you read what Rabbi Paul of Tarsus wrote of the Holy Temple? Do you not know that you are the temple of God if the Spirit of God dwells in you?" Abisha asked, watching the rabbi closely.

"But Abisha, I am familiar with many Christian writings and even a novel about the end times. Many of your people believe the temple is to be rebuilt and some even contribute financially to preliminary efforts to rebuild the Holy Temple.

"They say that antichrist must sit in the temple of God and declare himself to be god at the midpoint of a seven year tribulation. How could this be if there is to be no new temple?" Samuel asked.

He loved these discussions with Abisha, whom he found to be the most stimulating person he had ever met.

Abisha answered, "They don't realize that the man of lawlessness already took a seat on the throne of the temple in heaven on the day man was created. This rebellious one was at the throne, but now is not, being concealed and restrained until the church is raptured and taken out of the way. Then shall that wicked one be revealed and released from the bottomless pit to reign upon the earth for forty two months."

"But, Abisha, they also say this antichrist will take away the sacrifice causing it to cease. How can this be if sacrifices are not begun at a new temple?"

Abisha thought carefully before answering.

"Most don't know why they believe such things, and scholars who think they know don't truly understand Daniel 9:27. In this scripture, it is the Anointed One who confirmed the Holy Covenant with Israel for three and a half years. It was the Anointed One who caused the sacrifice to cease, as Paul wrote to the Hebrews, 'by the offering of the body of Jesus Christ once for all.' And the Anointed One will again confirm the Holy Covenant with the 12,000 descendants of the 12 tribes of Israel as they are protected in the wilderness for three and a half years. Some call this the second half of the seventieth week of Daniel."

Bernardi was engrossed in the conversation. It was exhilarating, and his voice trembled slightly.

"But Abisha, if there is no new temple, how can we possibly worship in the most pleasing way?"

Abisha touched the old rabbi's shoulder and looked intently into his eyes.

"New Jerusalem will someday come down from heaven. No temple will be seen there, for the Lord God Almighty and the Lamb are its temple, as written in Revelation 21:22. I do not say you must worship here or worship there but rather you must worship in spirit and in truth."

"Yes, Abisha, I long to worship in spirit and truth."

"Samuel, you have a heart that yearns for Messiah, the Anointed One. I am going to tell you plainly of these things. In the Jewish Bible, in the Ketuvim portion of the Tanakh, the book of Daniel 9:26, it is written that the Anointed One would be cut off or killed and after this the sanctuary or temple would be destroyed. Listen my friend, Daniel prophesied that the Anointed One would be killed before the temple would be destroyed. Recently the two of us were on the Mount of Olives, and we looked across the Kidron Valley at the city we love. The temple was not there. As you know, it was destroyed in 70 A.D."

"Yes, Abisha. Yes."

"And you, Samuel, believe that Messiah will stand on the Mount of Olives on the Day of the Lord, even as Zechariah wrote. So what must, therefore, have happened for these things to be possible?"

"Why, Abisha, for Daniel's and Zechariah's prophecies to be fulfilled, the Messiah must have been killed and then resurrected!" Samuel said. His eyes were glued to the young man's face.

"Yes, my friend," Abisha replied taking the rabbi's hands in his own as Samuel stared down at the deep scars on Abisha's wrists.

"I do trust you, Abisha. Everything shall be prepared to have the 12,000 of the twelve tribes of Israel assembled on the Mount of Olives as you have said."

Abisha held Samuel's shoulders in his hands, smiled and said, "I'll see you soon."

He turned and walked down the road. As Samuel watched his friend walking away, his mind returned to those scars, the scars that now seemed to haunt him. In his mind a glimmer of understanding began to form.

Chapter Thirty Six

It was nearly 5:00 p.m. and Tiero San Rilando, the secretary general of the United Nations was getting sleepy. He had been in meetings since breakfast and was looking forward to leaving soon and having a quiet dinner with his wife in their Manhattan condo.

Suddenly, the door to his office burst open, and Diablo charged into the room and went to Rilando's desk. His secretary followed the big stranger into the room, shouting that she had tried to stop him but he refused to listen.

"Sir, do you want me to call security?" her voice was trembling.

"No, that won't be necessary. Close the door please." The secretary general was also trembling because of the violence of the intrusion, but he was determined not to show it and bluff Diablo into settling down.

"Mr. Diablo, what do you mean rushing in here like a wounded water buffalo? Settle down and have a seat. What do you want to talk about?"

Diablo remained standing and moved to the back of the desk, next to the big chair where Rilando was perched. "What do you think you are playing at, little man?"

"Why I'm sure I don't know what you mean."

"Don't play games with me. Why haven't you sent troops to the Middle East? They should have been there and dug in by now. Do I need to talk to the newspapers about the embarrassing and illegal stuff you are mixed up in?" Diablo was angry which was unusual. He was usually very cool and collected.

Rilando blanched and began to perspire but tried to hold his ground. "Please calm down. There is no reason we can't discuss this like gentlemen," he said.

"Gentlemen! You want us to act like gentlemen? I'll give you gentlemen." With that he took off his Oakley sunglasses revealing his bulging yellow eyes with the vertical irises of a snake. He was standing so close to Rilando that the secretary was sure he could smell a faint odor of sulfur.

The little man cowered in his large chair, unable to pry his eyes away from Diablo's. "Ju…just tell me what you want." He stammered. "I'll do what you ask, just don't hurt me."

Diablo placed the glasses back on his nose and sat down on the edge of the desk. "Why haven't you moved troops into Syria and Jordan? I thought we had an agreement that you were going to order them into Israel."

"Mr. Diablo, these things take time. To do this, I need a vote from the Security Council, and I'm not sure how the United States will vote," he stammered.

"They will vote to send the troops. I have been working with the President. He will vote to send troops," Diablo responded.

"I'll still need to justify such a move. You have a great deal of influence. Perhaps you could organize a small incident between Israel and Hamas and Hezbollah on the West Bank. This would provide the excuse to move troops in as peacekeepers." Rilando eyed the handsome stranger closely to gauge how his idea was being received.

Diablo was quiet for a moment. He got up, took a cigar out of his coat pocket and lit it with a gold and diamond lighter. The fragrant grayish blue smoke rose lazily toward the ceiling. He sat down in a chair. He puffed and blew smoke rings but said nothing. "I actually think you have had a good idea. I'll just do that little thing tonight. It will be on the world news in the morning."

He got up and left without saying another word. Tiero San Rilando took out a handkerchief and wiped his face which was covered in sweat. He could feel his heart palpatating in his chest. He knew he had just faced death and was able to walk away alive. Well, he wasn't going to face that again. He was going to act right now. He called his secretary into the office. When she came in he said, "Get me the President of the United States on the phone right away. If they give some excuse, tell them it is an emergency."

In a couple of minutes, the phone purred, and President Steinmetz was on the line. "Hello, Mr. President. How good of you to return my call so quickly."

"Hello, Tiero, what's on your mind at this time of day? I was just on my way to a fund raising dinner for the ol' party." Steinmetz didn't care for the secretary general. He felt he was a wimp who avoided world problems.

"I am sorry to disturb you. We have a situation brewing in the Middle East that our intelligence tells us could blow up into a major confrontation," he said.

"Intelligence...the U.N.? Har, har, har! That's a good one. Never heard of the U.N. having any intelligence!"

Rilando tried to laugh at the awful joke, but he was too angry.

"It seems there will be riots in the West Bank tomorrow to protest the shooting of a young man by the Israeli police. This could escalate quickly so I am going to get approval to send peacekeeping troops to Jordan and Syria. I'm going to have a special session of the Security Council this evening. I hope I can count on the United States to support this effort."

"So Israel is at it again, are they. Yes, of course you can count on our vote. The sooner the better."

"May I ask for another favor?" Rilando asked.

Steinmetz was suspicious. He felt the secretary was going to put the arm on him for money. He didn't like the billions the U.S. gave to support the organization as it was. "I will try and be helpful. What do you want?"

"The peacekeeping forces will come from bases around the world. Could we use some of your Air Force's transport planes to pick up and move the men to the Middle East?"

The line was quiet for a minute. He had the feeling the President was talking to someone in the room. Then he came back on and said, "I think we can help you there. When you locate your troops, call me with location and how many you have to move, and I'll make the arrangements."

"Thank you, Mr. President. You have been most helpful. Good night."

He rang his secretary again. "Get the staff busy and have them arrange for a special meeting of the Security Council tonight at 8 p.m. Then come in and take notes for the materials I want presented tonight."

When the arrangements were beginning to take shape, he relaxed a little and poured himself a double shot of Johnny Walker. As he sipped his drink, he wrote himself notes about what he was going to say at the meeting. His secretary came in, and in an hour, his speech and supporting documents were finished and ready for copies to be made.

At 7:30 p.m., his phone rang. It was Diablo. "Yes, Mr. Diablo, what news do you have for me?"

"The problem we talked about is underway as we speak. There will be a number of young men killed. Israel is rushing troops and tanks to the scene. Hezbollah will be sending Scud missiles into the Jerusalem area in an hour. Get the vote and start moving the troops." Click! The phone went dead.

The whiskey had given him boldness, and he found himself daydreaming about killing the dreaded Diablo. But his revelry didn't last long. He contacted the general in charge of the United Nations troops world wide and ordered him to get troops and support equipment ready to move immediately.

"Give me the locations of the men and their supplies right after the Security Council meeting. The United States will be supplying whatever airlifting equipment you might need."

The Security Council was happy to rubber stamp his request to send troops to Syria and Jordan and spent an hour with each member venting his rage at the callousness of Israel in the slaughtering of boys throwing rocks.

As soon as the vote was recorded, Rilando got on the phone to the prime ministers of Syria and Jordan, asking for permission to land troops in their countries. In an hour, they had given the go ahead to land an invasion force in their respective countries.

The general in charge of the United Nations peace keeping forces called and gave the location of the troops to be transported and how many planes they would need. The secretary general called the President of the United States at midnight. Steinmetz was not in a happy mood.

"Yes, Rilando, what is it?"

"If you would be so kind to give us the use of as many C-130 transports as you can, plus four or five C5 Galaxies for lifting supplies. I will have our general contact your chief of staff with the locations and details. Syria and Jordan have both granted the use of their air space and landing privileges for your planes."

"Okay, I'll tell my guy to expect the call and to get the Air Force gassed up and going. You surely did a good job in getting this orchestrated in a short time frame. It will be good to slap Israel down a peg or two. Good night."

"Good night and thank you."

By late evening the next day, planes should be landing and troops moving to camp sites. In a couple of days, Israel would be looking at a military force of 25,000 men plus tanks and heavy equipment. Rilando was startled to learn that a trainload of Russian heavy tanks was already in Syria, ready to move.

At 4:00 a.m., he tumbled into bed, exhausted but feeling pleased that he had gotten that frightening Diablo off his back.

At 7:00 a.m., the world's news agencies were rushing to the area. Footage was already being broadcast showing young men throwing rocks and the Israeli army shooting rubber bullets, trying to quell the riot. There had already been many causalities and three deaths, all televised live around the world.

Scud missiles were flying in seemingly random trajectories, with most landing in orchards causing little damage but effectively frightening the people in Jerusalem who were stunned by the sudden events.

So great was the hatred for the Jewish people that the military operation, that would usually take months to organize, was granted approval by members of the United Nations Security Council almost overnight. The world condemned Israel for attacks they were not responsible for. They had simply attempted to quell a riot, which they had done many times in years past.

Mr. Diablo was sitting in his special suite in Las Vegas watching the events on television. He swirled brandy in a huge snifter and smiled at what he was watching. He was proud of what he had organized by pushing the right people with stacks of cash or the threat of blackmail. His demons in Jerusalem were doing an admirable job swirling around among the Palestinians, stirring them up to continue rioting. They were responsible for the three deaths. They had caused some Hezbollah soldiers to fire at some tanks, then pushed the young boys out into the line of fire, killing them.

As the news cameras jumped from one hotspot to another, some in Syria and Jordan noticed American Air Force transports flying overhead, apparently landing at military bases. Greek helicopters appeared and circled Jerusalem, finally landing a few miles from the Golan Heights.

Diablo lit a cigar and blew the soft grey smoke toward the television set. This was better than watching the losers at the craps tables.

Chapter Thirty Seven

Iranian President Muhammad Hafez was reviewing a parade of his military might put on to impress and intimidate the people of his country. The goose-stepping Revolutionary Guard was just marching by the reviewing stand, with eyes right to salute him. He stood as tall as he could and saluted the blocks of soldiers who took minutes to go by the reviewing stand where he stood. There were thousands of well-trained combat soldiers ready to do his bidding. He felt powerful and wise. He believed he would make a great king, which was his secret longing.

After the parade, Hafez was returning to his office when he received a call on his cell phone. It was the beautiful Dannah, his secretary. "Sir, the Russian minister of defense is here for your meeting. Will you be here shortly?" she asked.

"I'm about ten minutes out. Seat him in my office and give him some refreshment," he ordered.

"Yes sir," she cooed. Hafez knew for certain that he was in love with her. He was going to ask, and if necessary, demand that she become his bride. He would declare a holiday and have the most elaborate wedding since the great King Darius. He was sure that when the people of Iran were exposed to such a sophisticated celebration, they would be happy to embrace a return to the Persian Kingdom.

Back at the office, Dannah was the perfect hostess, escorting the Russian defense minster into the president's large and comfortable office.

"May I get you something to drink?" she asked demurely. Putnovich could not take his eyes off of her.

"Yes, please. Do you happen to have any Russian vodka?"

"I am afraid alcohol is officially forbidden in our country. But we have coffee or fresh lemonade to refresh you on this very hot day." She smiled and quickly exited the room.

The Russian seemed disappointed as he poured himself a glass of lemonade. He settled into a soft couch and took a sheaf of papers out of his briefcase and began reviewing them.

In the outer office, Dannah was finalizing her escape, scheduled for tonight at midnight. One of Tuck's men, whose code name was Lion, was scheduled to meet her near a truck stop. They would catch a ride with a man who despised the government, but there was no getting around the fact that this was going to be extremely dangerous. Tuck introduced Dannah to Jesus before she had left to begin this mission. Tonight, she whispered a prayer for protection during her escape. She was not going back to her apartment; she had some clothes in a paper sack under her desk.

Dannah, whose real name was Summer Montabon, loved the United States and had grown to love the people of Iran and felt sorry they had to live under such an evil tyrant.

Summer had no illusions about what would happen to her if she were caught by the secret intelligence monsters, Vevak. Being caught alive was not an option. She had a cyanide capsule that she would bite into if things went wrong.

Hafez scurried into the office and came over to her desk. She smiled at him, and he seemed to melt. She could smell the perspiration on him. It just added to the disgust she felt for this fool.

"Where is he, in the office?"

"Yes sir, that's where you advised I put him."

"Good." He charged into the office and found the Russian sitting on the couch with a big glass of lemonade. He hated these men from the north, but he needed them to supply his military and also help with the construction of his nuclear facilities and nuclear weapons. He rushed the Russian with arms outstretched to give him a big welcome hug. "Reggae. How wonderful to see you again. How are you?"

"I am doing fine, Mr. President. I hope you are well."

They spent a few minutes on nonsense talk, and then Putnovich got to the point.

"My government has instructed me to visit you in Tehran and update you and our common military goals. You are probably aware of the rioting taking place in the West Bank and Gaza," he said.

"Of course I am aware of it, I'm financing it," he said, a little miffed that the Russians never seemed to be impressed with how much world terrorism he was financing and how much of his budget it cost him.

"That is very good. Mr. President, my government believes it is very important that you remember your agreement made with my president, that you would not use nuclear weapons on Israel. The danger to the surrounding Arab states and the damage to the land for hundreds of years are too great. We realize your hatred for Israel is based on your religious beliefs, and a world catastrophe is of little concern to you because you believe some important personage of your faith will return to earth."

"You don't have to quote my religious beliefs to me. I know what they are. I want Israel and the Zionists who live there to be killed or pushed into the sea, or perhaps both," Hafez said with a rising voice. He was irked by the pomposity of the Russian.

"Well, whatever. The purpose of the visit is to tell you bluntly that my country and the rest of the world will be angered if you use nuclear weapons against the Zionists. There would be just too much collateral damage. I have been instructed to tell you that such a move by you would bring instant retaliation from the nations of the world. In plain language; don't do it."

Hafez raised himself slowly, like a corpse rising from a grave. "You dare come in here and threaten me! I am the president of a sovereign nation and will do as I see fit to an enemy of the state."

Reggae Putnovich didn't like this little twerp so he didn't try and conceal his contempt.

"Muhammad, I urge you to calm down and listen to me. The world is already moving to surround Israel and is prepared to intervene if she causes any problems with her neighbors or the Palestinians. Troops are moving into a peacekeeping role as we speak. It would be a good sign if you send troops to work with the United Nations in this effort."

"What did you say? Already underway? Why wasn't I informed of this before now? What are you trying to pull anyway? This is outrageous!"

"Calm down, Mr. President. You are being informed now, and we expect your cooperation and troops. In a few words, get your troops moving to Jordan."

"I'll move troops when I want and where I want them to go. No one tells a king how to manage his military." Hafez did not catch his slip of the tongue. Reggae did.

"King, what king? I'm talking to you. You need to remember you serve at the pleasure of the Supreme Leader. We can talk to him if you wish."

Hafez was scrambling to save face now, embarrassed by his mistake.

"No, no, that will not be necessary. I'll have my general of the Army contact the United Nations and see where our troops could be best used."

Reggae got up to leave. They did not shake hands. He turned and walked out of the office.

Hafez was so angry he couldn't think. He buzzed Dannah. He wanted her to call a cabinet meeting for tonight. The phone rang but no one answered. "Humph, she must be away from her desk," he murmured to himself.

Hafez was right. Summer had walked out of the building and was heading for a friend's apartment where she was going to stay until time to go to the truck stop. Always careful, when she stepped on the bus, she saw two men in casual clothes step on as well. They took a seat behind her.

She could smell their sweat and knew she was in great danger.

Unknown to her, Lion was seated behind the two men that he and Summer both believed to be Vevak agents. Lion was there because Langley had instructed him not to let her out of his sight until they made their escape. He didn't know what he was going to do, but he couldn't let this beautiful woman fall into the hands of these wild beasts. If they did, death would be a blessing.

Summer got up to leave the bus at the next stop. She was not going to get off near her friend's apartment. She would face these men alone, or die by the cyanide. She stepped down, turned right and headed for a clothing store. The men followed her. She did not notice Lion following all of them.

In the clothing store, she looked casually at some clothes, picked out some to try on, and was shown the way to the dressing rooms. Inside the little changing room, she fought back tears. She was terrified. She had no weapons. While walking to the room, she spotted a rear door, but if they were watching, they would see her run out. She could find no other option. She put the pill into her mouth, next to her cheek, ready to be bitten if necessary. Summer held her breath, and then made a mad dash for the back door.

Outside, she turned to the left into a large crowd of people watching a street vendor advertise his wares. She dove into the crowd and tried to become invisible. The two men burst out of the door, looked around, and headed for the crowd. Lion was right behind them. He had a six-inch knife hidden in his waistband. He had never used a weapon, but he was determined to learn fast. He got behind them just as they were closing in on Summer. He grabbed the closest man to him from behind, a hand over his mouth, and his right hand driving the knife deep into the man's back just above the kidney. Then he shouted at the top of his voice, "Look out, it's a suicide bomber, look out, run, police!"

The crowd erupted into a screaming mass of bodies tearing off in every direction. In the confusion, he grabbed the other Vevak and stabbed him in exactly the same manner. The man dropped like a stone. He had an automatic in his right hand. Lion grabbed the gun thinking it might come in handy later. Summer was staring back at him as she tried to run away. He caught her, and said, "It's all right, Summer; I'm Lion. Follow me."

They made their escape, finally settling in an off street café. They found a table in the gloom of the back and ordered coffee.

"That was a close one, my lady friend. I just happened to think about watching for you today. As soon as it's dark we head for the truck stop. With any luck, we'll be at the border by dawn. Then it's a little hike across the desert. The agency will have people there to pick us up. Then this horrible mess will be all over," Lion said.

"I'm thanking the Lord he protected me by sending you, and that I didn't resort to the cyanide capsule I had in my mouth. Whew, too close for comfort," she said to her new friend.

"I'm thanking the same Lord. Tuck must have talked to you, too."

"Yes, he did. If it wasn't for the Lord, I would never have had the courage to stay where I was and get as much information out as possible."

"You're right there. Come on, it's getting dark now. Let's start walking till we find a cab, then we'll hang out at the truck stop until it's time to leave. This is going to be a long night."

Twenty hours later, two tired agents of the Central Intelligence Agency in Langley, Virginia, were deposited from an army jeep by a transport air plane in the Green Zone in Baghdad. Twenty more hours found them in Charlene Lewis-Sloden's office, where they were engulfed by Charlene, Garrison, and Tuck, who broke down and wept when he saw his friend. He knelt on the floor and thanked his Jesus with all of his heart for delivering these fine people to safety. While on the floor, he felt arms around him and learned that everyone was on their knees in a circle with arms around each other, praising God and weeping.

Finally, Tuck got up, wiped his eyes and said, "I've got to get out of this business. I'm too old and slow and have too many friends in danger."

Charlene looked at him and said, "I'm afraid a number of us will not be here much longer. I made a fool of myself telling the President he was crazy for going against the nation of Israel."

"If we turn against Israel, I'm afraid this country is in for a very bad time," Tuck said. A chorus of "Amens" went up toward heaven. The group of old and new friends walked out of the office together.

Chapter Thirty Eight

Lt. Colonel Levi Cohen had commandeered a beat up '95 Toyota pickup from a friend. It was one part faded apple red and one part black primer. It would not attract much attention, which is exactly why he needed this truck. He was driving in a sleazy part of Jerusalem, which was part of the old Arab section, with few streetlights and lots of shadows. The darkness was welcomed by those who depended on the night to cover a multitude of sins.

After the '67 war, the government had promised to spend money to re-vitalize this part of the city, but somehow there was always another project that had a higher priority.

Cohen was glad he had his .357 Desert Eagle gas operated semi-automatic. The weapon carried a comforting nine rounds of ammo and was easily tucked into the waistband of his jeans.

The street corners were alive with people at this time of night. There were all sorts of sleazy characters hanging around, all of them trying to make a living by some illegal means. When he stopped for a street light, aggressive prostitutes and their skinny pimps descended on the truck. The drug dealers did not approach but did show what wares they had by opening their jackets, showing a variety of drugs pinned to the inside linings.

Cohen was a city boy and knew one could get anything illegal down here, including a hit man to take care of any pressing confidential problem, if that was what was needed.

He was glad when the light changed so he could get moving again. He was looking for a particular address, and it was tough in the darkness. Finally, he spotted the right number on the side of what looked like an old garage. He pulled the Toyota into the driveway and got out. He felt the Desert Eagle against his skin. He went to the door and knocked with confidence. A dog with a deep voice began barking loud enough to wake up the whole block.

A little hole opened in the door and an eyeball looked out at him.

"Yeah, what' cha want?"

"I need to talk to Devin Tontov. I have a little job for him." Cohen said.

"He ain't here, so beat it," the eyeball said.

"I'm willing to pay a lot of money for the job, but if he ain't here, I'll find somebody else." He turned and started walking away. The door opened a crack, and the eyeball said, "Wait up. I just wanted to check you out. What's your name?"

"Forget it! I'm not shouting my name around in this neighborhood. If you want to talk let's go inside," Cohen said. He was determined not to be pushed around by some creep in this filthy slumlord's dream project.

"Fair enough, come on in." The door opened and the colonel walked in. The building was full of the most sophisticated electronic equipment he had ever seen outside of the military.

"You have quite a business here, very impressive. But I need to talk to a guy named Tontov. You know him?" he asked.

"That's me," the young man said. He couldn't have been more that sixteen years old. His scruffy red hair was uncombed and evidently unwashed. He wore half glasses on his nose in front of two light blue eyes that appeared to have no irises. The colonel found the clothes the kid was wearing to be repulsive. The checkered shirt no longer had defined light and dark colors. His jeans were worn out at the knees and the pocket, where his wallet normally was housed. He had multiple earrings in his left ear and a little diamond sticking in his left nostril. The colonel yearned to get this loser into the military where he could have a shot at making a man out of him. But, he had daydreamed enough. It was down to business, regardless of his impressions of this young man, who most believed was a genius.

231

"Are you the guy who's supposed to be the best with a computer, and hacking information out of other people's computers?"

"You a cop?" the kid asked.

"Nope, I'm freelance," Cohen lied.

"If you're not a cop, why the gun?"

"Protection. This is a scary neighborhood."

"Now you're hurting my feelings; this is my home," the kid said with a slight grin.

"Okay, whatever you say. Can we get down to business?"

"Sure, but we need to get something straight. I'm just a little kid. You go back on your word or try to stiff me, I have a couple of very nasty friends who will rearrange your face and body so they never work well again. Capisce?"

Now Cohen was burning. "Don't talk to me like I'm some street bum, punk. You do a job for me, you'll be well paid. Now can we stop this crap and get down to business?"

"Okay, take it easy, old man. What can the genius do for you this lovely night?"

"I want to know if you can hack into the most sensitive and secret computers in the country?" Cohen asked, watching Devin closely.

"Hey man, take it easy; you're asking me to do something illegal, and I'm only a computer operator trying to make a living," Devin whined.

"You're a liar! You come highly recommended, and your work is the work of a genius. That's what I need; a genius," Cohen retorted. His eyes were burning as he stared at the young man.

"Okay, you need a genius. If the money is right, I'm your man."

"Let's have an agreement before we start talking serious stuff. I'm willing to pay you one million dollars for this job. When it's done, you will have to leave the country and live somewhere else. If you get caught, you will be hung as a traitor. I'll be dangling right beside you. After you do the job, you'll design a system so secure that another genius will not be able to crack it again. Agreed?"

Devin was thinking, but it was obvious he was greedy, and the sound of a million dollars was too much to resist. "So far it sounds like a good job for my retirement. What's the rest of the story?"

"Are you a patriot?"

"A what?"

"A patriot. Do you love your country, and would you do a dangerous job to protect her in her hour of need?"

"You've got to be kidding! I'm no patriot. I'm in business for me and no one else. You want one of those brave guys, get one of those suckers out of the army. They run around and get killed for nothing. You can save yourself all of that money," Devin yelled.

Cohen was stunned. He had not realized how shallow the younger generation had become. He pressed on. All other options had already been lost. He got up and leaned over the young boy as he sat with one leg on the seat of his chair, the other dangling near the floor. He yanked the chair out from under Devin, which threw him to the floor. During the fall, he had whipped out the Desert Eagle and shoved it into the kid's mouth.

"Now, young man, you are going to get a little lesson in citizenship. This mission is super secret. When I leave, I will have to be convinced that you will do the job and keep your mouth shut. If you don't agree to work with me, I'm going to scatter your brains all over this little hovel you call home. If you agree to work with me and talk to anyone, you will end up the same way - dead! Your only choice is to do the job I ask, and you will be a rich man. What say you, boy? Are you in or dead?"

Devin was white as a ghost. The automatic hurt his mouth, and he was bleeding a little. When he looked into the colonel's eyes, he saw a man very familiar with certain death. He motioned him to take the gun out of his mouth. Cohen took it out and wiped the barrel clean of the blood and spittle. "Sure, mister. Count me in. I want to get a little older. Put that gun away; it makes me nervous. What's the job?"

"It should be a snap for you, genius. All you have to do is hack into the prime minister's computer; get the numerical codes, sequences, passwords and ways to circumvent any failsafe program that's been installed. When you have them, I want you to send them to a number I'll give you."

"Are you, kidding? No one could get all of that information. It's super secret. They have the ability to track backwards to find anyone trying to hack in to those computers. I'll get killed no matter which way I move." There were actually tears in his eyes as he whined and wrung his hands.

"So, you're not the best. I guess I had bad information. I might as well shoot you now and go have dinner somewhere." Cohen knew the kid's ego would not let that go by.

"No man, I'm the best. You just scare me. Why do you want this stuff so bad? You're risking your life, too!"

"Here's the straight stuff, kid. The kook in Iran has sworn to kill all of Israel with nuclear missiles. It's been all talk up to now. But now we think he's got the bombs. If he fires them, the whole nation will be obliterated in a matter of seconds, including you, my young friend." Cohen watched Devin closely; he was paying attention.

"Man, that's bad news. But how can I help save the country? I'm just a computer geek."

"Our government is full of people who believe we can talk our way out of anything. They are blind to current world events. The United States is no longer our friend and ally. Our enemies left us alone in the past because of that long-standing friendship.

Armies from around the world are gathering in Syria, Jordan, Egypt and Iran. They are preparing for war, which the Iranians will start with a first strike missile launch against us. The whole bunch of them is not smart enough to realize that the radioactivity will infect most of them if he uses nukes. I and a few other men in the army believe the only way for us to survive is for us to launch a pre-emptive strike against their nuclear facilities and military bases. It is our only chance for survival, unless you're one of the people who believes God will somehow protect us." Cohen stopped talking.

"Naw, I'm not religious. God's never done anything for me, except kill my parents and put me on the street to survive the best way I can. I like your plan better. So you need this stuff to be able to launch the missiles, right?"

"Right, and we need it yesterday. Can you do it?"

Devin thought for a moment then said, "Count me in, General. I'll need some data you can give me, and then we start to work. It will take me a day at the outside."

Cohen smiled for the first time and stuck out his hand. They shook hands and got down to the business of trying to destroy Iran before it destroyed them.

Chapter Thirty Nine

Hiram Meier, the Israeli Prime Minister sat in his black Cadillac limousine which was parked in the lot of an amusement park in North Jerusalem. He was eating a vanilla ice cream cone with great relish. Ice cream was his real weakness. He would eat it at every meal if he thought he could get away with it.

It was just getting dark, and the park's neon lights were coming on, filling the dark sky with color and excitement. He wasn't sitting here to watch the lights come on, however. He was having another clandestine meeting with Abram Weiss, director of the feared Mossad. Every enemy agent working against Israel worried about being captured and tortured by this agency, which had the reputation to go any lengths, anywhere, to find those out who would destroy their country.

Meier hated these meetings, but Weiss insisted on them. Rooms could be bugged. New technology allowed listening to people talking in a room, in a car, even outside walking. Meier knew that Weiss was going to drag him into the amusement park with all of its wonderful noise.

Suddenly, someone tried the car door. It was locked. The person outside knocked on the window. Meier loved this trick. The door was supposed to be unlocked so Weiss could jump into the back seat. But now he was standing outside knocking and cursing something awful. Meier didn't like Weiss, and this little pay back gave him immense satisfaction.

Finally, he gave in and unlocked the door. Weiss boiled into the car and shut the door. Apparently, spies dislike being outside for any length of time.

"The door was supposed to be unlocked. What's the matter with you?" Weiss complained.

"Don't talk to me like I was one of your spooks. I'm your boss, remember?"

Weiss swallowed hard. He felt the prime minister had the backbone of an eel.

"Yes sir. I beg your pardon. Will you join me by the show tent? There is lots of noise there. We can talk without the fear of being overheard."

"Just don't stop by the entrance, where they have that recording of a fat lady laughing her head off. That thing gets me every time. She laughs, and I laugh!"

Both men climbed out of the limo and headed for the park. Weiss stopped by the roller coaster because there were shadows plus a great deal of noise.

"Sir, I have disturbing news. I know you have been watching the buildup of United Nations troops in our friendly neighborhood terrorist countries. Our intel says they will be moving into a position about ten miles from our border very soon. As of last count, we have no friends who will stand with us when the war breaks out.

"A real worry is that we have learned someone has hacked into our government computers. He has gotten through every firewall we had installed. We're working on backtracking to see if we can find him and give him a lead stomach ache." Weiss smiled at his little attempt at spy humor.

"Where do you think the cyber attack is coming from?"

"We think its coming from Iran. Big surprise there."

"What computers have they compromised?"

"They're working on the defense force computers. Probably trying to anticipate what our military response will be if they attack," Weiss answered.

"If? Don't you mean *when* they attack?" Meier asked.

"You're right. Things don't look very good for us. I have not seen such world hatred of the Jewish people since World War II."

"Are you able to do some counter-intelligence work that might slow their plans?"

"I've got every man working on that right now. If we get an opportunity, we'll go after the general of the United Nations army. Believe it or not, this guy's name is Israel

Garza. He's from Spain and a pretty good military man. But the troops aren't much to worry about. If there weren't so many of them, we could beat them hands down in a battle. These armies are from twenty or so different countries and speak that many different languages; most of them are with the U.N. because they're losers, and their own army wants to get rid of them."

"Still sounds like the whole world is excited about having a war with us, even though we have not done anything to warrant such hatred. It's as if some cosmic force has signed a death warrant for our nation," Meier said sadly.

"You ever read the Christian Bible, Hiram?" Weiss asked casually.

"I'm a Jew. I don't read Christian writings."

"Well, this might be a good time try reading it. They have a book called Revelation which talks about the end of days for us. It's pretty tough reading. This could be such a time."

"Phooey! I don't even read the Torah, why should I spend time in such a book of heresy?" Meier huffed. He didn't like this line of discussion. He wanted to talk about how to conduct the war.

"Well, do you read the prophets?" Weiss asked with some exasperation.

"I have in my youth, but that memory left me ages ago." Meier looked absentmindedly at some young children getting on the roller coaster. They were shouting and laughing, without a care in the world. It was his job to protect them, but he wasn't doing a very good job at that.

"You should read the prophet Zechariah, chapter 14. I read it last night as we were working on the hacker. It says the Day of the Lord is coming when our enemies will plunder our cities. The Lord will gather all nations to battle against Jerusalem. The city will be captured, the houses ransacked, and our women brutalized. Half of the city will be taken into captivity. Only a remnant will escape the city alive. Pretty bleak, huh?" Weiss waited to hear the response.

"That's one of the reasons I don't believe in religion; nothing but misery."

"Well, there is some hope. Another sentence says, 'Then the Lord will go out and fight against those nations, as he fights in the day of battle.' So maybe there is hope for us yet. God rescued our people over and over again in the Torah. Perhaps he will again."

"Will you stop reciting ancient texts that have nothing to do with us and our perilous situation? When are you going to find that hacker?"

"If he stays online, we should have him tomorrow. I'll have my best people working on new firewalls for all government agencies. We should be protected."

"Should be! There you go again; nothing helpful. I'm going back to the office. This carnival music is giving me a headache."

He turned and walked back to his car and driver. He looked around but did not see where Weiss went. "Spooks!" he mumbled to himself. "They love that disappearing stuff!"

Chapter Forty

Damascus and Amman were a mess. Flights of American Air Force transport planes were landing around the clock, carrying troops from many nations. But there were problems. No one in the United Nations command had anticipated how efficient the American air lift would be. Nor did they foresee the enormous number of men walking around without truck transport to their staging area. The airports around both cities were clogged, and General Garza had been forced to call his staff to stop any more planes from coming in, except those carrying transport vehicles. He had to get these men out of the cities before trouble started.

General Israel Garza, the commanding officer for this "peace keeping" force was a career officer with a proven record of accomplishing difficult missions with the United Nations.

But this assignment was different. He wasn't going to be a peacekeeper, and he knew it. He was commanding an invasion force that would eventually number about 70,000 fighting men and another 20,000 in support roles.

He didn't have any particular feelings about the Israeli army one way or another. One thing he knew, however, was the fact that the Israeli forces were tough and would never give up while defending their homeland. This was going to be a fight to the death.

But right now, he had to get these troops out into the field, and he had to do it right away. He barked orders to subordinates who scurried around trying to get organized. He went to his headquarters, which had been set up in the Syrian army base where he had better communications.

He spent most of the day trying to find the location of his transport vehicles. He was told by the Americans that four C5 Galaxies were flying in from Germany with twenty trucks. Twenty trucks! He needed hundreds, but if all he could get right now was twenty, he'd take them. His men had to get the airport on the military base cleared out and get as many planes into the air and off the tarmac as possible, to give the giant C5's room to land and maneuver.

In Damascus, four men dressed in casual clothes were trying to find a cab to take them to a hotel close to the army base. Finally, an old junker bounced to the curb, and the men clamored in. They told the driver in broken English they needed to go to a hotel close to the army base.

In forty minutes of fighting the streets full of uniformed soldiers, they arrived at the hotel. They paid the driver and went inside. To call it seedy would be a compliment, but the men seemed not to notice. They registered and were given keys and directions to their rooms. Each man carried a large, thin suitcase which contained an M24 Sniper rifle, a military version of the Remington 700. They went to their rooms in silence. One motioned the others to his room where they gathered in a small circle to whisper to each other.

"Gentlemen, we are running out of time very quickly. The U.N. General is on the base. We have to figure a way of getting close enough to get a shot off. If we are unsuccessful, I wouldn't plan a vacation this year." The others snickered.

All were plain-looking men, but a closer examination would have revealed they were heavily muscled. They had long ago given up any hope of retirement. They were trained killers for the Mossad, and their assignment to assassinate General Israel Garza had to be carried out immediately. It was hoped his death would cause enough confusion that the invasion might be stalled for some time.

They took out maps and aerial photographs of the base, with close up shots of the general's tent. One tall man called Samson, who was in his early sixties said, "There's so much confusion and such a crowd milling around, I think we should just get Jordanian Army uniforms, walk into his office and shoot him."

"Not much chance for escape in that plan. I would kind of like to get within sniper range with a silencer and give it a shot. No pun intended."

The third man said, "Okay, let's just get going. There is no time left. These jerks will be in Jerusalem in two days."

"Alright, you two take off and try and find a place for a sniper shot. We'll get some Jordanian Army uniforms. Let's meet back here in three hours."

Three hours later, they were back in the hotel. The scroungers had found four uniforms that could be used immediately if that became the plan.

The big one, named Adessa, said, "I found the perfect sniper shot. It's across the street. It's a big warehouse that doesn't seem to have anyone around."

The agent in charge was called Timmy. "Good job. Both of you set up right away. Don't use the radios unless absolutely necessary. We are going to see if we can walk right into their headquarters. I doubt that many will look too closely at our rifles, which we'll use if we can't get close to him. You all know the escape route out of here. Remember, Israel is counting on our success."

Adessa bowed and prayed out loud, "Great God of Israel, remember your people now, and help us to be successful." The other three just moved out. None were believers in anything but a good rifle.

An hour later, all four were in position. Adessa was hidden behind some boxes piled high in front of a window. Now, all he could do was wait. Timmy and Samson were walking slowly toward the headquarters tent. So far, no one was challenging them although there were guards at the door of the tent. The guards were Irish, so when the two Mossad agents walked up to them and started showing them some documents and yelling in Farsi that they had papers the general must sign, the Irish soldiers just shook their heads and held up their hands. A soldier came out of the tent to see what the noise was all about.

The Mossad agents started to give the same story, when, of all things, General Garza walked out and stood looking at the men arguing. He shook his head. He would never understand Arabs. Then, out of the blue as he stood staring at the men, a hole appeared in his forehead and the back of his head disappeared. His eyes were wide, unbelieving. He collapsed on the spot without making a sound. No one heard a shot.

The camp erupted into chaos as everyone ran around trying to find a shooter. Timmy and his companion simply turned around and walked out of the camp, caught up in the confusion. Once again, the remarkable Mossad had accomplished their mission.

Chapter Forty One

Devin Tontov had been pounding the dirty keys of his computer for twelve straight hours. He was tired and hot and dirty, but he was making progress. He was mad at himself for not making arrangements to have his million dollars deposited in a bank in the Cayman Islands before he gave the colonel the codes. It occurred to him that, if he gave them the codes, they might just kill him and save the money. He determined he was not a very good spy or traitor.

Devin made a couple of clicks on the computer, and his face lit up like the strip downtown. "I'm in!" he yelled. "Tell me I'm not a genius!" he laughed and danced around the crummy room. After a few minutes, he settled down and got a beer out of the fridge and started to get to work - before someone was notified that a hacker was making a run at the biggest computer in Israel. He had to get in and out quick and leave a false trail.

In ten minutes, he had the codes, electronic challenges, passwords, and order of connection for the computer. He exited the computer and called the number Colonel Cohen had given him. The colonel answered immediately.

"I've got the numbers you wanted," Devin said proudly.

"Don't give them on the phone. I'll be at your place in fifteen minutes."

"Well, don't come without the money. You don't get anything until I see the cash," Devin said.

"Don't be stupid. You think I'm going to haul that kind of cash around in that rat hole neighborhood you live in. Find yourself a nice bank that has numbered accounts. When I get there, you give me the account number. I'll have the money transferred into your account. You hold back one launch code until the deposit has been verified. Just don't try and get cute with me, or you'll end up buried in the trash downtown."

Cohen was talking as he was getting into his car. He was a dope for putting all of his trust in this little creep, but he had no choice. In a couple of days, the U.N. would be in position and would have their surface-to-air missiles set up and operational. He had to get Israel's missiles in the air immediately.

In twenty minutes, he knocked on the kid's door. Devin didn't answer right away, which made Cohen nervous. He got the Desert Eagle out of his waistband and chambered a round. He stood to one side of the door and knocked again. The little peep hole opened and an eye looked out. One blink and the door opened, and the kid was standing there with a big grin on his face. Cohen jumped into the room and looked around as he closed the door. "Why did you take so long to answer the door?"

"I was in the john. Good grief! Settle down and take it easy will ya?"

Cohen was in no mood for chit chat. He took out a special, secure cell phone. He laid the Desert Eagle on the table within easy reach. "Give me the codes."

"What about my money?" Devin tried to sound tough.

"Give me the account number, and I'll have the money transferred in the morning. It's night time in the Cayman Islands, hot shot."

Devin had not even thought about a time difference. He would have to trust this guy with the ugly disposition. He thought for a minute about changing one of the codes but looked at the automatic on the table and decided that might not be a good idea. He took out a piece of paper and handed it to Cohen, who immediately repeated them on the cell phone. "We launch as soon as I get back," Cohen said.

"I hope you didn't hold back any numbers, my friend. If you have, I will surely kill you."

"Naw, I gave you everything. You haven't said thanks for the great job I did. No one in the country could have done what I did," Devin bragged.

"You're right, kid. I'll see you in the morning to show you the money has been transferred. Then I suggest you get out of the country - very, very fast."

Cohen drove like a maniac to the Palmachim Air Base which was located just south of Tel Aviv. General Ezra Korach would meet him there. With the codes, they could launch the missiles, some of them targeting the Nari Plain in Iran.

Their plan was to launch twenty-three Jericho IIB missiles in a pre-emptive strike against Iran. The army had already targeted their missile sites and where their intel indicated were the best locations of the hidden nuclear facilities. If any Iranian missiles were launched, Israel would depend on the Arrow surface-to-air defense missiles to knock them out of the sky.

Colonel Cohen got through Air Force security at the base. It was coming up on 2300 hours, so the base was very quiet, with only a minimum number of security patrols moving around. He met General Ezra Korach just inside the main gate. Their passes cleared them through to the most sensitive and secret area of the base, the missile launch center and control room. Inside, they got to work. Korach had recruited four of the most patriotic enlisted men he could find. They would assist in the launch, which should be almost automatic once the process was started.

Korach asked, "How much do you trust the kid?"

"Not much. He's a freaky geek, but he is the only one we could get so were stuck with him."

"Are all the codes here but the one number he's holding as security until we deposit the money in his bank?"

"We should do that now," Cohen said.

Korach said, "I'll take care of that right now. It should take about twenty minutes."

"Good. I'll call the kid and have him check his account when you finish."

Twenty-five minutes later, Cohen called Devin. He answered on the first ring.

"Yeah."

"Call your bank, and then call this number with the last code. Take a second before you do and look out your front room window. You'll see two rather large men in an old Plymouth. You try and stiff me, and they'll pay you a very unpleasant visit. They should be getting out of the car about now. If I don't call them off, they'll be knocking. The bigger guy really hates nose rings. He enjoys ripping them out of people's noses."

"Okay, okay. Give me a minute to call and check the bank." Devin made the call to the Grand Cayman's and was told that the money was on deposit.

He dialed Cohen's number. It was answered on the first ring. "The code number is 666! Somebody in your office has a sense of humor."

"What do you mean?" Cohen asked.

"666, the mark of the beast. The end times. Haven't you read Revelation in a Bible?"

"Never read the book. Get out of town now, and keep your mouth shut. Got it?"

"Yeah, I got it. Good bye, and thanks for the cash."

"Good bye Devin, and hey, you really are the best geek in the country." As he said the last word, he could hear the crash of the door to Devin's apartment being forced open. Devin screamed and shouted, "Wait a minute. We've got a deal. I gave them the right code." There was the crash of furniture and more screaming, then the muffled "poof" sound of an automatic silencer. A man picked up the phone and said, "Everything's been taken care of sir. Good night." And the phone went dead.

Cohen immediately made a call on a secure line to Abram Weiss who answered the phone. "Abram, everything went according to plan. Thanks for your help. You can get your money out of the Caymans," Cohen said.

"I am glad the plan worked well. I wish you much success in your efforts," Weiss said and hung up the phone. His plan was to play both sides of the field. If things went well and Israel was saved, he would forget all about tonight. If things went badly, he had everything taped and could say the military forced him to cooperate. He smiled and went back to sleep.

In the control bunker, everything was ready. The codes from the prime minister were in, the targets programmed into the guidance systems of the missiles; all they had to do was turn the keys.

General Korach was at one station; Lt. Colonel Cohen was manning the other.

The general glanced at the computer screens that told him all was ready. He glanced heavenward for a split second, then shouted, "Ignition!" They both turned their keys at the same time. Missile silos from Tel Aviv to Haifa opened and the giant missiles raised slowly, each on a huge plume of fire and smoke.

In seconds, they were roaring through the atmosphere toward their targets in an unsuspecting Iran, where alarms would be going off in radar units all over the country. Hafez was going to get his war, just a little earlier than he planned.

Chapter Forty Two

President Muhammad Hafez was asleep in his apartment, dreaming about the beautiful Dannah, who had mysteriously disappeared two days ago.

The phone purred just loud enough to jangle his nerves and wake him. "Yes, what is it?" he snarled.

"Sir, this is the duty officer at Jardat Defense Force base, south of Tehran. Our radar shows twenty-three incoming missiles headed for our country. They will be arriving in about fifteen minutes."

"What did you say?" Hafez was awake and jumping out of bed.

"There are twenty-three…"

"I heard you, idiot. Get me the commanding general now!"

The phone clicked, and a sleepy sounding voice came on the line. "General, this is President Hafez. We are under attack, you idiot. Get up and launch our missiles at Israel. Kill them, kill them all, wipe them off the earth!"

The general was startled but fully awake. "Yes sir, it shall be as you wish." He hung up and began dressing. He had his aide start notifying the army missile sites to launch immediately.

Five minutes later, Iranian Shahab 6 and some older Scuds were climbing into the black sky. None had nuclear warheads. They would be raining down on Israel in just a few minutes.

Hafez clamored to get into some clothes while phoning members of his cabinet and getting the warning sirens going, even though he knew there would be no place for them to go to get away from the incoming death machines. He couldn't believe this was happening. For years he had dreamed of this very surprise attack, but it was to be against Israel, not his country.

The phone jangled as he burst into his office. His aides were just now pouring into the building in various stages of getting dressed. He picked up the phone and heard words that chilled his heart.

"Sir, missiles are now dropping on the site at Nari Plain. First reports say they have nuclear warheads which are causing cataclysmic damage."

Hafez sat down, holding his head in his hands. He managed to whisper, "Are there any reports of damage to our other nuclear sites?"

"No sir, none have come in yet. I'll call you as soon as I hear anything."

Hafez could hear some explosions in the distance. Twenty three missiles were coming. He tried to count the number of blasts but was soon overwhelmed. As he sat at his desk, a thought came to his mind. This could still start a world war, which was what his objective had always been. This might just be what was necessary for the Mahdi to come. Surely he would be rewarded with riches of great value, and he would rest in heaven forever! Now that he thought about it, his plan to start such a world war was working. It just wasn't working in the way he had planned.

Chapter Forty Three

The Israeli prime minister was apoplectic with rage, "What do you mean someone launched missiles without your knowledge? That's impossible you fool, it's impossible!"

The poor army corporal who had the misfortune to be on the other end of the line was frightened out of his wits. All he could do was stutter and stammer and give a few "yes sirs" when Meier stopped cursing to breathe.

"Get me General Korach immediately. I'll give you one minute, and if the general isn't on this line I'll have you shot, you worthless pile of garbage!" In two minutes, General Korach came on the line.

"Yes, Mr. Prime Minister, what is it you want?" the general said calmly without any emotion.

"What do I want? Have you gone mad? Are you the one responsible for launching the missiles?"

"I am," the general said quietly, his voice barely audible.

"Where are they going?"

"They will be arriving in Iran in just a few minutes. President Hafez is going to have a rude awakening."

"You must be insane. You are a maniac! Who gave you permission to launch anything?" Meier screamed into the phone.

"I gave myself permission. You are a spineless politician dithering around while our enemies plot our destruction. A pre-emptive strike may destroy enough of the Iranian missiles that we will survive the attack which will surely come," the general said, emphasizing "spineless" as he spoke by spitting out the word.

"Are you so unbalanced that you think Iran will not attack now, with everything they have in their arsenal? And what do you think the United Nations troops gathering on our borders will do when they realize we initiated an attack on another country? General, were these missiles equipped with

251

nuclear warheads?" Meier asked. His eyes were bulging from his head, and he was drenched in sweat.

"Of course they have nuclear warheads. It's the only chance we have of destroying their nuclear facilities buried around the country. What's the sense of starting a war if it doesn't change anything? If we are successful, we should set their nuclear capabilities back five years. They're going to attack us anyway. Launching missiles is not going to change the world's mind about wanting to wipe our nation from the earth.

"May I say, Mr. Prime Minister, that you should be giving orders to sound the civil defense alarms around the nation to warn our people about the coming attack? Before you fire me, I'll alert all branches of the military and get them organized to defend ourselves, including calling up all of our reserves," Korach said.

The prime minister was calming down, but his blood pressure was at stroke level, and he began to realize that time was running out quickly. He needed to use this maniac now. He would punish him later, if any of them survived.

"Yes, initiate all civil and military defense plans. I will alert all police agencies and the members of the Knesset. General, I fear that you have killed us all. Before I have you shot, you must tell me how you got around our security systems to enable you to launch the missiles."

He slammed down the phone and then grabbed it again and began calling all of his aides to get to the office immediately, notifying people that they were in a national emergency.

Meier's secretary raced into the building. When he saw her he yelled, "Get me the President of the United States on the phone as fast as you can." He could hear sirens going off around the city. He wondered if he would even have time to call the President before the Scuds began raining down on Jerusalem.

In a short time, his phone purred, and he was told the President was on the line. "Hello, Mr. President. I must tell you that we are in crisis here, a crisis brought on by a rogue general who launched missiles without authority and without my knowledge. The missiles are in flight as we speak. They are programmed to hit various targets in Iran." There was silence on the line.

Finally, the President spoke. His voice was as cold and without emotion as a serpent. "Are you telling me that Israel has attacked Iran after you people have whined for sixty years that the whole world was against you and that all you wanted was to live in peace? And now you are the aggressors. This reveals the true attitude of the Jewish people: attack and kill innocent civilians whenever you wish and then ask for military and financial help from us to continue your immoral government." Steinmetz could hardly keep from laughing. What a wonderful turn of events. Now the whole world will be happy to attack Israel and break up that wicked country.

"Mr. President, I do not need a lecture about world opinion from the country that dropped two nuclear bombs on cities in Japan during World War II and brought the world into the nuclear age. I called you to give you a heads up as to what is transpiring in this part of the world. Forgive me for believing you might be helpful." He slammed down the phone and let out a string of obscenities that startled those who had arrived at the office.

His phone rang, it was General Korach. "The Arrow missile defense system is up and ready to shoot down incoming missiles. We still have around a hundred Jericho II B's ready to fly. Give me the order, and we'll pound Iran back into the Stone Age."

Meier was stunned into silence. More missiles? What could the man be thinking? But, a thought began to creep into his mind. The damage has been done. The whole world's armies were moving into position to attack his beloved country and wipe it off of the map forever. Why not finish

Iran off? Why not kill more of our enemies before we are killed ourselves?

"All right, general. You have my permission to launch. I presume you have no need for my initiating the security system override."

"No sir, there is no need. The missiles will be on their way in sixty seconds. If we ever meet again, I will be honored to shake your hand before the firing squad ends my life," he said sincerely.

"God help us both, General."

Chapter Forty Four

Tiero San Rilando, the Secretary of the United Nations was in his bathrobe preparing to share some champagne with a beautiful translator when his phone rang.

"Pardon me, my dear," he said smiling with his most charming smile.

"Sir, this is General Horst Gunderson with military command. As you are aware, General Israel Garza was killed today in Damascus."

"Yes, of course, I know that. What do you want?"

"Sir, it appears the State of Israel launched a missile attack against Iran a few minutes ago. Our troops are in a state of disarray, with a few hundred breaking loose and walking toward Israel. Trucks are moving as many as possible. We are moving men and equipment around the clock. Our problem is that no one is in charge to issue the orders we need to get things moving toward the rogue state of Israel."

Rilando was trying to take everything in. Israel had sent a pre-emptive missile strike to Iran! What did the idiots hope to accomplish? They can't fight the whole world. Well, this was the very thing needed to solidify world opinion against them. He liked what the general had said, "rogue state." Yes, that was good; he would order that all communications to the media use those terms.

"General, what did you say your name was?"

"Gunderson, sir."

"Well, Gunderson, what did Iran do about the missile launch?"

"Iranian missiles are in the atmosphere as we speak. If they're shooting Scuds, then I'm worried about our troops in the field around Israel. Those missiles are notoriously inaccurate, and they may land on our people. But, it won't take long to find out."

"Use your head, General. If the missiles kill any of our troops, we'll tell the press they were fired on by Israel. Publicity, General, publicity. The world turns on publicity.

"You are a very lucky man. You are going to be the commanding general who finally brings the state of Israel to its knees. You are now in charge. Get the troops moving immediately. Don't stop at any borders. Move in and occupy all towns and villages. But Jerusalem is headquarters of the hated Zionists. It must be punished. Destroy the city. Burn it to the ground! We're going to teach the Jews a lesson they will never forget."

"Sir, there is a lot of animosity toward the Jews in our forces. If we burn Jerusalem, I fear there will be ransacking, looting, and the killing of women and children," the general said.

"Well, war is hell, boy," Tiero responded with real joy in his voice that the general found strange coming from the head of the United Nations.

"Yes, sir. All troops should be in-country within the week. I'll call in air support tomorrow. It will be a good test of our pilots. The Israeli pilots are the best in the Middle East. The only problem will be coordination and the different languages, but we'll press on.

"Oh, Mr. Secretary, I must bring to your attention the huge mosque in Jerusalem, the Dome of the Rock. It's sacred to Muslim people all over the world. If we destroy it, we might be facing a world-wide uprising."

Tiero hadn't thought about that. But then, the wheels in his head started again. "Hmm, you're right, General. Tell your people to spare it if they possibly can. But it they can't and it is damaged or destroyed, we'll tell the world press that the Jews destroyed the building in retaliation for the bombing of the city!" He smiled. He was actually beginning to like being in charge of a war. It was against the UN Charter, but hey, you do what you have to do.

"Yes, sir. I'll take care of everything. Thank you for the promotion. Good bye."

"Quite all right, General. Do a good job, and the sky's the limit for your career."

He hung up the phone. "This should make that wretched Diablo happy and get him off of my back."

Chapter Forty Five

In the Saudi Arabian desert near the small village of Al-Turayt, which was close to the Jordanian border, a few Bedouins were camped near a small spring. They had watered their goats and the camels wandering the desert with them. The evening meal of boiled camel meat and bread was finished, and the men crouched in a circle around the fire to discuss the day's events. The desert chill forced the men to gather their multicolored robes around themselves. If they were fortunate, someone would start a healthy debate. The subject was unimportant. The squabble was what mattered.

The women were busy repairing clothing or tents. They became amused as the men struggled to find the grounds for a heated argument. Children were running and playing in the cooling desert sands. Two of the oldest young men were standing watch over the herd, which was beginning to settle down for some relaxing cud-chewing.

Jabak Tencholah was the elder of the group and, as elder, he had a number of assumed rights that went with his office. He sat in the group and was discussing the route they were to take in the morning as they set out in search of vegetation. He knew there was an old well about a day's journey due east of where they were camped. "Mosule, will your camel make it to the next water before she drops her calf?"

"I believe so, but it will be close. She's so big now that she has a hard time walking." He imitated the walk of his pregnant camel. The whole camp joined in the laughter.

"Then we water the animals just before dawn and travel due east." He pointed with great confidence even though he had no instruments to show direction. A keen sense of direction came from his Bedouin background and was never wrong.

Jabak got up to go to his tent. It was time to sleep. As he was walking toward his sleeping area, he glanced up at the black sky with thousands of points of light. He knew the stars and recognized them. He had navigated the desert many times using these heavenly guides. But as he looked up, he was startled to see so many moving points of light.

"What is happening?" he shouted. Everyone in the camp came out to see the reason for the shouting. They looked up and became instantly startled by what they saw. Numerous points of lights were rapidly moving from west to east. "There is great movement in the heavens. What can this mean?"

These Bedouins did not know they were witnessing Israeli missiles on their trajectory to Iran. They did know an amazing sign was taking place above. Something dramatic was happening.

Chapter Forty Six

The push to get the United Nations military forces into position east of Israel had been on going for several days. The missile launch had surprised everyone, and when General Horst Gunderson was awakened by his aide, he knew that his army was in the unenviable position of being in the middle of a missile war. He sent out orders to make preparations for an immediate attack on Israel when the death machines stopped raining down on the country. He smiled to himself. At least they now had justification for attacking the little country. Israel had fired first!

Gunderson left his command tent and ordered a staff car to take him to a place where he could see the battlefield. When he arrived at a small hill overlooking the plain area east of Haifa, he was horrified to see errant Scud missiles dropping on the U.N. positions.

"Those stinking Russians! They never could design anything that was accurate," he yelled to no one in particular. Two Scuds slammed into the earth, and then the area became quiet. He could hear explosions coming from the Haifa area.

His troops were now on the move again, trying to get to their assigned positions. Gunderson grabbed the radio and told his commanding officers to meet him in the command tent in an hour. He had made up his mind that he might just as well take advantage of this mess and move up his attack plans to start as soon as the missiles stopped raining down. He wondered how many Hafez had sent. It was rumored he had hundreds at his disposal.

In twenty minutes, the missiles stopped. His officers reported heavy damage in Haifa, Tel Aviv and Jerusalem. The Hezbolla and Hamas fighters had taken the opportunity to send some of their own Scuds into Israel, which was then under attack from two directions.

Gunderson's officers arrived, and he got right down to business.

"This missile attack by Israel on Iran changes our plans. We no longer need to maintain a diplomatic effort to establish our position as peacekeepers along the Israeli border. All bets are off. You are to employ your attack plans as soon as your men are in position. I understand all of them are out of the staging areas making their way to the front. Where are the Russian tanks?"

"Sir," the officer said, "the tanks are being unloaded and fueled up in Damascus. They can be on station late tomorrow at Haifa. The tanks from Amman can be in Jerusalem in three hours going down Highway 40 to the border."

"Good. We'll have our major push into Jerusalem begin the day after tomorrow. See that all of the army units are in place."

One of his commanders spoke up. "Sir, the Israeli army has launched attacks against all of our positions with tanks and infantry. These are almost suicide assaults. I'm sure they realize they are greatly out numbered and must have decided to throw everything they have into hitting us before we start our attacks. They also have air support and are attacking the Russian tanks being unloaded in Damascus and Amman. They are not worried about the violation of Syrian or Jordanian air space. Their Arrow missile defense system worked very well. We don't know how many missiles Iran sent, but our men on the front lines report that only one out of five made it to a target. The others were destroyed in the air. None of the missiles appears to have been carrying a nuclear warhead."

"Great Caesar's Ghost, we've got to get moving and launch attacks of our own, or they'll crush our forces before we get started. Where's my Air Force commander?"

A colonel from Greece stepped forward and saluted. Gunderson was furious and shouted at the unlucky officer, "Well, where is my air support? We're getting murdered out there! We need you fly boys to go after their tank and artillery units. Well, get going man; don't just stand there!"

"I do beg your pardon, general. There is a slight political problem."

"Political problem! What are you talking about?" Gunderson was steaming.

"Sir," The colonel was very nervous and averted his eyes from Gunderson's blazing orbs. "it seems that before a warplane from any of our member states is sent into battle, we must have permission from their government. This is taking considerably more time than we expected. I should have planes available tomorrow morning."

"Tomorrow morning! What do you think we're doing here, playing games? You get me some airplanes up within the hour or you're fired! Got it?" Gunderson screamed.

The Grecian colonel saluted and hurried away as an Israeli jet roared over their tent, barely 30 feet above the deck. The noise was deafening, and men dove for cover or ran away, which was what the pilot wanted to happen.

"Where are my surface-to-air missiles? We need to knock some of these boys out of the air to teach them a lesson," Gunderson seethed.

He had the uncomfortable feeling that he had lost control of the battle. His men were unprepared for the fight. Gunderson pondered the urgent situation. *"Blast the Israeli army for sending those missiles on a first strike. This throws the entire timetable totally off kilter."*

Chapter Forty Seven

Muhammad Hafez, the president of Iran, sat alone in his administrative center. A breeze was blowing through a broken window, carrying smoke and dust into his opulent office. He stared out of the window watching plumes of smoke rise to the sky from one of many fires in Tehran. *"How could this happen?"* He asked himself. *"How could this happen?"*

His phone purred, bringing him back to reality. "Yes, what is it?" he asked.

The voice on the line carefully said, "Sir, I am afraid that I must report to you that the nuclear research center at Nari Plane has been destroyed. Radiation is too strong for us to search for survivors. If they are alive, they won't be for very long."

Silence. "Sir, did you hear me?"

Hafez whispered, "Yes, I heard you." He hung up the phone. An aide came in and reported that most of their military bases had been destroyed. A check of the air bases revealed a scene of devastation. Hundreds of jet fighters were now nothing but tangled heaps of metal. Thousands had been killed in the army bases. Much of Tehran was gone; there was neither water nor electricity and there were reports of looting. The police feared that riots would soon break out because of the shortage of water and food.

How could this happen?

Hafez looked up with bleary, blood shot eyes. "Get out, all of you. Get out!"

The phone rang. An aide answered it and listened as the person on the other end spoke in a loud voice. He put his hand over the receiver and spoke quietly to his president. "Sir, it is a United Nations coordinator. They are battling the Israeli army and want to know if you will be contributing any men and equipment for the struggle."

Hafez sat for a moment, then his shoulders began to shake and quiver, but he was not weeping, he was laughing.

Soon he was laughing so heavily that tears ran down his cheeks. "Ha, har, har, whoey, that's a good one; that's a great one. Let me talk to that funny man." Hafez grabbed the phone away from the aide. "Hello, who is this speaking? General Who? Ha, ha, har, General Who, that's a great one! Very funny. So you need some of my men for the war, do you? Well, General Who, it may interest you to know that I have no army left. I don't even have an air force. I sent all of my missiles to you boys last night, so I guess you will have to win this war on your own and not depend on me. Good bye, Who, have a nice day!"

He was still chuckling when the office doors were thrown open so hard they banged against the walls, and Tieman Koumani, the Supreme Leader of the nation of Iran swept into the room. His face was contorted with rage. As he stormed into the room, his summer robes ballooned out behind him, giving the impression he was gliding in air.

"Well, Hafez, what to you have to say for yourself?" he roared.

"I have nothing to say for myself. I prepared the nation for the time of war, but no one would listen. The one thing I did not plan for was Israel using a pre-emptive strike against us," he murmured. He was a beaten man and stood there with his shoulders sloped, his chin nearly touching his chest.

"How is this devastation possible? Have you been outside of this office? Have you seen our beloved Tehran? It's in shambles! I believed you when you said no missile could get through our defense shield. Where was the shield?" Koumani demanded.

"It appears the demonstrations we held when we were testing the anti-missile equipment were faulty. We manufactured the surface-to-air missiles in cooperation with the Russians, who let us use their designs. I must call President Propochnik and let him know that there are problems. I'm sure he would appreciate the call."

"He would appreciate the call…why you damnable fool; you have destroyed our nation with your maniacal fixation on killing Jews. You may get your wish if the United Nations conquers the Zionists, but we will not share in the celebrations. We'll be fortunate if some country doesn't invade us now that we are defenseless."

"But you are the Supreme Leader. Surely you believe that the Mahdi will return to earth when the whole world is at war. Now, he must come, and we all will receive his blessings and will live in happiness in his heaven."

Hafez recited the mantra he had been preaching ever since he was elected president… with the strong and secret influence of the Supreme Leader.

"Oh, shut up, you fanatical idiot! When the Mahdi comes, it will be to bring peace and justice to the earth, not nuclear destruction. Your egotistical incompetence has destroyed our nation. We are being wiped off the map by the Zionists, and it's your fault. If the Mahdi did come today, his first act of justice would be to execute your miserable life!

"You wanted to be a world leader, a man of importance because you were going to have a nuclear bomb to threaten people with. Well, what has happened? Are you a world leader? Does anyone fear you? The answer is no! We are a pariah in the eyes of the world's leaders. You are made fun of on the world's late night comedy shows. They laugh at you strutting around, acting important. Well, go out and strut now. I could use a laugh!"

There was a knock on the door. It was opened and the fearsome silent giant, Sasheen, was standing in the room. His dark face, black eyes, black beard, and black robes made him appear to be an apparition from an Edgar Allan Poe novel.

"Sasheen, what are you doing here? I didn't call for you. Leave at once, this is a private meeting." Hafez was not only nervous, but he was frightened … very frightened.

"I asked him to come to your office. I'm afraid your political career will have to be, ah … shall we say 'terminated?' You have led this nation to ruin. Now you are required to pay for the damage your bloated ego has caused. Sasheen, you know what to do." He swung around with his robes swirling around his body and stormed out of the door.

Sasheen walked toward Hafez who backed away, crashing into furniture in his terrified retreat. "Sasheen, you are my friend. I've always taken care of you. Please, let me get away. No one will have to know, please!"

The giant remained mute as he moved ever closer the fleeing president. Hafez leaped over a chair and tried to reach one of the tall windows and escape. He failed. Sasheen moved with the speed of a striking snake. He caught the president by the arm and pulled him to the ground, nearly yanking the arm out of its socket. He bent over until his face was near enough that he could smell the fear. He unsheathed a huge, curved knife from the sash around his waist. It was a beautiful thing, gold hilt encrusted with jewels and polished steel blade. Hafez knew resistance was futile. They walked from the office together, arm in arm, like old friends.

Later that night, standing on the edge of an old wadi, the former president of the nation of Iran accepted his fate. He prayed to Allah that he would be received into heaven with honor and praise and live in happiness forever. As he finished his prayers, the great knife pierced his throat and in seconds he was dead. His body was unceremoniously pushed over the edge where it rolled to the bottom, disturbing desert adders on the way down. He who would be a world power was no more.

Chapter Forty Eight

It was a splendid, if not glorious, sunset over Israel. Even the wounded looked up and remarked on the beautiful scene in the heavens.

General Gunderson finally got his Russian tanks unloaded, fueled, and moving toward Israel. He had lost a third of them to Israeli aircraft. The political mess about permission for jets to fly had been overcome, and French and British jets patrolled the border of Israel almost unchallenged.

Troops were in the outskirts of Haifa and Tel Aviv. His tanks would be in position outside of Jericho in a few hours. It would be a short run into Jerusalem, and he planned an all out invasion of the Israeli capital for sunrise the next day. He anticipated an easy assault that would include tanks, artillery, and rockets softening up the target, and then thousands of infantry would be turned loose to mop up the capital.

In fact, things were going so well that he decided to find a cot somewhere and take a nap. He hadn't slept in 40 hours.

While General Gunderson began snoring loud enough to irritate those working near to him, Hiram Meier, the prime minister, was meeting with his generals in the war room hidden below the Knesset building. The room was silent, morose. The men in the room knew what was coming in the morning. Some were thinking that this must have been how the Jews in Jerusalem felt before they were conquered and taken into captivity by the Babylonians.

Jerusalem was dark, blacked out. The streets were empty of traffic, but strangely, no one had thought to turn off the traffic lights. They dutifully switched from green to yellow to red over and over again, giving a surreal feeling when someone looked down the street and saw the lines of color disappearing into the blackness.

Meier asked General Singleton for an assessment. "I think we are in a hopeless situation. The U.N. will certainly attack in the morning, and they have an overwhelming superiority in tanks, artillery and infantry. Our pilots were heroic today and inflicted great damage on the enemy forces, but they were just out-numbered and were either shot from the sky or bombed into oblivion when they landed for fuel." He paused and looked around the room. Faces were haggard and gray from the stress and lack of sleep. He continued speaking in a low voice. "At dawn I expect an attack from the east. They are going to throw everything they have at us. Our tank corps will fight until they are out of gas or ammunition. They will make the world pay a fearful price for the land they conquer.

"It is possible that the Palestinians will pour across the border with a tremendous blood lust to kill everyone they see. I have ordered the soldiers on that line to open fire when they rush the fence, and to keep firing until they have no bullets left. I also have the evil feeling that all of our enemies are going to be intent on killing us; there will probably no offer of peace or taking of prisoners."

He began to weep, and with great tears running down his grizzled chin, he looked into the prime minister's eyes and said, "Sir, I think this is the end of the nation of Israel forever."

Meier looked at his weeping general. He tried to sooth the man's pain by putting his arm around the general's shoulder and quietly whispered, "There, there, my friend. You've done all you could. All of us are determined to die bravely and not be taken prisoner, particularly by the Palestinians." He looked around the room and saw nothing but foreboding and gloom. He spotted Abram Weiss, head of the Mossad, sitting against the wall. He was finally getting to meet Abram in the light. "What news can you give us, Abram?"

"Nothing good. We're going to fight as bravely as we can. I've instructed my snipers to scatter around the city and take out any officer they can get in their sights. I can tell you that some citizens are sneaking out under the cover of darkness. They are going in various directions, even out into the desert. There is not much hope for them. The old ones remember their parents talking about the pogroms in Europe and the death camps in Poland. They say they'll die fighting, not being herded like cattle to the slaughter."

"No one can condemn them for that. Gentlemen, tomorrow has the potential to be the end of the Jewish nation. What are your thoughts? Shall we send a delegation and sue for peace, or do we dig in and fight?"

Weiss spoke up first. "My people fought the Arabs for this land in 1948 and 1949. The whole world was against us then, but we fought all of them. Many died, but many lived and brought about the greatest nation in the Middle East. I'm not prepared to just lie down in front of a Russian tank. I want to make them pay a heavy price for their hatred." There was a light applause.

"All right, gentlemen. Try and get some sleep. All of our civil defense plans are in effect. We will do everything we can for our people." He hesitated before speaking again. "Ahh, would someone like to close this meeting in prayer to the God of Israel, or any god that you would prefer?"

A voice from the back of the room whispered a simple petition, "God help us, your children!" No one else was moved to pray.

Chapter Forty Nine

Half a world away from the Israeli conflict, where it had just gotten dark, it was the dawning of a new day. Del Rio was braced for a hot one. The old men who sat on benches at gas stations and the convenience store were already looking for the shade and dreaming of a cold beer. They gathered in a small group to discuss the war going on in the Middle East and watch people coming into the store. Their brown faces were deeply lined from years of working in the unforgiving sun of the Southwest. They smoked or chewed tobacco.

The store owner didn't mind them sitting around on old chairs and benches, but he would not tolerate the men throwing their cigarette butts on the concrete, and he went absolutely wild if one of the men spit tobacco juice on the cement floor.

In another part of Del Rio, little Pedro Ramirez was still asleep. An amazing thing had happened during the night. A smiling angel came to visit.

The angel had said, "Pedro, do not be afraid."

"Hey, I know you. You're the man standing behind Jesus when he touched my arm!" Pedro exclaimed.

"You're right, my small friend, and I want to tell you that I have been sent by the Lord Jesus to tell you a special secret, a secret that only you will know," the angel said.

Pedro rubbed his eyes and sat up with interest. "I like secrets; tell me, please tell me the secret. Is this a game?"

"No, it's not a game. It is more like a wonderful trip."

Pedro was now excited and wanted to know more from this kind and friendly person. "Am I supposed to keep the secret?"

"No, my young friend, this special secret is for you to tell. You get to be the special one who tells your family, your neighbors, and your friends."

"Okay, that sounds like fun!"

"You're right, Pedro. Now listen carefully while I whisper in your ear the special secret about tomorrow. Tomorrow is a very special day. It is known as the Day of the Lord, and Jesus is coming back to take you and your family to heaven. You will get to fly up to meet him in the air!"

Now Pedro was very excited and was bouncing on the bed. "Really?"

"Really! It will be a wonderful trip to your new home in heaven. But, early tomorrow the sun will get very dark, and you may even see the moon turn dark red. The earth will start shivering and shaking like this," the angel explained by shaking his shoulders up and down.

"Like this?" Pedro responded laughing and shaking his shoulders in rhythm with the angel.

"You've got it," the angel laughed. "When you hear a big trumpet sound, many people will be afraid, but you are not to be scared. You will be outside, look up in the clouds, and see Jesus coming. Every person on earth will see him. Lots of people will be afraid and run away and hide, but you will not be afraid. I know you will be happy to see Jesus coming. Then, I will come and pick you up and carry you to Jesus way up in the clouds. Pretty neat, huh!"

"You mean I get to fly?" shouted Pedro excitedly.

"Yes, you will get to fly away like a little bird to a wonderful place, and I will be carrying you."

"I don't want you to carry me. I want to fly on my own. I can do it. Wow, I can hardly wait!" Pedro said as he was bouncing up and down while still seated cross legged on the bed.

"Hey, take it easy little one. Tomorrow will be a big day. Rest now and finish sleeping."

When Pedro woke up, he walked into the kitchen. His mother Maria and his father Emilio were sitting at the table having coffee and tortillas.

"Hi, son. Sit down and have something to eat."

"Guess what, Mama. I have a secret."

"Ohhh! You do, do you? Well you better be careful and keep the secret," his mother teased.

"No, Mama, this secret is for me to tell! The angel last night told me to tell everybody that today is the Day of the Lord, and Jesus is coming back to take us to heaven today. We will get to fly up to meet him in the air!"

"Wow," Maria said smiling. "Now that is a big secret."

"The boy has been traveling too much Maria," said Emilio. "He is over-tired telling his story with the preacher man. We have to do better and watch his health. He's too tired, I tell you."

"No," Maria responded. "Pedro is just fine." She took Pedro into her arms, "The boy was just dreaming that's all. Just a dream."

"But I must tell the neighbors and my friends, Mama. The angel said to."

"It was a dream, Pedro. That is all. Just a dream, child."

"No, no Mama. This was real."

"Just a dream, Pedro…only a nice dream."

Pedro forcefully took his mother's cheeks in both palms and looked her in the eyes and said, "Mama, the man Jesus touched my arm, and I can use it. That was real, and this is real, too. I go tell the neighbors now. Okay, pleeese?" said Pedro with a pleading smile that routinely melted the heart of his mother.

Maria seemed a bit flustered not knowing what to say; it seemed so impossible. How could she let Pedro go and tell the neighbors such a thing? Yet something was stirring in her heart, a glimmer of something she knew well … a moving of the Spirit in her heart.

She stood up, leaving the table. "One momento, Pedro, I must ask the Lord something."

She retreated to her special prayer closet, which was really the broom closet, shut the door, took a seat and picked up her Bible.

"Oh, Chihuahua!" sighed Pedro, pressing his wrists into his temples. "She might be in there for hours! And I needed to go tell the neighbors." Pedro plopped down at the table as his arms flopped swinging at his sides.

"You might as well eat, Pedro," instructed Emilio while putting a tortilla and a dab of beans on Pedro's plate.

Behind closed doors, Maria was desperately seeking God's help. "Lord, what am I do? Pedro seems so certain. And after all you have done for him, how can I forbid him from doing what he believes you tell him to do? Will you please show me the truth? Was it just a little boy's dream?"

As she prayed, a tear dropped from her eye. One single tear fell on the casually opened Bible lying in her lap. The tear fell, staining a word in the text. "Secret" was the tear stained word in the text of Amos 3:7, which read, *"Surely the Lord God will do nothing, unless he reveals his **secret** to his servants the prophets."*

"Oh, my Lord. Could this be true, that you are really coming today? Pedro said he had a secret of what you are about to do. Is this the secret? The secret you needed someone to know and to tell?"

Maria felt a familiar moving in her heart. It was the Spirit of the Lord assuring her that she should support her son in this small but special ministry. She grabbed her sweater from the shelf, and stern-faced, she marched quickly from her prayer closet. Pedro seemed surprised to see his mother so soon and quickly gulped down the bite of breakfast in his mouth.

"So can I go, Mama? Like the angel told me?"

"We go now, and I go with you!" Maria said with an authority in her voice which startled Emilio who could do nothing but wave goodbye as Pedro smiled leaving the room.

Maria walked briskly down the cracked and uneven sidewalk trying to keep up with Pedro who was jogging on ahead and turning back frequently to motion for his mother to hurry and keep up. The yards in front of the old houses were unkempt and filled with tall weeds. Cerveza bottles and an occasional abandoned, worn-out tire littered yards, sidewalks and parking lots. Maria was a bit nervous, wondering if she was really doing the right thing to allow her determined son to walk through this particular neighborhood. There had been a lot of reported crime and drug trafficking in the area over the past few months. A meth lab had been broken up by the police last month in the block ahead, and Maria knew of the violence meth heads were capable of. She whispered a prayer with each step as she became a bit breathless pacing quickly to make sure she stayed close to Pedro.

The sun was beginning to burn down on their heads, and both of them began to sweat. She was sorry she had not thought to bring both of them something to wear on their heads.

This part of town was a sad place. People who lived here had given up. They were hooked on booze or drugs, or they were just plain worn out from a lifetime of struggling to get by. As Maria and Pedro trundled down the broken sidewalk, they noticed someone two houses ahead. He was a gray-haired, burned out alcoholic perched on the grease covered front porch step. He was slumped over as if all strength had been sucked out of him. It was all he could do to puff on an unfiltered Camel which brought on a hacking cough that threatened to topple him off of the porch completely. A half empty bottle of cheap whiskey joined him, sitting next to him on the step. The bottle was his only friend in the world. Maria hoped in her heart that Pedro would not try to talk to this guy. Fear started to plead with her to grab her son and run the other direction.

Pedro strode confidently toward the old man who scolded, "Get out of my yard, kid!"

"But, Señor, I have good news. Last night an angel sent me to tell you that Jesus is coming today. We get to fly and go to heaven!"

The man looked up scowling as he pulled a piece of loose tobacco from his teeth left from a drag on the unfiltered cigarette that had been hanging on his lip, "Jesus, huh! Well, he sure ain't gonna want me to go with him."

"Why not?" Pedro said with a puzzled expression on his face. "He wants everybody, Señor."

"Boy, I can't even tell you all the bad stuff I've done in my life. It wouldn't be polite to talk that way in front of the missus and you being a kid and all. Even ran off my own family. Jesus sure ain't gonna want me. Now git!"

"No, no," replied Pedro while waving his index finger from side to side as if scolding the old man. "Pastor Gabby tell us story. When Jesus was on cross, there was very bad man being punished on cross right next to Jesus. The very bad man looked at Jesus and say, 'Lord, do you want me?' And Jesus say 'Yes, I want you. Today you will be with me in heaven.' Jesus wanted that bad man, and he want you, too!"

The old man hung his head, and a tear began to flow down one cheek and dropped to the concrete. Pedro boldly put his hands on the old man's cheeks and raised his face forcing him to look straight into Pedro's eyes. "Look, Señor, I only see two kinds of people today. Some saved, and some about to be saved. Which one you?"

Pedro's determined eyes were melting the old man's heart. He was quiet for a moment, then he mumbled, "Well, I guess I'm about to be saved."

"Here, take my hand," commanded Pedro, "and repeat prayer."

The old man stood up on weak skinny legs and took Pedro's hand slowly repeating every word, "Jesus, I want you. Jesus, I want you. Will you take me to heaven with you? Amen."

The old man looked at Pedro and Maria with eyes that showed a glimmer of life for the first time in many years. The air was still and quiet, but in the distance was the distinct call of a trumpet.

Chapter Fifty

It was after midnight at the secret farm where the Red Angus herd had been kept for so many months. The night was a little chilly, and a wind was blowing in from the Mediterranean Sea. The breeze cleansed the air from the smell of cordite and gun powder, mixed with the smell of diesel exhaust forced out of a thousand motors during the preceding day of battle.

Around Haifa, the Israeli tanks had fought heroically. They inflicted heavy damage on the multi-national United Nations forces, which were hampered by language problems and confusion about the chain of command. In battle after battle, the Israelis fought viciously, using their latest hit and run tactics. The Russian tanks were behemoths with great firepower and only one weak spot - the rear end of the tank.

The Israelis would find a tank that was busy destroying as much property as possible. Three of the Israelis tanks would surround the Russian, with one acting as a decoy weaving back and forth in front of the giant's gun. When there was an opening, the other two would pour shell after shell into the back side which had less armor and take it out of action. Brave men would leave their tank and run to their victim and plug its exhaust system and its air intake system. Soon the men would bale out of the tank coughing and gasping for air, only to be mowed down by Israeli tank machine guns. This technique worked time after time, but there were still heavy losses in tanks and infantry.

The Israeli Air Force fought like wild men, filling the skies with falling planes and parachutes. They were outnumbered five to one but still flew as long as they had fuel. They inflicted heavy damage on the U.N. ground troops and artillery pieces, even bombing an occasional tank.

Now, in the darkness, there seemed to be some safety, although there were screams from Haifa as troops moved into the city to ransack it. The troops were more like madmen than members of a trained military unit. There was pillaging, and the killing of men, women, and children.

Rabbi Bernardi was frantic. He had to get the Miphkad Altar to Jerusalem and on to the Mount of Olives. He had constructed it to biblical specifications and designs listed in the Torah. It was located in the barn, and as the fighting had died down somewhat, this was the time to get it out of here. A friend had a tractor-trailer that could haul the altar, but he had not shown up, thus the anxiety for Samuel.

When it was nearly two in the morning, he finally heard the throbbing of a diesel engine coming toward the barn. This was either his truck or men from the United Nations on a killing spree. It was the truck. The driver parked it across the barn door, so the fork lift could put the altar in the center of the trailer.

He jumped out and ran to the forklift, gently picked up the altar, and carefully put it on the truck. When it was aboard, the driver carefully strapped it in place with the heavy cloth straps.

Bernardi thanked the driver for risking his life to make the red heifer sacrifice possible. The truck idled down the driveway and took the highway towards Jerusalem. Bernardi prayed to God that he would protect the driver and the altar during this dangerous trip.

Now there was only one more thing to do. He and the farm hands and security guards needed to load Alice in a livestock trailer that would take her to Jerusalem. She was in a pen inside the barn and had on a bright black leather halter with pure gold trim. But all of the noisy things happening around the barn in the darkness were making her nervous, and she kept pulling against the rope tied to the halter and a post.

"Okay, men, let's get this over with. One of you grab her halter and lead her into the trailer. The rest of us will stay behind her and push if she becomes uncooperative." There was a rustling and snickering among the men who felt that this was going to be a snap.

One of the men untied Alice, who pulled back and tried to get away from the men. They cornered her in the pen, grabbed the rope, and two men proceeded to try and lead her into the trailer as planned. Alice was having none of it. She balked, bawled, threw her head and tried to hook the men with her horns. She was full grown and weighed nearly a thousand pounds. She could do considerable damage if she felt threatened.

The posse surrounded the furious bovine and began to muscle her toward the trailer; the man with the rope went through the trailer and out the front so he could pull her up into the trailer. Alice was upset. She bawled and danced and shook her tail. One man who believed he was quite the clever fellow found an electric cattle prod. He got behind Alice and prodded her viciously in her back leg, jolting her with a high electric charge. This not only frightened her but enraged her at the same time. She could see the man with the stick that hurt her. She let fly a back leg kick that was as swift as a lightning bolt, striking the man straight on his knee cap. He screamed and went down like a sack of sand.

"Stop, stop this before someone gets hurt. This is a spirited animal, but she has always been given special treatment. Everybody get away from her and go to the front and pull on the rope when I put some grain in the trough," Bernardi said.

Alice smelled the grain and stretched her head toward the trough. The men pulled, and she walked into the trailer. The back was closed, and she was ready for the final trip of her life.

"Thank you, men. You will never know the service you have given your country this night." He climbed into the cab of the truck with the driver, glad to be able to sit down. They drove to the freeway leading to Jerusalem. The perilous journey to the Mount of Olives would be complete in a few hours if all went well. But there was little certainty of that among the two men in the truck. The old rabbi thanked God for helping them get this far and prayed they would not meet any U.N. soldiers.

When they approached Jerusalem, Bernardi made a call on his cell to a friend who ran a huge warehouse business. He had arranged previously to have his friend bring one of his huge fork lifts, capable of lifting several tons twenty feet into the air.

A sleepy voice answered the phone. "Yeah, what is it?"

"It's Bernardi, my friend. Do you remember you said you could help us unload a heavy altar?"

"Yeah, I remember, but I didn't know you wanted to do it in the middle of the night with a war going on. What are trying to do in secret, fly off to heaven and leave the rest of us here?" The man chuckled at his little attempt at humor.

"Now, Simon, don't be difficult. What we are doing will save the lives of thousands of people. So get that big machine to the top of the Mount of Olives. We'll be there in half an hour."

"Yeah, yeah, I'll be there, but you owe me, Bernardi!"

They arrived in time to see the fork lift rumble up the slopes, its big diesel roaring slightly. Bernardi had paid a man to smooth a place wide enough to give a level place for the altar to rest. The tractor trailer stopped parallel to the resting place. In five minutes, the fork lift had the altar in the proper place.

It was shaped like a large rectangle, with one end left open. This open end was facing the spot where the temple stood so many years ago. Inside this opening was where Alice would meet her death as the final red heifer sacrifice that would bring about the arrival of the Jewish Messiah.

The most important part of this sacrifice for the nation of Israel was tied to a tree a few yards from the altar. She was standing quietly watching the movement of the men. Someone had remembered to bring her some high quality hay which she was enjoying. The trip in the trailer had been exhausting and frightening, so it was not long until she lay down to rest, but she kept her ears moving from front to back to warn her of any danger. Somehow she knew danger was close by.

Chapter Fifty One

The volcano Sharat Kovakab was covered in a low mist, with the breeze making the air a bit chilly. Basil Hyde-Newton and Lydia Hannity were hauling armloads of gear toward the top of the mountain. They intended to do research on how dormant the volcano really was. They stopped to rest at what looked like an old vent. They set down their packs, and Lydia was given the task of lighting their small kerosene stove to make some tea. "If you want to conquer the British, just boycott tea deliveries," she murmured to herself.

While they were enjoying their rest, a world-shaking event was about to change the planet forever. All of a sudden, a great bolt of lightning streamed from above striking the ground near the summit of the volcano. The bolt was so powerful and deafening that the two academics were knocked backwards onto the rocky ground as the kerosene stove toppled over, ruining the tea.

"Good God!" cried Basil as he slowly stood back up dusting himself off.

Lydia also was regaining her footing and looked Basil in the eye. "I didn't think you believed in God."

"Of course not. I am a scientist. It's obvious that we are merely the result of evolution. Darwin is the only sanity a true scientist could believe in."

"Yeah," responded a shaken Lydia, "But sometimes I wonder, but never mind, there couldn't be a God in this tragic world. But, Basil, did you hear something that sounded like a trumpet and the sound of a voice shouting something? It sounded like I heard a voice shouting something in the distance about Jesus. Sounds crazy, huh?"

"Give me a break, Lydia. The shell shock of the lightning must be giving you hallucinations or maybe you hit your head too hard on a rock."

The final call of grace from Gabriel flying high above fell on deaf ears, not so much because of the great thunder clap when the lightning struck but rather a life time of being hardened to many presentations of the gospel routinely rejected in the name of academic elitism. Their last chance had just passed over without either of them realizing it. Massive numbers had just been saved and raptured across the earth and especially from the Islamic, the Asian, and the African nations, where the gospel had rarely been heard but where the hearts of the masses were ripe to hear the final harvest message delivered by the great angel Gabriel.

Also unknown to the two scientists, the evil god of this world, Satan, had struck the earth a mere 150 yards from where they stood. This evil one had been hurled down from heaven with great force, falling as a lightning from on high. He had somehow managed to tightly hold in his sinister hands a small chest during the long course of his fall. The chest looked like a small treasure chest. It contained a key.

Satan stood dusting off his suit and looking around. "Where is that door? It must be around here somewhere. Abaddon is powerful," he thought, "very powerful, indeed, but is a bit weak-minded. I have swayed his actions in the past so why not again? He should be more than willing to help rid the earth of those pesky Jews and submit to my command."

Deep in the utmost depths of the bottomless pit, heavily chained for eons, were the ten demonic rulers, powerful kings in the kingdom of darkness. Abaddon had little to do with them since the rebellion in heaven, except that he had visited on occasion, every thousand years or so. He encouraged them that one day they would be released from this dreadful pit. Abaddon knew this for good reason. The pit had a door with a key hole. Abaddon had seen it himself. He intuitively knew without a doubt that any door with a keyhole will someday, given enough time, be opened.

He tried to keep up the morale of the ten kings, knowing their great power which had been displayed in allegiance to him in his thwarted attempt to take the throne of God in heaven. These were not ordinary fallen angels, but some of the highest elite warriors. By deception, Lucifer had drawn them astray and now they were held in strong chains in the deepest confines of the pit.

At each visit Abaddon preached to them about that low life, Lucifer, who had caused the problem and their great misery through the centuries. And he also inflamed them especially toward the hated mankind who had the favor of God, usurping the great rulership they all deserved on the earth, at least in their own wicked opinion.

How they hated Satan! Most of their time in bondage was occupied with dreaming of the day they would attack Satan and inflict terrible punishment, stripping him of all power and authority. For God had put it into their hearts to fulfill his will, and to agree, and to give their kingdom, the kingdom of darkness, unto the beast, Abaddon, until the words of God should be fulfilled. Then, Abaddon would reign supreme on the earth for forty-two months. The ten demonic rulers were Abaddon's key to victory, not only over Satan but in his warped mind, ultimately over the Lord Jesus.

Suddenly, outside the massive iron door to the pit, there was a great commotion as lightning crashed to the ground. The two angelic guardians could not see anything because of the mist and the brightness from the great lightning flash near the door they guarded. What they had heard and seen was Satan arriving on the scene, falling from heaven as lightning.

The two warrior angels looked at him with open hostility. "Do you have the key, evil one?"

"Don't get snippy with me, wise guy. Just remember you are only a warrior angel, and I don't take orders from you. Now get out of my way." He attempted to shove the warrior angel, but he didn't move. His bronze face drew close to Satan's, and he looked without a hint of fear in the evil one's eyes.

"I asked you if you have the key."

"Yes, I have the key. Now beat it and go back to your job of helping little old ladies across the street in Hoboken."

The two angels moved back to the sides of the great door that had been closed for eons. Satan moved carefully to the door and waited. He pondered the key, tapping it in the palm of his hand, trying to decide if it would really be in his best interest to release Abaddon. But, then, his great pride took over. Of course he would release Abaddon!

"I am the ruler, the god of this world, and Abaddon will simply have to obey me as I command him to go forth and kill every Jew on earth. This will totally thwart the so called Messiah. Some Messiah he will be … Messiah of the dead!" he said to himself, but loud enough for the two angels to hear him and be impressed.

He was trying to see if he could hear anyone on the other side. Hearing nothing, he put the key in the lock and turned it. The door exploded open, and Abaddon roared out sounding like a racing freight train. He was followed by the False Prophet.

The mist had been replaced by low roiling, ominous black clouds with intermittent flashes of sheet lightning. Deep in the bowels of the earth, the chains on the ten rulers dropped away, and they were freed. They came swirling up with great passion and power to the throne room in the volcano at the time the massive iron door swung open, having been kicked by Abaddon's great bear foot.

"Freedom! I am free at last from this place of horrors. Never again will I submit to such punishment. Never!"

Then the leaders of the demonic horde saw Satan standing to one side of the door.

"You! You're the cause of my suffering. You deserve a preview of what's in store for you in the future." Abaddon charged Satan, and there was a terrible struggle. Dirt and rocks and plants were uprooted and thrown about.

The two volcanologists were startled, not knowing what was happening. The professor, full of his own wisdom, casually said, "This is just a little dust devil. Nothing to worry about."

Abaddon, the false Prophet and the ten kings surrounded the terrified Satan. They grabbed him with their talon-like hands and began to flog him with their wings. They bit him with their protruding teeth and punched him without mercy.

Satan screeched and fell whimpering to the ground as Abaddon roughly placed his great bear foot on the deceiver's head with enough pressure to bust it like an overripe boil at any moment. Satan screamed, pleading with them to stop. This one who so enjoyed seeing others suffer and die had no tolerance for pain.

"Don't hurt me, please don't hurt me. I can help you. I can show you how to make war with Jesus and defeat him. But you must listen to me. I have dealt with him for thousands of years. I submit to your command great Abaddon. I give you my seat. I give you my power. I give you my great authority as ruler of the earth … just don't hurt me!" Diablo pleaded like a wimp under Abaddon's powerful and massive foot.

Abaddon glared at Satan as he scratched his lion like chin and looking down at the pathetic little man under his great foot.

"Stop whining. Perhaps I will spare your miserable life as you do have some experience in deceiving the masses. But don't forget for one moment that I am the one in charge. You answer to me!"

Abaddon looked over at the prophet who nodded his great ram's horns in approval. "My friend, Prophet, are all of the demons and the creatures with the scorpion tails up to speed as to their assignments?"

"They are anxious and ready to begin when you give the word."

Abaddon stood and gazed around the mountain at the vast openness to the horizon. There was so much to do, speed was imperative. "Loose them all, now!"

285

The Prophet gave a word, and there was a great 'swooshing' sound as uncounted wings beat the air. Millions of demons came out of the mountain and moved away in orderly columns that spread out to every point of the compass. The noise reverberated around the world. Many thought they were hearing a tornado or hurricane. Next to escape the prison of darkness were the creatures with the scorpion tails. They were roaring and growling and raging so loudly that the noise of their beating wings was lost to the listener.

One came out so angry that he drooled with anticipation. He wanted to hurt somebody, and he wanted to do it now. He spotted the two volcano explorers sitting near by, astounded by what they saw because all of the creatures were now visible to humans.

The giant creature did not fly; he walked casually and slowly toward the man and young woman. His face was contorted, full of evil joy. The two victims were speechless with fright. They wanted to run but were unable to get up. It was as if they were chained in place. The creature stopped in front of them and growled, with his eyes bulging. His breath foul, a combination of garbage and sulfur.

He exploded into action, grabbing the professor first and holding him tightly in his steel-like grasp. His big scorpion tail moved slowly over his back and zeroed in on the man's forehead. The black poison-filled stinger with a little red tip repeatedly pierced the professor's forehead, indelibly marking the name of the beast on his soul for all eternity.

The pain was unimaginable, mixed with the dread of total eternal hopelessness. It was like liquid fire burning in his flesh and a black hole melting through his heart. The burning of the mark took a lot of time because the creature relished every moment.

He released the man and grabbed the young woman. She screamed at the top of her voice. There was no rescue. The pain was too intense for her. She fainted while calling for god to rescue her, but it was too late.

Like the five foolish virgins in the famous Bible parable, she was now left outside the door of the wedding chamber for all eternity. She had never used the Lord's name in any manner except while cursing in her whole life. Both marks were oozing pus and smelled putrid.

Chapter Fifty Two

General Gunderson was up before dawn. The excitement of the upcoming battle wouldn't allow him to sleep. The tankers were already warming up the massive diesels in the Russian tanks, preparing them for the day that promised to be a massacre of historic proportions.

The general had spent the night in Jericho with some tanks and infantry. He had in mind that he would ride on the lead tank to enter Jerusalem, just like General Patton entered conquered German villages over sixty years ago.

He had a quick shower and put on a clean uniform in preparation for the grand entrance later today. Just as he walked to the mess tent for some breakfast, an unseen Israeli fighter strafed the camp, forcing him to dive for cover. When he got his face out of the dirt and looked at his uniform, he let off a string of obscenities that turned the air blue. The fact that two of his men had just been killed around him was of no interest. He stomped back to his tent to change. To him, image was everything, especially when leading men into battle. The fact that he had never led men into anything before yesterday did not register in his mind.

After a breakfast of French toast and scrambled eggs, he made his way to the tank he had designated to be the lead tank for the thrust into Jerusalem. He climbed aboard and sat in the turret. Looking around to see that everyone was ready, he gave the "hand pump" so familiar to movie goers, signaling to move out. The big diesels roared and put up a cloud of black exhaust as they clattered forward. It should only take an hour to reach their objective.

Israeli planes dove out of the clouds in single line formation. One at a time, they dropped their bombs and strafed the tanks and infantry with 50-caliber machine gun fire that was accurate and deadly. Troops from the nations of the world balked at seeing their comrades dropping like flies and turned to flee back the way they had come. They had never seen combat, having been only used in peacekeeping missions, mostly in Africa.

This was different. Men were dying all over the place.

"Hold your positions!" Gunderson shouted at his fleeing army. "Hold your positions, or I'll kill you myself."

The men stopped but grouped around the tanks for protection. Finally, U.N. air support jets screamed onto the scene and broke up the attack formations of the Israeli Air Force. Two U.N. jets were immediately shot down and another damaged. One Israeli jet put out a plume of black smoke, indicating it was badly damaged. Instead of heading for friendly territory, the pilot banked his aircraft and headed for a Russian tank. With incredible bravery, the pilot steered his wounded jet right into the tank where it exploded in a huge, yellow ball of flame. The men inside were vaporized.

"I'll tell you one thing," Gunderson said to the tank driver next to him. "These guys have a lot of guts."

"Yeah, well we're goin' to spill their guts all over the place when we get to Jerusalem. That was my brother in that tank. Somebody's going to get paid back in spades."

The battle raged on. The Israelis attacked and withdrew with heavy losses, but they attacked again and again. Surface-to-air missiles had taken down a large number of fighters, so threats from the air were becoming less costly.

At noon the UN tanks and troops were entering Jerusalem itself. They were like crazed warriors, destroying buildings as they went. Soldiers trying to hold a rear guard position were captured when they ran out of ammunition. They were hacked to death with bayonets. Many women were hiding in their homes rather than attempting to flee the city. Perhaps they believed the enemy soldiers would take them prisoner without harm. They were badly mistaken. The screams from the houses told what was really happening.

Few events in history could be compared to the viciousness and evil loosed on the city. The Massacre of Nanking, China, by the Japanese in World War II, was similar. It was as if all of the evil and hatred on the planet had come to Jerusalem for vengeance.

Most of the city was in flames. The roaring of the fires, the blasts from guns, and the screams of the helpless finally sickened General Gunderson. He had tried to control his men, but they were like animals gone wild. Nothing could stop them.

A spotter plane flying over the city reported to him that there were streams of people leaving the city going east, to what the pilot thought might be the Mount of Olives. "If you pour it on, you can trap them before they can escape. It should be good pickings for the boys on the ground. Wish I was down there. The infantry always has all the luck," the pilot said sadly.

Gunderson looked around at the carnage that was visible in every direction. Flames were everywhere. Beautiful buildings destroyed and looted. He could hardly believe his own eyes. Some people were being led away as slaves!

"My God, what have we done?" he whispered to himself. "What have we done?"

Chapter Fifty Three

Days before the destruction began, Rabbi Bernardi was pondering over the task Abisha had given him, to find 12,000 people from each of the twelve tribes of Israel and have them gather at the Mount of Olives when the destruction of Jerusalem begins. Such a gigantic problem! He didn't know where to begin. He prayed for guidance from God. Soon a thought began to flourish in his brain. There were at least twelve young men that went to his synagogue who could be described as computer "geeks". The fact that there were twelve young fellows who would even go to synagogue was in itself a miracle.

He called them to meet in his home in the evening. They came out of curiosity rather wanting to help him with one of his schemes to get more people to come to services. He had ice cream and chocolate cookies for a snack but then began to explain the problem he faced.

"Here is the problem, my young friends. By the way, thank you for coming out tonight. Here is the difficulty I face. I am hoping one of you might have an answer. I need to get in touch with 12,000 people from each of the ancient tribes of Israel, and I have to do it tonight. How can I do it?" he queried.

"Go on television with an appeal," one young man said.

"Yeah, and the radio as well," said another.

"No, I must keep the whole project secret. I can't have the government snooping around," Bernardi explained.

"Oh ho, so you're up to something illegal are you?" the boys laughed.

"No, no, I just have to get this done now. Come on, think," he said impatiently.

One skinny boy stood up. He had glasses that looked like the bottoms of Coke bottles. Bernardi could see no flesh on his bones. "I think we could do it on our computers. Each of us take one tribe and then key into the computer at the national archives. We type in the tribal name and click on "search". It should kick out the names of family members who are alive now. If and when we get 12,000, we send a "spam" email to all of them, giving them the message you want them to have. There might even be an organization with the email addresses in a "list" form. If there is and we could get our hands on it, *"Bam"* we're in like Flynn. It should be possible, and I think it could be done in a matter of hours."

Bernardi jumped up and hugged the boy, nearly cracking his boney frame. "Wonderful, just wonderful. Will you do it, gentlemen?"

"Sure, it might be fun. What do you want us to say in the email?"

"I want you to say, 'Dear friend. Our nation is in great peril. In two days, our beloved Jerusalem will probably be attacked. If and when that happens, you must go to the Mount of Olives, east of the city. You must be there to save your lives. On the mount, the ancient red heifer sacrifice will be performed as directed in the Torah. These directions are from God and were mentioned by the prophets to save you from destruction.' I believe Messiah will meet us there as he promised so long ago."

"Okay, we'll get right to work on it. Your message is too long but we'll get by somehow," one of the boys teased. "By the way, Rabbi, there is no way that we can tell how many people will respond. This might all be for nothing."

"Yes, I know. The number will be up to God. The hands of man have done all they could when you finish. By the way, you and your parents make sure you are at the Mount when the city falls. It will be the only safe place to run."

"Thanks, Rabbi, but my parents don't believe in this religious stuff, so they won't be there, but I might wander up there to get away from the war."

"Good, my lad, good! We'll see the Messiah together!"

Chapter Fifty Four

The morning of the final assault on the city of Jerusalem, the fighting started early. The Israeli army was fighting house to house but losing ground by the minute. Everything was burning. The slaughter of the people was horrific and brutal. The ancient ones were quick to say that this was just like the Nazis in World War II, when the people were packed into cattle cars and shipped away to be slaughtered. It was like all of the world's evil was in this place, and the Jews were being targeted once again for extermination, though not in death camps, but in their very homes.

Rabbi Bernardi was on the Mount of Olives waiting to see if he should perform the red heifer sacrifice or if Messiah would come and finish it. The Miphkad Altar was ready. Men had led Alice into the altar then tripped her and she fell over on her side. The wood in the altar hurt her and she bawled out her complaint. These same men tied her feet together so that she could not move.

She looked around in terror and continued to struggle to get free of the ropes. Bernardi looked at her struggle and was filled with compassion for her. He had watched her grow, and she was his pet. But now, she would be required to allow herself to be sacrificed for the people of Israel.

During the early morning hours, people fleeing the fighting began arriving at the mount. Nearly all said they had received the "spam" message. Others said friends had called them and told them to be here. Family members made sure that children were there. There was such fear and sadness in the crowd, there was the continual sound of mourning and wailing. There was nowhere else to go. For them, they believed this was the end; they would die together with some semblance of dignity.

They continued looking back at Jerusalem and the devastation that was taking place as they could also see that the attacking armies would soon reach them. They stood in faith, believing that the Messiah, their only hope, would come to complete the red heifer sacrifice and deliver them from this attack. There was no thought of running; there was nowhere to go. They would soon be totally surrounded by enemy troops on all sides.

As the brutal armies drew closer and closer to the base of the Mount of Olives, the rabbi held the knife to kill Alice, the perfect red heifer for the sacrifice. He was uncertain what he should do next. Should he step up and slay the red heifer himself? "No." He shook his head. He decided he must stand in faith hoping for the Messiah he had longed to see for most of his life.

All of a sudden, the sky above them changed from blue to near total darkness. Clouds formed and reached towards the heavens. They were dark and menacing, and great winds blew in, filling the crowd with both fear and wonder. The sun was darkened. The moon was visible; it had turned blood red. A clear space between the two tempests was in the middle of the sky, and from it a great trumpet sounded, so loudly that their ears hurt and the ground under them shook with the power of the heavenly blast.

Then, as the crowd looked skyward, they saw *Him* in the clouds. No one had to be told who the great person in the clouds was. They knew who it was, and most fell to the ground weeping and wailing and tearing their clothes. It was Jesus, the Son of God, who stood before them in radiant splendor. The great Creator God was looking down on his creation. He raised his arms into the air and said in a loud voice, "Come up, my children, come up with me!"

Some in the crowd were Christians or Messianic Jews, who shouted, "Yeshua, my Savior!"

These people began to rise up into the air as they called out the name of the Lord. They left the 144,000 behind as they met Jesus in the air. Those left behind watched with a mixture of awe and sadness. All of the things they had been taught about Jesus were wrong, and they now knew it. Their wailing grew even louder.

Those being raised stretched high their hands and cried out in joyful rapture, "Jesus! Jesus!" As they ascended to meet the Lord in the air, they knew exactly what was happening. They had been taught that this day would happen, and here it was at last. This was the event of the rapture which was taking place over the entire earth.

Gabby, Tuck, Pedro and countless others, who had led souls to Christ, were being raised up to meet the Lord in the air. Rising with them were great multitudes who were the fruit of their labor of love. The sufferings and sacrifices the laborers had endured were now a thing of the past – not being worthy to be compared with the riches in glory of this joyous Kingdom they were now entering.

After a few moments, the 144,000 could see the Lord continuing to descend, coming right toward them. His feet touched down before them on the Mount of Olives. At his side were two witnesses. The Lord Jesus stood in such bright radiance, it was difficult to look upon Him. The two witnesses were Moses and Elijah, one on each side, a re-enactment of an event seen long ago on the Mount of Transfiguration.

Rabbi Bernardi approached the Messiah he had been looking for all of his adult life. He bowed in reverence, but there was a smile on his face. He was now sure that he had seen Jesus before: Abisha, the man with the terrible scars. Bernardi approached Messiah and held up the knife for the sacrifice of the red heifer on his outstretched palms, expecting him to take the knife and complete the sacrifice.

The Lord Jesus took the knife and placed it in Elijah's hand, who stepped towards the altar of sacrifice. The red heifer was tied, lying on her side and looked wide-eyed with fear as Elijah approached and held the knife high, ready to make one decisive stroke of the razor sharp blade. The knife fell but did not strike the heifer's jugular; but instead cut the rope binding the legs of the heifer.

She struggled to her feet and bolted off of the altar and trotted quickly through the olive groves and out of sight. As she was moving away, she turned and looked at the one who had spoiled her by scratching behind her ears. He smiled at her, and she was gone.

Elijah tossed the knife on the empty altar and looked up into the heavens. His lips moved and suddenly the crowd jumped back as a bolt of fire fell and instantly consumed the altar and even the rocks near the altar. The Lord Jesus clothed in radiance held out his arms in the shape of a cross before the crowd. His wrists and feet displayed the deep scars of his sacrifice, the final sacrifice for sin.

The Jews looked upon him who was pierced, their Messiah, the Lord Jesus. Then, as prophesied in Zechariah 12:10, a wailing cry began to move through the crowd. Those gathered on the slopes of the Mount of Olives began to weep bitterly. The rabbi was weeping while on his knees before the Lord Jesus. His tears rushed down his beard and fell on the feet of the Lord in a stream as his new faith in Jesus Christ as Lord cleansed his spirit.

Bernardi had longed to see the Messiah, and now he was worshipping him in spirit and truth. The Lord then gave a slight nod to Moses, the giver of the law. Moses stepped forward, raised his hands and staff toward the crowd and proclaimed in a supernatural booming voice, "It was finished!" The law had been nailed to a cross with the sacrifice of the Lord Jesus 2000 years ago.

Moses then faced the east, away from the city and stretched out his staff as he did long ago when he parted the Red Sea. The Mount of Olives began to crack open, and just as the Red Sea parted, the mountain was parting, making a way for the escape of the Jewish remnant. The Lord Jesus stepped toward the narrow valley and motioned for the crowd to follow to safety. The crowd quickly began to follow Jesus who led them briskly through the valley toward the east, away from the conquered city of Jerusalem.

As the last of the people entered the valley fleeing the advancing armies, Moses and Elijah stood shoulder to shoulder. These two heroes of the Old Testament were guarding the retreat of the remnant of Israel. No one would pass into the valley to chase the fleeing nation of Israel.

These two witnesses were facing a great army. But greater were those with them than all the armies gathered against them. The Archangel Michael and his battalion of angelic host were providing air support. And the two witnesses each possessed tremendous power granted from on high. The first of the battle tanks approached as Elijah opened his mouth. A great stream of the fire of God shot out of his mouth for over a mile. Soldiers stood as the flesh fell off their bones, and their eyes melted in their heads before their bones could hit the ground.

Then Moses stretched forth his rod and tremendous hail began to fall from heaven. The huge hailstones were mingled with fire and with blood, as it fell on wide areas across the earth but concentrated on the advancing armies.

After a few moments, only one-sixth of the original attacking armies remained alive. The rest turned tail in full retreat.

Moses and Elijah took a deep breath and prepared for their next foe that would be arriving soon. They would battle this fearsome visage for the next 1,260 days. No man had ever faced such a destructive and terrifying opponent. Soon they would stand face to face against the fallen angelic beast, Abaddon himself!

As the 144,000 began their flight through the valley of the Mount of Olives, Michael's special company applied the protective seal of God to each of their foreheads. Far in the distance, at a special place in the history of the earth and of mankind, there is a place of nourishment east of Jerusalem near the Tigris and Euphrates rivers.

The two great angelic guardians knew it was time as they set aside a flaming sword and swung open the great gates to the Garden of Eden, which has been protected from man since the beginning of time. Now the garden is prepared to receive the remaining 12,000 members of each of the twelve tribes of Israel.

In this special garden, protected since the time of Adam and Eve, the remnant of the nation of Israel will be nourished for three and a half years as Abaddon the Beast unleashes destruction, torture and domination to the inhabitants of the earth, opposed only by the two great witnesses.

The End

Afterword

A number of characters in our story were filled with joy being heavenward bound when the great trumpet sounded and Jesus Christ was seen coming on the clouds in power and glory. These, who had made a decision for Christ, came to experience the joyful rapture of the Church as they were raised off the earth to meet the Lord in the air.

As co-authors, Lyle and I hold a deep desire in our hearts that, those who may read these pages will make that important decision and call on the name of Jesus for salvation.

Considering the unique eschatological framework woven into our storyline, the reader may ask, why the event of Jesus standing on the Mount of Olives is depicted to occur at the beginning of tribulation rather than at the end of tribulation as most theologians teach? The 144,000 would have no reason to flee from Jerusalem through the valley formed in the Mount of Olives if tribulation were at an end.

Another factor in the equation is the fact that Jerusalem, the Holy City, is prophesied to be trodden underfoot by the Gentiles for 42 months as seen in Revelation 11:2. This three and a half year period is the same time period that the 144,000 will be nourished at a secret location away from Jerusalem. Thus, their flight from Jerusalem must occur three and a half years before the end of tribulation.

A key in this equation is that Zechariah chapter 14 states that Jesus will stand on the Mount of Olives on the Day of the Lord. Paul states in 1 Thessalonians chapters 4 and 5 that the Day of the Lord will come as a thief in the night, and this will be the day that the dead in Christ rise, and those alive in Christ will also be lifted up to meet the Lord in the air, an event frequently described as the rapture of the Church.

Additionally, the reader may ask, why is the tribulation depicted as lasting only three and a half years rather than seven years? Why can no one left behind be saved after the rapture of the Church? Why will the two witnesses be the only tribulation martyrs? Why the Temple is not rebuilt? What is the fulfillment of the abomination of desolation?

These and many other important questions are answered in detail from the scriptures in my first book.

Escaping The Mark Of The Beast
by Dr. Terry Gage
www.biblemystery.com

Other novels by Lyle A. Way
Betrayal at Heaven's Gate
Edge of Disaster
Murder in Shades of Gray
Junta
www.lyleaway.com

Visit
www.dayofthelordbook.com
Participate in the
Joel 2:1 Project.

Blow the trumpet in Zion, and sound an alarm in my holy mountain! Let all the inhabitants of the earth tremble; for the day of the Lord is coming... Joel 2:1

LaVergne, TN USA
16 July 2010
189771LV00003B/5/P